ENCOUNTER PROGRAM

ROBERT ENSTROM

New Myth Publications

Encounter Program
Copyright © 2017 by Robert Enstrom
All rights reserved
Published by New Myths Publishing
www.NewMythsPublishing.com

ISBN: 978-1-939354-07-5

Cover art:

© Innovari | Dreamstime.com - Alien Spaceship Photo

© Nopow | Dreamstime.com - Stars Photo

Cover and interior design copyright © 2017 Knotted Road Press

Originally published by Doubleday & Company, Inc. 1977
Library of Congress Catalog Card Number 77-74300

Contents

PREFACE

Many years hence when the reaction of the past shall have left only the grand outline in view, this perhaps is how a philosopher will speak of it. He will say that the idea, peculiar to the nineteenth century, of employing science in the satisfaction of our material wants had given a wholly unforeseen extension to the mechanical arts and had equipped man in less than fifty years with more tools than he had made during the thousands of years he had lived on the earth. Each new machine being for man a new organ—an artificial organ which merely prolongs the natural organs —his body became suddenly and prodigiously increased in size, without his soul being able at the same time to dilate to the dimensions of his new body.

—Henri Bergson

From *Source Records of the Great War*, Charles F. Home, ed., Copyright, 1930, The American Legion. *Indianapolis.*

PART I

STRANGE BEGINNINGS

CHAPTER 1. THE LAW

Herman's Intergalactic Law for the Layman, 2.2nd Edition:

TITLE 1246: The Encounter Clause.

Section 1. The Encounter Program: No ship is legally equipped with Hommont Drive, or any subsequent development thereof, without simultaneous installation of an *Authorized Encounter Program* in the Ship Computer. No Ship Computer capable of, or designed for, coupling with such a drive is legally manufactured without the inclusion of an *Authorized Encounter Program.* Evasion of, or incomplete compliance with, this section will result in a charge of *Criminal Evasion of a Primary Directive.*

Section 2. The Recognition Program: *ALL ABOVE STIPULATIONS APPLY* (see Section 1, Title 1246), with *Authorized Recognition Program* substituted for *Authorized Encounter Program.* All data on known interstellar drives (Hommont Drive or any derivative thereof) is contained in the *Authorized Recognition Program.* By law the Recognition Program *must* be augmented at every *First Class Port of Call.* Recognition Program loses its *Authorization* on failure to comply with this section. Failure to comply with augmentation of Recognition Program will result in a charge of *Criminal Negligence in the First Degree* against either Pilot, Port of Call, or both.

Section 3. The Manual Trigger: *ALL ABOVE STIPULATIONS APPLY* (Section 1). The Encounter Program can be triggered manually *only* through a properly identified *Manual Trigger*. The *Manual Trigger* is operative only during a period, two hours in length, following any encounter with any interstellar drive in deep space.* False or unjustifiable use of the *Manual Trigger* will result in a charge of *Criminal Nuisance in the First Degree*.

The Encounter Clause was enacted shortly after the disastrous Hursk encounter of 4180 a.d. and was designed to prevent other unregulated encounters with aliens of any sort. The Encounter Clause has lately fallen into general disuse due to the proliferation of Commercial Regulation Beacons and the construction of inexpensive ships capable of travel only within two light-years of, or along, the connecting strings of these Beacons, which now exist between all human settled worlds.

Ships of this newer type are exempt from the clause because they are technically always within the field of another interstellar drive (the Commercial Regulation Beacon), which is itself equipped with all of the proper programming. Few ships today are even equipped with coupled computer drives capable of operation or navigation in deep space, and these few are mainly for use by the IXT. (The IXT is a military branch of the Combined Governments, and it is charged with enforcement of the Encounter Clause and related articles.)

—D. F. Herman

* Deep space: Any point at a distance of greater than two light-years from any *Beacon* (Commercial Regulation, Navigational, or Habitation Beacon). For further information see *Technical Definitions (Legal)*; Vol. 18, by R. Ew Burger.

CHAPTER 2. PLEASURE CRUISE

Somack paused in his examination of the ship and allowed himself to smile. The years of effort and frugal living were behind him now and in their place stood the culmination of a lifetime of work and desire. He reached out his hand and under a fine layer of dust he could feel the cold, firm strength of *his* ship. He seemed to gain strength himself from the contact and for a moment the weight of his years left him.

Down he climbed into the bowels of his ship, with a brisk step long absent from his walk. All of those years working for the Company he'd never seen his goal as anything but a mistiness off in the distance. Now, walking among the massive coils and shining storage banks, he wondered how he'd lived so long without her. So silent and so strong, she'd make up for all those years and toil, taking him into the dark loneliness of deep space.

Forty long years she'd lain in storage, as if waiting for him to free her. Now, at last, he'd come. In a few more days she'd taste vacuum again.

Beauty and perfection had drawn him to the battered little ship. The pocked and pitted hull were signs of aging and infirmity to others, to him they showed character. The *R. B. Ambol* was unpretentious and bore her history unconcealed by the gilt and polish of the day. She proudly carried the name of a man long dead and forgotten. He would never change that name. It was part of her now, as much a part as the scarred exterior she'd earned in that man's service.

How well he knew the perfection and quality of her interior belied the face she gave the world. Her drive was nothing new and in this lay its advantage. Nor was it fast, but it worked—it *always* worked. Nothing could go wrong which he could not easily fix. She even took the cheapest, lowest quality fuel; fuel so poor others considered it only an intermediate stage in refining the real thing.

Slow, yes—and with very limited cargo space too, but she was what he wanted; she could take him where he wanted to go with an absolute certainty of getting there.

He sobered suddenly, remembering the passengers. Only two, thankfully, for the *Ambol's* quarters were cramped; little more than a control room and hall joining five tiny sleeping compartments. Still, it was a shame he had to let them come. If only his money had lasted. Then he'd never have offered her up for charter. But this would be the last time, the last time he'd be following someone else's orders. Then he'd be free. Free to search for a dream.

Even now after so many years he could still recall the smallest details of that dream. It had come to him only once, and he remembered the date well because it had been the eve of his fifth birthday. Rain beat against his window and he lay awake, waiting for the morning and the fun to come. Meager presents scraped together by his poor family sat hidden in their nooks and crannies, hideouts he knew by heart. They were pathetic little gifts doomed never to be opened and still waiting, even now, in their dusty places for a party that would never come.

That night, through the rain and the storm, a man came to their house. How clearly he could still hear those sloshing feet, the urgent pounding on the door, and the hushed and frightened faces of his parents as they let the stranger in. And the harsh and ragged breathing of the stranger who, wet and bleeding, lay down to die on their living room sofa.

Then came the running feet, the shouting and searching. For the stranger had been a criminal, a fugitive from justice, bearing with him something of value. And so his family lost their home and what little they had in the world. The searchers searched them one after another, and not finding what they sought, had tossed them into the rain like so many empty bottles until only he remained. Cowering in his bed, hidden ineffectually beneath the sheets, he waited for them to come and search him too. His fear grew with every passing second, knowing in his child's mind that he had what they were after. And they had come, ripping him from his bed and the clothes from his back. But they searched him in vain, not knowing that what they sought he held in his mind. Naked, they tossed him out to join his family in the rain. In their frustration the searchers sealed the house, vowing that if they could not find what the stranger had possessed then at least no other would. They never knew that in his room, listening to a stranger die, little Billy Somack had dreamed a dream; a dream that brought a smile to a dying man's lips and unshakable resolution to a little boy's life.

The young man glowered down at the shadowy hulk sitting in its storage bunker.

"Is that it?" he snapped. "You expect me to gamble my life and my wife's in that derelict?"

"You answered the ad," Somack replied calmly. "You've seen all its papers. The ship's condition is good and all its papers are in order. It's old, I grant you, but it's still the only one around that'll take you into deep space. Age," he smiled, "is not always a handicap."

The young man shook his head doubtfully. "I'll see those papers again."

"As you wish," Somack replied with strained patience, and for the third time he smoothed out his purchase contract for inspection. For the third time the young man read the section guaranteeing an ability he doubted. He finished reading, shaking his head again. The previous owners, Black and Co., a well-known holding company, would never risk a triple penalty guaranteeing the impossible. With a great show of reluctance he took out a pen and signed a draft for expenses, as well as the deposit payment for the trip.

Somack added his signature to the charter agreement and the thing was done.

The young man turned to go, then seemed to change his mind about something. He turned and called over his shoulder, "We'll leave as soon as possible. If anyone gets in your way or causes you trouble just tell them you work for me. If they persist, let me know and I'll take care of it."

"I'll remember that," Somack replied, and he would. He watched Brodrick's figure dwindle into the distance, noticeably small for the first time all day. There went a big man, big in money, big in power, and someone he was already beginning to dislike.

As the days passed Brodrick came around often, prodding and

pushing in his "expert at everything" way; advising the dock workers how to load this or store that. It was a measure of his power that these hardened men took it all calmly, with quiet "yes, sirs." But there was nothing in the world to stop them from going back and doing everything exactly as they pleased when Brodrick was gone.

Somack's unease grew and he noticed that with all his comings and goings Brodrick was never accompanied by his wife. He began to wonder if there was one. Only at the last minute was he informed that the wife was really "the bride" and that the trip was to be a honeymoon as well as an expedition.

The day of departure came and Somack was up early. Wisps of ground fog blew across the field obscuring the ship for seconds at a time as it was being raised from its storage bunker. Fully loaded and equipped for six months in space, she looked down over the grooves and stains of her many years, making their colors and shapes distinct in the morning light.

Great handling machines gripped her carefully, holding her poised above the field as they transported her to the center of the nearest launching grid. In less than an hour the grid would be activated. In co-ordination with the *Ambol's* auxiliary drive it would push the ship into space under a near constant acceleration of four gees. Seven short minutes later they would be free of the planet's gravity, in orbit around the sun, and ready to throw in the main drive.

Somack waited impatiently now for his passengers to arrive. He scanned the field with little hope as the fog continued, clinging stubbornly to the cool concrete. With a swirl the fluffy white mass parted and an impossibly large car emerged, shining black in the waxing light. The impressively built chauffeur popped out, opened the door on Brodrick's side, and stood stiffly at attention as the young man stepped forth. Brodrick climbed the ramp briskly, leaving the chauffeur to hurry around to the other door and help his wife out.

Dressed in a flowing white gown, she seemed little more than a child on the arm of her muscular escort. The driver hurried her up the ramp after his master, at times nearly lifting her feet from the metal steps. Brodrick turned at the top of the ramp and waited for the pair to catch up. He took his wife's arm and led her inside while his employee descended two and three steps at a time. Within seconds of its arrival the car disappeared into the fog, leaving Somack to stand at the head of the boarding ramp wondering exactly what had happened.

Not a word had been spoken. Somack shook his head and knelt to disengage the ramp. In his brief, partially obstructed view of the young lady, Somack had come to a few quick conclusions. She was too young, and although pretty in a moody sort of way, she was not what he'd envisioned as Brodrick's choice. In a few years, perhaps, but not yet. Self-possessed and calm, serious even; she was hardly the stereotype of a blushing bride. Somack shook his head again, determined to keep his nose where it belonged.

He slammed the hatch shut, securing it manually. The ship blinked a confirmation at him. Smiling, he stepped into the small control room and the air-tight door snapped shut behind him. Inured as he was by the routine of a thousand take-offs, Somack could strap himself into a launching harness in a few seconds. But passengers were another matter. He stood watching to see that they did it properly. Brodrick made a careful ritual of it, step by step; by the book all the way. The girl bride, although striving bravely at the tangle of harness, was getting nowhere.

Bending to help, Somack got a dark look from Brodrick. He ignored it and concentrated on his job. Suddenly, with an almost physical shock, he realized that this girl, despite her outward calm, was scared stiff. Her hands gripped the straps with just a little too much force, releasing only when he pried at them. It took several minutes to straighten the mess and all the time Somack was thinking furiously. Something was not at all right with this trip. Again, and this time with more difficulty, he restrained his train of thought.

He settled into launch preparation, letting the ship take over when it indicated a knowledge of the procedure. He utilized the few minutes' freedom this gave him to check the charter agreement. It stated that he was to transport Brodrick and his wife into deep space and go anywhere Brodrick wished for a four-month period, at which time he would return by the most direct route to Palverde, the planet they were about to leave, and receive full payment. Included was a penalty clause which made it impossible for him to terminate the trip early without losing his ship.

Well, that settled that idea. He slipped the papers back where they belonged and resigned himself to several months of discomfort. A warning light flashed and Somack relaxed. The ship lifted and his weight quadrupled under its acceleration, pressing him into the comfortable cushion below him. Seven-odd minutes later he was free of the excess weight and turning on one of the ship's six fields of view. The wall before him dissolved into starlit space with only a faint pattern of control lights superimposed on the scene. The view and the grid imposed on it were adjusted to his position. To the others in the room it didn't look quite right, but was still recognizable as a star field.

"Can't you give us a better view than this?" Brodrick asked, scowling faintly. The slight distortion seemed to bother him.

"It's an old ship," Somack answered, making it clear without being too blunt that he was running the ship. By the contract Brodrick could tell him where to go but not how.

"I see," Brodrick said, turning to unstrap his wife. "Perhaps we should discuss our first objective over dinner."

"As you wish," Somack replied, watching the rough handling Brodrick was giving his wife's harness. She made no protest, only watched her husband's hands with large dark eyes. Finally free, she sat up slowly, carefully straightening her dress as she did so.

Brodrick leaned forward, whispering something in her ear. Her eyes darted up, searching his face, then turned to Somack and quickly back again. She shook her head; no. Brodrick forced a smile and lifted her into a standing position. Still smiling, he led her from the control room, down the short hall, and into the small room already fitted for them.

"When will you be ready?" Brodrick demanded, when he and the girl were alone. "I want you to finish with him as soon as you can. I want this job done with."

"Not yet," the girl pleaded. "It takes time. I can't see his whole mind —not so fast—not without hurting."

"You do it," Brodrick commanded. "You do it *tonight*!"

The girl looked at him with defiance.

"Bah!" Brodrick spat. It disgusted him having to work with people closely associated with the Quaker—and this girl was certainly that. She had special talent—she operated under the Quaker's protection.

Brodrick preferred his independence. He'd take the Quaker's money —and he'd do the job, but he hated interference. There were other methods of getting information from a subject like Somack. Quicker methods.

Brodrick returned to the control room alone and found Somack busy at the controls. "My wife is not feeling well," he stated flatly. "She'll be eating alone tonight."

"Anything wrong, anything I can do?" Somack asked, knowing the answer.

"No. She's just not used to space yet, that's all," Brodrick replied, ending the conversation.

Over their meal the two men discussed the general direction of their first day's flight. Brodrick wanted to leave beaconed space as quickly as possible, and with this at least Somack agreed. A direction was finally set and Brodrick too retired to the room at the end of the hall.

With Brodrick gone, Somack punched the hall door closed and kicked in the other five viewscreens. In every direction now the stars blinked at him from the walls of the darkened control room. The ship's navigation computer, active for the first time in more than forty years, hummed to itself. Another grid appeared on the all-pervasive control room screens, this one a course and distortion indicator. Now, since they were traveling at a speed less than that of light, it looked no different from the inertial grid except that its axes were aligned with the projected course and not the galactic plane.

The ship, having received its instructions, took matters out of Somack's hands. He relaxed in his chair and watched things happen. The main drive ignition fired once and caught. Power throbbed through the ship, vibrating everything, then settling down to a smooth rumble. A brilliant display of lights flashed onto the screen, each one representing another interstellar drive operating within *Ambol's* distortion range, about two light-years in every direction. The color and size of each dot in view showed the type of drive it was and its distance from the *Ambol*. For a frantic moment the *Ambol's* long unused recognition program received and classified the source of each incoming distortion. Some were beacons with their characteristic green and pink, stringing off in two directions—like dots in a highway divider. Others were ships with old and familiar drives: blue and yellow moving slowly across the star field. But most were ships with a newly developed drive and for a moment they showed a brilliant red. Then, one by one, the *Ambol* recognized them with the data provided just before take-off by the Port of Palverde. In seconds the red dots were gone, replaced on the screen with milder colors. Satisfied with its work the recognition program subsided into quiescence, releasing control of the ship to the navigation computer's more mundane functions.

Swinging in space, the ship aligned itself and Somack found himself looking directly down along their projected course. Almost perceptibly stars began to shift on the screen as the *Ambol* began to move. Somack turned, watching as stars began bunching and dancing toward the rear. The light-blue course grid stretched and bulged, conforming to the changing pattern. The ship was moving faster than the speed of light.

The screen soon presented a strange sight. The front half remained nearly unchanged while the stars in the rear were now clumped into a small disk directly behind him. Palverde's star, the brightest on the screen, slid over the invisible barrier separating the two halves of the screen. Almost instantly it joined the clump in the rear, dancing at the edge a moment, then sinking slowly to the center where it would remain until a course change was made.

Somack smiled at his ship's perfect performance. He leaned back in his chair, half closing his eyes in anticipation of a long watch. He was prepared to spend the next two hours watching the signs of civilization disappear. In that short time he would leave behind, for the first time in his life, the colorful array of dots and spots: beacons and his fellow space travelers. Already most had fallen into the disk behind him. Soon they would blink off as he reached the limit of their distortion.

He nodded forward in his chair. Something seemed to converge and surround him for a moment. He shook his head and blinked. There was a bad taste in his mouth. Somack realized with considerable irritation that he had napped. It had never happened to him like that before and he didn't like it.

The screen was already free of all blips and he shut it off, irritated at himself. His head began to ache, or rather he noticed that it was already aching, and he decided that a good night's sleep would do him some good.

He lay in bed trying to sleep, only his headache grew. This restlessness was not like him and in desperation he took something to help him sleep. It only made things worse. He dreamed. Not the special, private dream, but about that night. Only something was wrong, something was terribly wrong. He forced himself to open his eyes, but the dream continued. Instead of the metal of his small sleeping quarters he was seeing the peeled yellow paint and white plastic of his boyhood home. Lightning lashed through the window above his shoulder and sheets of water washed against the cold glass. Footsteps sounded on the walk. He groaned, twisting in his small bunk. In seconds there would be no turning back, *it* would start, unwilled and unwanted.

He landed on the steel floor with a thump, shaking his head savagely, driving away the last remnant of sleep. He dressed in a hurry and splashed a little water in his face. The agony in his head diminished to a pain he could tolerate. He left his room quietly and paused in passing the Brodrick's door, listening to the silence within, not really expecting to hear anything through the air-tight seal. He passed on. At the end of the hall he carefully opened the hatch leading down into the ship's vital spaces. He wandered there among the machinery, pulling himself through a few maintenance tunnels just to feel that he was doing something useful. But he'd really come for the restful thumping of the drive and the cool strength of the ship, hoping they would lift him from a troubled mood. He moved about, making needless adjustments and passing the time. Slowly the weight on his mind lifted, leaving him relaxed and tired in a nice sort of way, feeling much better.

With the morning cycle approaching, he packed away his tools and began his climb up through the length of the ship. On each level he dimmed the lights and secured the hatch. It was an old habit with most spacers, handed down from a time when an air-tight door was often all that stood between life and death. Now it was just a habit.

On the last level, the one right below the control room and sleeping quarters, he halted. All about, neatly packed and strapped in place, lay the baggage. Every thing that did not belong, not intrinsically a part of the ship, could be found here or on the level above. He bent to the hatch and very carefully locked it. Now the ship at least was safe. Feeling better for his precaution, he crossed to the ladder leading up to the passenger level, dimmed the lights, and started to climb.

"Hello."

With that softly spoken word Somack missed a step, nearly fell. It came from the semi-darkness below him. He eased himself back to the solid deck and there she was; sitting on a low packing crate with legs drawn up beneath her, elbows on knees and chin in hands. She seemed even more the child than before. Still dressed in a now slightly crumpled wedding dress, she looked so small. Her eyes were shadowed with fatigue and in the light thrown from above they appeared caves from which two bright flashes of light shown.

"Mrs. Brodrick?" he asked, at a loss. He was struck by the contrasting youth in body and age in voice. How many sorrows must lay behind those dark eyes, beneath those long luminous strands of dark hair.

"My name is Anna," she said, now looking directly at him, "not Brodrick." A slow smile spread across her face, transforming fatigue into a sad beauty, then it was gone. She was very serious again. "Thank you. I came to thank you. Not just for your consideration, but for something you made impossible, something I would have done and regretted."

Somack glanced at the locked hatch.

Her smile came back as she saw what he was thinking. "Yes, in a way. You locked something away from me—where I couldn't get it." She stopped suddenly and cocked her head to one side, her smile gone. She stood, no longer thinking of him, and walked to the foot of the ladder. Climbing a few steps quickly, she turned and looked back. "Thank you."

He stood with his mouth half open, wanting to say something, and watched her bare feet disappearing through the hatch above. He climbed after her, only to find the hall and control deck as still and quiet as he'd left it hours before.

Somack spent the rest of his time slumped in the command chair, thinking. The day came and he was still thinking. He ate his breakfast in the silence of his small room, ignoring Brodrick, who entered with a new course in his hand. Somack frowned down at his food as if it was somehow responsible for a growing problem.

To break the silence Brodrick finally commented, "My wife's not feeling well. She slept badly last night."

Somack looked up from his meal, wondering just what kind of bait this was. But Brodrick's face showed nothing but a lewd grin, an expression that said just what it was meant to say. Somack turned away and poked at his cold food. He no longer felt like eating.

"Here's the new course," Brodrick continued. He was still grinning hut his eyes were darkened, searching Somack's face for some sign.

Somack took the course without comment, without looking up from his congealing meal.

"I expect that course change to be implemented at the exact time noted," Brodrick snapped. "And followed for exactly twenty minutes. Is that clear?"

Somack looked up with an expression of mild surprise. "Certainly, sir," he said in a properly fear-laden and respectful tone.

Brodrick's smile returned and some of the tension left his shoulders. "Good," he murmured and added jovially, "I'll meet you in the control room in a few minutes."

With that comment he departed and Somack was on his feet immediately. He watched Brodrick disappearing into his room at the end of the hall, and stepped into the control room when he was gone. The door slid shut behind him and sealed itself quietly. He glanced at the course change and punched out a halt order.

Three quarters of an hour later, at the time specified, the *Ambol* came to a stop, reoriented itself, and started in a new direction. Somack watched the change with all the screens on. He was curious to see if his guess was correct. Sure enough, when the ship had completed its reorientation a star blazed brightly, directly ahead. For twenty minutes he watched the ship plunge toward this unknown star, wondering all the time if he should turn back. Brodrick was no newcomer to deep space; no one could navigate that well by accident. He would face the loss of his ship if he turned back, and perhaps more if he continued. Curiosity and determination had brought him this far and he would see it through.

The ship halted finally and Somack blanked five of the six control room screens. For the first time in just over an hour he let himself hear a faint pounding on the other side of the control room door. It slid open reluctantly at his command. Brodrick entered, his face livid with a rage that vanished when he caught sight of the twin yellow star on the screen and returned when he looked at Somack.

"What's the idea of locking me out of the control room? You could lose your ship for this."

"Locking you out? Why, that's incredible. Do you mean to tell me that the door wouldn't open for you? And I thought I'd fixed it."

Brodrick sputtered, turning a shade of purple. His ears seemed to glow for just a second and then, quite suddenly, he was in control again.

"Well, at least we're here," he commented grudgingly and then added, rubbing his hands together as he watched the screen, "Excellent! Excellent A friend of mine gave me the co-ordinates of this pair a long time ago. He said they were beautiful, absolutely beautiful. Now why don't you drop into normal space, so we can get a better look."

Somack nodded and cut the drive. The view on the screen popped once, then steadied. The stars were the same, only now they were surrounded by a distended ring of debris, the nearer edge of it nearly reaching out to their position. The light from the twin star gave the tumbled rock and ice an eerie sparkle and the beauty of a truly unusual sight. Intricate patterns of white and rose twined themselves around and between the two stars, a spiderweb of light and color against the dark background of space. Tenuous streamers of rock reached out beyond the main flows, only to fall back into the beautiful tangle further on. It was something completely beyond Somack's experience and he gaped at it, completely absorbed.

The ship, oblivious to the grandeur of the sight, was unobtrusively matching its speed with nearer objects. Somack felt this quiet activity and it brought him back to reality. He realized he was seeing something few people would ever view. Time and two greedy stars would reduce this wonder to a scattering of metallic debris and a few fragmentary planets. It couldn't last, nor could it be very old.

He turned to his companion, and seeing an expression of satisfaction, strangely lit by the color-strewn screen, wondered if in some sinister way Brodrick was responsible; the creator of this beauty. He studied that rapt face with distaste. The drooping eyelids and perpetual sneer were missing for the first time in this brief moment of appreciation. It was a handsome face. But it carried with it a warning. Somehow the mind behind projected through and made itself clear to him with all its malignancy and evil intent.

Somack's silent study ended when he caught sight of movement from the corner of his eye. Anna too had been drawn out by this spectacle and her face showed an awe and innocence missing in their first encounter. She was dressed in a simple long robe and her hair was disarrayed with the sleep she had missed during the night. Her eyes shifted to him and she smiled, but her face was guarded, hardened again.

Brodrick chose this moment to glance at Somack and followed around to see his wife. She stiffened, but he surprised them both with his mild reaction to her presence. "Feeling better?" he said, and smiled sardonically. "Perhaps you had better get ready for our little excursion."

She looked at him blankly.

"Surely you remember, dear. The walk we're going to take, to find stones for your collection."

Somack frowned. "You plan to leave the ship?"

"Certainly," Brodrick replied cheerfully. "The equipment is all there, right below us," and he tapped the deck with his toe.

"Isn't this kind of sudden?"

Brodrick's friendly smile froze into place. "I was going to let you in on it, but your sticky door there prevented me."

"Well," Somack said, realizing the man had a point, "perhaps I can make up for that by helping you two get ready. I can do that and get my own things on in plenty of time."

"No," Brodrick said slowly, "we can manage . . . alone."

Half an hour later the *Ambol* cautiously closed with a sizable rock, about three hundred feet long and a hundred across. It tumbled slowly along its short axis and represented a perfect course for interesting finds. Located far out from the main body of the belt there was little or no chance of stray material threatening the safety of the ship or out-board personnel.

Brodrick nodded at the screen in satisfaction. This was just what he was looking for. He slipped his helmet on and crossed to the control room hatch. Anna followed him hesitantly, adjusting her suit and holding an awkward array of unfamiliar mining equipment and sample containers. Brodrick punched the hatch's control. Nothing happened. The bulky figure turned on Somack slowly.

"Patience," Somack said, struggling to contain his smile. "This ship is an old design, remember. She holds only half an atmosphere in her exit chambers. It reduces structural strain over long periods of time."

As he was speaking, the hatch opened with a tiny puff from a residual pressure difference. Brodrick pulled his wife after him without comment.

The hatch closed after them and the air cycled away, giving them both plenty of time to test their suits and stop the process if anything was wrong.

Somack watched with all screens on as the two figures diminished into the distance. They approached the rock slowly, paused to make a few halfhearted pounding motions against an outcrop, then slid under and out of sight on the other side. So much for what I'm going to see from here, Somack thought, and began to suit himself up. He was just about to close his helmet when the ship buzzed at him. He turned around and stared as a stream of words flowed across the small command console.

ENERGY SOURCE XA663 COMMENCED OPERATION 16.17.23 THIS DATE. TARGET SOURCE BEARING 89.436°; 03.772°; RANGE I.602 KM.

Somack stood stock still. He was not surprised to find that the *Ambol* was equipped with a weapons system of some type; there were a few closed-off spaces he'd wondered about. But he was surprised that it should choose this moment to put them into operation. He watched cross hairs with a tiny grid appear on the screen, swing through two arcs, and come to rest on the midsection of the tumbling asteroid. XA663 must be a mining tool. But why would the ship consider it a threat?

AWAITING INSTRUCTION.

Somack ignored the comment. He was watching a lone figure approaching the ship. It was Brodrick, moving fast. The suited man scrambled into the ship's outer hatch as it opened for him. Air flooded into the small space and as the pressure equalized the ship's screens disappeared.

Brodrick's helmet was coming off as he stepped out. He was panting heavily from his exertion, and words came in broken gasps. "My wife . . . an accident . . . there's been an accident."

"What?" Somack shouted, pushing his way into the exit chamber. "Where is she?"

"Wait!" Brodrick panted. "She's got her leg caught in a crevice, wait until I can get a cutting tool." And with that he dashed out of the control room and down the hall.

In seconds he was back, running hard, with a small laser torch clutched in his hand. Somack motioned at his head and Brodrick slid to a stop. His helmet was gone and he finally realized that this was what Somack's frantic gestures were striving to convey. His hand went to his sweaty forehead, brushing back a tangle of hair. A slow smile spread across his face and the small torch in his hand flashed. The front of Somack's suit charred, blackened, and began to smoke. The hatch door snapped shut, cutting off the beam and isolating Somack in the small exit hatch.

Dumfounded, Somack looked at the smoking ruin of his breastplate and the pain finally came. He gasped explosively, and backed convulsively against the outer bulkhead, trying to get away from the burning heat of his suit front, but it followed right along with him. He rebounded, ripping at the charred fabric as he fell. Chunks of smoldering weave came away in his gloved hands, revealing hideously blackened flesh and one gleaming rib. A darkening tide of pain washed through him and he dimly heard a tooth splinter as his jaw tightened and he felt the taste of blood in his mouth. The wound itself refused to bleed. He lay on his back now, breathing as shallowly as he could, trying to keep the pain from knocking him out.

The intercom crackled and Brodrick's voice came through. "Hey in there. Answer me! I can hear you breathing."

Somack squeezed tears from his eyes, trying to focus on the intercom.

It crackled again. "You're going to tell me something, Somack, or you're going to die. It's as simple as that. I want to know, and I mean now, where and what *it* is. Some friends of mine are going to be along shortly and I'd hate to disappoint them. Spit it out before I deflate your little bubble of air in there." Brodrick's hand moved to the out-cycling switch in preparation.

Somack wriggled his helmet off, coughed once to get the blood out of his throat, and then held his breath against the wave of pain that followed.

"I can hear you," Brodrick repeated. "Why doesn't this hatch door open? I can't get in to help you."

Somack smiled weakly.

"You're being foolish," Brodrick said, reasonably. "Don't you know that you've been watched all your life—and the rest of your family too. You're the only one left. The only one who scraped and pinched away for enough money to buy this ship. So you must know. I'll give you thirty seconds. Tell me and we'll do our best for you."

"Anna?" Somack gasped. "What did you do with her?"

"She's in cold storage, you might say. Just in case you don't come through, we'll get the information from her. . . . Anna? So you do know her name. I thought so. You should never get chummy with a telepath. If you hadn't convinced her to keep quiet about what she learned last night, things might have worked out differently for you. But now you're going to die and she's going to have her pretty little brains scraped clean."

"Why?" Somack croaked. "Why?"

"You stubborn fool."

Brodrick punched the cycle button in disgust and heard the satisfying sound of the ship's pumps laboring to empty the tiny exit chamber where Somack lay of air. He realized too late that the control room—the room where he stood—was being emptied of air instead. He gasped for breath and his eyes bulged as he tried to hold that last breath against the growing pressure in his lungs. His eardrums burst audibly and his hands came up, but the air was already gone with a whistling sound.

The pumps stopped and Brodrick's dead body slumped to the deck. Air streamed back into the control room and the command console came to life.

HAVE TAKEN UNAUTHORIZED INITIATIVE. SERIES #1389-DF. CONTINUING PURSUANT COUNTERMAND. FILED FOR JUDGMENT.

With this said the ship spun to its left and spiraled around the cigar-shaped asteroid. Burning on the far side was a bright light, a XA663 to be exact. It hung in space about twenty yards from the asteroid and was tied down by a thin guy wire. Also bound to the wire was a violently struggling space suit. The ship closed on this wriggling body and despite efforts to the contrary by the body, managed to maneuver it into the open cargo hatch. The cargo hatch closed carefully, cutting through strands of wire in such a way as to free the suited figure.

Back in the control room the command console began flashing again. **awaiting instruction,** it said. And the ship ceased to act.

S omack was still alive. He realized that when he felt something tickle his face, and he opened his eyes. A long strand of black hair brushed his chin and two dark eyes looked into his.

CHAPTER 3. THE QUAKER

To some he was the Quaker; to others, simply Quaker. The origin of the name—like the rest of his life—was lost somewhere deep in the past. He knew and he remembered, but no one else did—not that it really mattered. When he spoke, men moved. They moved not so much out of fear, although it was a factor, but out of the habit of a lifetime. Recruited young, employment in his service was all they knew. He cared for them and they did for him. It was an arrangement that suited them all.

Today was special. The Quaker was actually on the bridge, an occurrence which was becoming rare with his advancing age. Of course, age is a relative thing and it would not be fair to compare the Quaker's with that of a normal man. With the advances in science most lived close to two centuries, but the Quaker was different. He himself measured age in multiples of the short span enjoyed by his companions, and surprisingly this longevity caused no resentment among the crew. They accepted it as they accepted everything about the Quaker. It was just another of the things that made him different—and not one of them, even the lowest, would have traded humanity for what he had. At times, times like the present, the Quaker almost enjoyed the life he lived. He was stirred in mind and body with an anticipation he seldom felt. His body, the giant quivering mass that it was, weighed on him less than it had in years.

Close by a voice spoke, breaking the long silence. "We've picked up the visual beacon, sir."

The Quaker nodded and allowed his officer to continue. He was content to sit and observe for the moment. He watched in silence as the great ship he had built maneuvered toward the tiny *Ambol*. The *Ambol's* image was magnified and projected on the screen for his benefit. He saw the scarred and pitted hull; the squat football shape and strange discolorations marking the little ship. The sight set him to rocking gently. Ridges and folds of flesh contracted around his eyes.

"Prepare all weapon systems," he said, smiling in his lopsided, ironic way.

"Yes, sir!" the duty officer responded, springing into action at this unexpected order. Within seconds the big ship was prepared to meet the combined attack of five other ships, comparable in size, and come away undamaged. The *Ambol* seemed a forlorn speck in space next to the giant it faced.

A message winged its way from the little ship and displayed itself on their screen: **this is *R. B. AMBOL*. what ship are you?**

The communications officer glanced at the brooding Quaker and receiving no instruction he sent the prearranged message: THIS SHIP IS EXPECTED, and then added, VISUAL COMMUNICATION REQUESTED.

There followed a long pause. The Quaker leaned back, joining his hands across the ample expanse of his mid-section. "Prepare the forward launch," he said quietly, closing his eyes.

Finally the screen flickered and the *Ambol's* reply came: **acknowledged.**

With that one word the visual channel opened between the two ships. Anna appeared, looking confused and not a little frightened. Her dark eyes were rimmed with red and smudges of dirt and grime covered would-be tracks across her cheeks. With one look at the Quaker her confusion and fear vanished, replaced by something else. The Quaker noticed and smiled gently at this change.

"Anna dear, where is Harold?" he asked, careful to keep any hint of reproach from his voice.

At the mention of Brodrick's first name her face twisted and she glared at him, almost defiantly. "He's dead," and she looked away from his calm regard, her momentary defiance gone.

"And the subject?" he asked gently.

"Dying!" and she was looking at him again, her eyes sharp with unspoken accusation. "He was hard. Harder than you thought. Brodrick wouldn't believe me and he died trying to kill"—and she choked on the words—"the subject."

"I see," the Quaker murmured sympathetically. And indeed he did see, more than he cared to. He knew all of his people in a personal way. Their lives and their thoughts; these were his constant worries from the moment he acquired them to the moment they died. The ones with talent were especially difficult, temperamental and unpredictable. It was a constant risk to employ them on the outside, and yet a necessary one. Anna was something special. The best and at the same time the worst of her kind. She could not only read a mind's surface in the ordinary sort of way, but she could make her subjects want her to—make them want to tell. She could go deeper and see more clearly than any he'd ever seen before. He could remember the trouble he'd gone to in recruiting her. The effort had required his personal attention and careful direction. Now, with one act of stupidity, all of that was in danger; about to be thrown away. It was just as well for Brodrick that he was dead.

"Shall I send help?" the Quaker asked carefully. The ice was thin and he was treading softly.

Anna looked away from the screen and back again, her mind torn between the necessity of getting medical help and the cost getting that help would be for Somack. She could trust the Quaker. She had to. He'd been the major influence in her life since the day her parents' deaths had orphaned her at the age of three. He was always there when she needed help and, more than that, he was the only father she'd ever known, the only adult who'd ever believed in or encouraged the strange power she carried inside. She had never questioned—never before. But now she stood, torn with indecision.

The Quaker remained quiet. He watched the emotions and arguments crossing the face on the screen as clearly as if they were being broadcast aloud. His long, long experience with people had made him as nearly a telepath as sharp eyes and a sympathetic nature could make a man. What his eyes told him this time was not good. Persuasion and simple trust were not going to be enough. He made a small motion with his hand and the duty officer issued hurried orders out of sight of the girl.

The *Ambol* stirred into sudden life. First it cut visual communication with the Quaker's ship, then brightened its own screens and console.

ARMED VESSEL, TYPE (9-B), SEPARATING FROM LARGER

VESSEL OF UNKNOWN TYPE. APPROACHING. YELLOW ZONE PENETRATION WITHIN TWENTY SECONDS.

Anna watched without comprehension as target co-ordinates, distances, and a welter of other data flashed at her. Grids and cross hairs appeared here and there on the screen and the ship continued to mumble to itself for several seconds. Finally it quieted.

AWAITING INSTRUCTION, it said.

Anna stepped back from the screen and looked at the battle display surrounding her. The walls were alive with stars, grids, and shifting colors, all of which meant nothing to her.

AWAITING INSTRUCTION, the console repeated, and if words flashed on a luminous screen could express impatience these certainly did. The words began to flash on and off, terrifying in their silent urgency.

"What is it?" she pleaded. "What's happening?"

INSTRUCTIONS GARBLED, PLEASE REPEAT.

"What?" she cried, clamping her hands over her ears against the rising wail of a siren deep in the ship. "What are you?" she begged.

GARBLED, it flashed, **GARBLED, GARBLED, GARBLED.**

The siren increased in volume and pitch.

"Stop it," she moaned and sank to the floor. "Please stop it and go away."

INSTRUCTIONS RECEIVED AND UNDERSTOOD, COMMENCING ACTION.

Incandescence filled the screen. Streaks of color flashed and subsided. A converging web of light and energy engulfed the launch which had been edging toward the *Ambol.* For a brief second the launch twisted and turned convulsively, then it was gone.

Anna covered her eyes. What had she done, oh God, what had she done?

FIRST INSTRUCTION COMPLETED. CONTINUING AS INSTRUCTED.

The words flashed into empty space, no one was looking. But the ship continued none the less.

The Quaker watched without a word or a change of expression as twenty of his men and a space launch vaporized into the hungry emptiness of space. He held up a hand and the men on the bridge stared at the gesture in disbelief. Only a lifetime of complete obedience kept them from pressing home the switches and controls which would have turned the giant ship into a killing machine of the highest magnitude.

They watched impotently as the *Ambol* twisted away, increased distance, and winked into high drive.

"Shall we follow?" one man asked, hardly able to keep his voice steady.

The question seemed to break into the Quaker's train of thought and he looked at the man for a few seconds and then blinked twice.

"Yes," he said, "we shall follow."

The *Ambol* moved away quickly. The stars on its screen were again falling into their familiar pattern, clumping more and more to the rear as the ship's speed increased. There was only one among the many objects clustering there which was not a star. It hung there, quietly reminding the *Ambol* that it could not stop.

Anna came to her feet slowly. Her gaze fell to Brodrick's body and beyond to Somack, still lying quietly in the small exit hatch. Her problems were just beginning. She'd already used half the medifoam aboard in her first hasty treatment of his gaping wound. When the rest was gone there would be nothing to keep it closed and free of infection.

She crossed the room and knelt. He was breathing easier now and the swelling and bleeding in his jaw gone. He would live. She was sure of it. If only he could stand the shock of the wound and her uncertain treatments. She reached out reluctantly and touched his forehead. It was hot, terribly hot, and her concern grew. She was no doctor. Her one talent, her one ability seemed so useless. All her life she'd used and developed it in the place of formal learning. There was always someone who knew, someone else's mind where she could look and find the answer. But not here and not now. There was only her and, for better or worse, what little she could do.

Somack stirred, moaned quietly, and opened his eyes. Seeing her he was reassured and lapsed back into unconsciousness with a slight smile on his lips. And she was smiling back, gratefully. For a while, at least, she would not be alone and her tears fell to the deck unnoticed. She leaned forward and kissed him lightly, very lightly, on the forehead.

Half an hour later, after much care and toil, Somack was asleep on the floor of his small room. She dared not lift him and the blanket she had sledded him on would have to remain as his only bed. Only when he was comfortably covered and settled did she take the time to dispose of Brodrick. His body lay in the control room airlock now, where it would have to remain until the ship cut the main drive. And the ship alone knew when that would be.

The *Ambol*, it seemed, was content to co-operate with her in small ways, opening doors and such, but it steadfastly refused to stop or do anything that would help her get in contact with the Quaker. The console remained lit with the one word, **CONTINUING.** It was still "going away." Still following her orders. There had to be a way she could stop it, somehow get the ship under control. Once again she went through each control on the small console, trying every position without success. Then, when she'd almost given up, she saw a small lump on the edge of the console. She hadn't noticed that before. In fact, she was sure it hadn't been there before. She'd checked too carefully for that.

She ran her fingers over the smooth protrusion. It was like a shell, a covering of some type. She poked at it and squeezed until finally it popped to one side revealing a small switch. Directly above the little switch a small plate glowed a warning at her. **MANUAL TRIGGER** it said; **DO NOT USE.**

Do not use? Why was it there if it wasn't supposed to be used? She considered the question. Would it cause the ship to self-destruct, or something like that? Or would it merely stop the main drive? There were any number of things it could do, but it hadn't been there before and that seemed to be the only clue to its function. Perhaps it was a safety device of some kind to give the pilot control if the ship went mad.

As if to confirm her suspicion the console began flashing rapid instructions at her: **DO NOT USE. DO NOT USE. EMERGENCY ONLY, WARNING, MANUAL TRIGGER. USE SUBJECT TO IXT INVESTIGATION. RESULT OF USE UNKNOWN. DANGER. DO NOT USE.**

Whatever it was, the ship certainly did not want it used. She moved her hand away and let the covering fall back into place. As rapidly as the agitation had come it died away and the console cleared of its profuse warnings.

It took her less than a second to remove the cover for a second time and depress that little switch. She did it so quickly that the ship's protest died in mid-line. For nearly a full minute nothing seemed to happen. Anna rose from the command chair, disappointed at yet another failure. Then, quite suddenly, the console lights flickered out. The screens died next, then lights and power throughout the ship. Every lock and port slid closed and locked into place. A thick oily brown gas jetted from the vents. Anna, frozen in mid-stride, held her breath. The gas swirled closer and touched her exposed skin. She choked at the contact and fell. She floated down toward the deck but never quite made it.

The main drive of the ship sputtered and wavered. A very special ripple of distortion moved out and away from the *Ambol*. Almost instantaneously that ripple reached and washed over the Quaker's ship. Had that ship been built strictly according to law (as it certainly was not) it would have been equipped to respond correctly to the signal it had just received from the *Ambol*. Instead it merely recorded the disturbance and reported it to the men in command.

Receiving no reply to its test pulse, the *Ambol's* encounter program now knew it was in contact with another ship which, although it was equipped with a recognizable drive, had no encounter program of its own. Then, and only then—after making sure—it took control of the ship. All power not going directly to the drive was cut. All internal compartments were sealed to give the ship a maximum probability of surviving its encounter. Any compartments containing life were filled with a gas which had seen its last commercial use back in the days before light-speed-plus drives. The gas would keep personnel in a safely suspended state of life.

With this taken care of the encounter program was free to consider the problem at hand. It was in contact with a ship which by its very nature must be classified as of the utmost danger. Instructions were explicit. *Ambol* must proceed at once to the closest IXT disposal point and do so without passing through any area of human habitation or frequent travel. Calculations began immediately.

The Quaker was patient. He had infinite patience. The prospect of following the *Ambol* for a year until it finally ran out of fuel did not impress him as difficult. It was simply a matter of time. But things were not going to be that easy. Present calculations showed the *Ambol* reaching populated areas long before it ran low on fuel. Areas where he and the ship under him could not follow. Somehow, its course would have to be interrupted.

There was only one way to influence the *Ambol's* course and that was to place another drive or a star (whichever was easier) directly in its path. A difficult task, since course changes could be made only when the ship involved was at a dead stop. At the moment the Quaker's ship was following the *Ambol* on a course as close to exactly parallel as the finest navigating computers could make it. If he came to a full stop and spent enough time to calculate an accurate intercept, the *Ambol* would be long gone. To avoid this, he came to a stop, dropped out of drive, set a second launch free, and got back on the *Ambol's* trail before it was gone. Using the launch like an extra length of leash, he could give his computers the time they needed.

Everything was set up for the delicate maneuver when the *Ambol* itself came to a stop and changed direction away from the populated lanes of its own accord.

The *Ambol* led a merry chase for several days. They were days which brought the *Ambol* closer, and finally to, the area it had been seeking. A tight cluster of stars lay directly ahead. The *Ambol* plunged into their midst and the other two ships followed, preparing themselves for yet another attempt to dislodge them. But this time as the *Ambol* came to a stop it did not change course, as it had so many times before. Instead it dropped out of drive altogether.

It was a move for which the Quaker was well prepared. Once before he'd been led a chase like this and it had ended in the same way, in an IXT trap. He had backed away that first time. Destruction of the IXT did not interest him, but this time they were going to get something he wanted. Something he wanted desperately. They would have to fight this time. And if they drove him away, he would get back what he wanted in another way. He could not be stopped. Not when he really wanted something.

There was nothing, nothing, which could withstand the power of the ship he now rode. It was handmade—by him. It had weapons. And they were weapons the greater part of the human race had never seen, nor faced before. Where had they come from? Well, the Quaker knew, and perhaps someday he would let someone else know, but not until there was no further need, not until the last alien creeping imitation of life had been cleansed. Until that day came they had a use.

Anna woke with a start. A bare light bulb stared down at her from a bare ceiling. Something gripped her arm with a hold like a vise. Croaking noises came to her ears and only gradually did they resolve themselves into words.

"Get up, deary."

She turned to the source of the voice and what she saw was straight horror. A face lashed with scars and a patch where one eye should be. There was hair hanging in irregular patches; a stringy remnant which strove unsuccessfully to cover the ravaged scalp and deformed ears. And below this, in unbelievable contrast, was the crisp clean color of a uniform with the unmistakable IXT insignia. Too late did Anna realize that her reaction to the face was all too clear. The grip on her arm increased in magnitude and the deep croaking voice harshened with impatience.

"Get up!" There was no longer a pretense that the order was a request.

She found herself standing, being propelled toward a cell door, all without any effort on her own behalf. The matron, a scowl hardly improving the condition of her face, held Anna by the right arm and was pushing her forward, through the door and down a long aisle. A single row of roof lights disappeared into a distant haze along the incredibly straight and featureless corridor. She could feel now, a strange mixture of hate and pity coming from her solidly built guard. Perhaps in the past she'd been attractive. Yes, Anna could see that now. And she could see the burning resentment directed at her, a resentment which only partially masked an underlying sympathy and pity for what she was about to face.

The matron stopped abruptly, with a jolt that painfully loosened Anna's shoulder. "In here," she commanded, thrusting Anna toward a panel which parted only just in time.

Inside there was a table, a chair, and an otherwise empty room. She was pressed into a chair and her hands were securely taped to the smooth metal of the table top. The matron, apparently finished, stepped back and stood directly behind her, settling into a position of parade rest.

Anna sat perfectly still facing a blank wall and wondering what would happen next. She didn't have to wait long. The wall in front of her slid up and away and she found herself looking into two hard slate-blue eyes. To say the man's face was grim would have been an understatement. He also wore the IXT markings on his collar and the rank of commander. The one word "Jennings" was posted in plastic above his right shirt pocket. Aside from these few items his uniform was bare, empty of the usual plethora of ribbons and badges. His face and uniform were not all that marked him as different. His right sleeve was empty, carefully folded and pinned at the shoulder. His left arm lay on the table between them and it wasn't until he lifted it and waved a small piece of paper in her face that she noticed the polished steel of its three prongs. They held the paper delicately so as not to crease or bend it.

"These are the charges being made against you, young lady," he said, and laid the paper down facing her. But the print was too fine and crowded to read. She looked at it briefly and then back at the commander without saying a word.

"Now," the commander said, and he picked up a writing tool, poising it over a tablet set into the table. "What is your real name?"

"Mrs. Helen Brodrick," she replied, smiling hesitantly.

"Your real name, please," the officer repeated without looking up. He scribbled something on his tablet. "You are under oath. Perjury will not be tolerated." And the way he said it, with absolutely no emotion, sent a chill down her spine.

"Anna Bey."

"Date of birth?" he droned.

"I don't know. I'm not sure."

The officer looked up and for the first time interest lit his eyes. He looked over Anna's head at the matron.

"Between sixteen and twenty," the matron supplied.

"Humm," the officer said to himself. "Do you consider yourself to be an adult?"

"Yes," she answered, trying for the first time to see what this was leading to. But the officer, unlike the matron, was not loosened at the moment by emotion.

"Good. Then we may proceed." He said this while adding yet another notation to his pad. "Did you or did you not kill a man known to you by the name of Harold Brodrick?"

"No."

"Thank you," the officer said, and a block of the fine print on the paper lying in front of her disappeared. "Did you assault and attempt to kill a man known to you by the name of William Somack?"

"No," she answered again, and another block of fine print disappeared.

"Did you or did you not activate a device, known to you only as a 'Manual Trigger/ without knowing the function or under what circumstances this device could be used?"

"Yes."

Jennings looked up from his tablet. For a long moment he stared at her. Then he was writing again and as he wrote the remaining fine print smoked and burned indelibly through the orange-tinted paper lying in front of her. Jennings finished writing and detached the tablet he had been using from the table. He removed a sheet of paper, the fourth one down, and pushed it at her. It was a printed form, marked in places with a well-controlled hand, and signed at the bottom. It read:

IXT (145-L6) RECORD OF CRIMINAL PROCEEDINGS
COPY: PRISONER'S
SUBJECT: ANNA BEY
AGE: ? ADULT
SEX: FEM
CHARGES:
I. DELETE
II. DELETE
III. GUILTY
SENTENCE: HARD LABOR
TERM (IF ANY): LIFE
REASON(s) FOR LENIENT SENTENCE (IF GIVEN):
MITIGATING CIRCUMSTANCES
SIGNED: *R.L. Jennings, Com.*
OFFICER OF THE COURT

"Keep these with you at all times," Jennings was saying as the matron picked up the two pieces of paper and pinned them neatly to the front of Anna's shapeless prisoner's blouse. "You will be questioned later concerning the circumstances of your capture and your use of the Manual Trigger."

As Jennings finished speaking, Anna noticed for the first time what she was wearing. The plain fabric and rough texture of it brought home to her the reality of it all. It was really happening. It was really happening. She was alive when she hadn't expected it. She wasn't in a brown foggy sea any more and the *Ambol* was gone. For the moment these unexpected facts overshadowed what lay in the future.

"Somack?" she asked. "He's alive. You said he's alive."

Jennings, in the act of reaching for a switch, stopped and looked again at the young girl he had just sentenced to a life of misery.

"Miss Bey," he said, "since you did not waste the Court's time with pleas of false innocence and injured rights, I will answer that question for you. Yes, Mr. Somack is alive and he will recover to normal health, something for which he can thank you, I suspect. You may even see him again when you are both delivered to our penal colony on Hollenglen." With that he ended, touching a switch, and the wall descended.

CHAPTER 4. THE IXT

From the *Cadet's Manual:*

The IXT is an organization unique to its time. Although some will compare it to the U.N. of days gone by, there is really very little resemblance, except perhaps in their origins. Both were born of wars which had nearly disastrous results for the human race. But the Hursk Encounter and the war of extermination which followed differed from any other in human history. The Hursk, in their sustained and nearly successful attempt to destroy the human race, managed to bring our scattered populations together and united us for a short time. When, after years of effort and war, the Hursk were finally overcome, the overriding reason for this unity (survival) disappeared with them. But this eventuality had been foreseen early in the conflict and provided for; an unusual example of foresight which has proven to be of lasting importance in human affairs. The bulk of this foresight is contained in a single document prepared during the darkest hours of that great conflict. In it are the guidelines under which the IXT still functions.

The original cover sheet for this document hangs today in the General Library of Man, located on Earth, and it reads:

TOP SECRET

Proceedings of the Select Committee on External Affairs
Concerning

THE HURSK ENCOUNTER
and Its Aftermath

Included Are Committee Recommendations
on Future Procedures for
Initial Contact

TOP SECRET

And resting beside this cover sheet is another from the censored report which was released to important public officials. The censored cover sheet differs in only one way from the original. The three bottom lines, starting with "Included Are . . have been blocked out in solid black. The intention was to make these lines completely unreadable, but somehow the overprinting for the last line had been made too short—missing the I in Initial and the tail-end *t* in Contact. These two letters and the intervening bar became a popular catch phrase and eventually the official designation of an organization which was supposed to remain wholly secret: The IXT.

As it is, the IXT remains two-thirds secret. Its public branch, Intelligence, is charged with overseeing and enforcing certain laws—all of them dealing with spaceship design, engines, ports of call, beacons, etc. It is Intelligence's unenviable job to work with the local authorities on each planet in an attempt to prevent unauthorized exploration; or *any* kind of exploration which could result in another encounter like the Hursk Encounter.

There remain, however, two other branches of the organization about which the public knows nothing. These are Enforcement and Justice. It is Enforcement's job to deal with any alien intelligence which might come sniffing around human space; to trade with these aliens if they are peaceful, or to destroy them if they are not. But, regardless of any other consideration, Enforcement is to keep aliens at an arm's length—and very secret —from the mass of the human population. This it has successfully done for many years now.

Justice has a much simpler task. All it has to do is deal with individuals who gain access to the secrets of the IXT or in any way attempt to contact aliens illegally.

Intelligence, Enforcement, and Justice are three branches on the same tree. The failure of one means the failure of all.

Commander Ralph Jennings was thinking of those words right now. They had been his first introduction to the structure he was devoting his life to and he realized how deceptively simple Justice's task was.

In the three long years Jennings had been with Justice, he'd never before had a case. They were so rare that it was considered something of a privilege to preside on one when they did show up. Some privilege. The trials were just a formality—something to convince the unfortunate prisoners they'd had their day in court. It made them accept their lives of labor and exile.

Suddenly tired, Jennings rolled and deposited his documents. His work was done. He produced a cigarette and began to tap it absently against the desk. There was something more to this case. He could feel it in his bones. He had only one arm and a mechanical hand at the end of it, but his instincts were still good. There was something about the girl—something that made him suspect that she could tell a lot about things the IXT wanted to know.

He lit his cigarette against a small plate in the wall and smiled ruefully. It was going to be a challenge questioning this one. Something he would enjoy doing. Just as he was sinking into these pleasant thoughts there was a tap on his door and a worried face poked in at him.

"Ralph, we've got problems. The admiral wants to see you in K Section Conference immediately."

Merrick's face was gone before Jennings could answer. He winced at the thought of having to face Admiral Keel this early in the day. The admiral was a notorious abstainer; couldn't stand the faintest hint of tobacco, and Jennings disposed of his. He could sympathize. The admiral's lungs just weren't the same after that brush with Elfine gas.

It was funny how every alien caught in the IXT's trap had a different way of fighting. Some of the weapons they'd learned about were quite intriguing. It was unfortunate that the lessons were so often painful. Everyone in Justice knew how painful they could be. It was the only way you could qualify for the job.

Hurrying, he caught Merrick halfway down the corridor and slowed to keep pace with the other's slight limp. K Section Conference was the map room. Exactly what Justice had to do with containment and tracking was something Jennings would like to see. The admiral was already there, waiting next to the central sphere with two bedraggled-looking aides from Enforcement.

Admiral Keel looked up as Jennings and Merrick approached and mumbled a quick introduction of the two men with him. "They are with Enforcement," he continued, stating the obvious since both men were wearing the distinctive black and silver of that branch. "They have a problem which they want us to solve for them."

Admiral Keel paused for breath and the elder of the two Enforcement men took advantage of the moment to speak.

"As we were telling Admiral Keel, we had two Initial Contacts yesterday. Both ships were following closely the contact vessel, *Ambol*. The *Ambol* was no problem. We simply picked it up and brought it in after it dropped out of high drive. The other two were another matter however. They made no attempt to communicate when they dropped out of drive and seemed intent on only one thing—getting a hold on the *Ambol*, We classified them as hostile immediately and activated a ring of drones, just in case they got back into drive and tried to get away. Then we initiated our standard capture procedures. The two unknown ships continued to ignore us completely. They went straight for the *Ambol* and the tow we had on her. Here, let me show you what happened."

For a moment he stopped talking while the other Enforcement man activated the central map sphere. The sphere stood nearly eight feet high and its crystal interior was lit now with a tight cluster of star pips. A small green dot appeared at the top of the sphere moving slowly toward the center. "That," the man continued, "is the *Ambol*, coming into the map field." Jennings followed the action on the screen closely. Two red dots appeared. They were the two alien ships and it was clear that they were following the *Ambol;* paralleling its course and staying a short distance behind. The group penetrated into the cluster of stars and approached the center of the map sphere.

Everything was going just as it should. The *Ambol* was leading the other two into a trap, just as any other human-built ship would have done. Its Encounter Program was functioning perfectly.

Jennings watched as each ship in turn cut drive and dropped from the star map. The scale of the map sphere adjusted instantly to compensate for the change. The stars streamed outward, disappearing from the screen and ship dots returned. Now each dot represented the mass of the ship instead of a functioning drive. The *Ambol* and the small tow which had already hooked onto it were small green dots, an evidence of small mass. One of the aliens was also small, but its companion ship appeared as a bloated red ball on the screen. The mass of a battleship at least.

Jennings swallowed hard. His mouth dried as he watched. From every direction blue dots entered the field and converged on the strange ships. They were Enforcement ships, waiting on station for months or years at a time for a moment just like this. It was their job to see that none of the intruding ships escaped intact. They were to capture if possible and destroy if necessary.

Incredibly the target ships made no effort to escape. Instead they continued to close on the *Ambol*, grappling it and trying to pull it away from the Enforcement tow already holding it down. The encircling Enforcement ships drew closer and threw constraining webs of energy around both of the alien ships.

The reaction was immediate. The smaller of the two alien ships suddenly broke from its entanglements and disappeared into the bulk of the larger ship. And, in turn, the larger ship snapped its bonds with an ease that was frightening. The pair, now a single mass, turned their attention back to the *Ambol*, attempting and almost succeeding in pulling it from the grasp of a tug and five other Enforcement ships.

The struggle continued for a second and all the Enforcement ships not engaged in holding the *Ambol* began to rake the alien ship with hellfire and damnation. Nothing happened. The huge red mass simply ignored the destructive energy being flung at it by a score or more ships its mass and larger. Then it seemed to give way, breaking off its struggle for the *Ambol* and jumping into drive.

There was an audible sigh around the room and Jennings noticed that even the Enforcement men—already knowing the outcome of the fight —were just as relieved as he was. The alien ship had done the impossible and Jennings licked his lips.

His eyes returned to the map projection and he watched as the scale shifted again and the stars reappeared. This time the stars were not alone. Twelve orange lights fitted in a perfect pattern around the lone alien-red glow. The orange lights were drones—drives fitted for only one purpose and that was to seek and destroy the alien drive they surrounded. The single red dot hesitated for a second as if contemplating the impossibility of escape, then it began to move outward toward the ring of drones.

For some time the drones remained motionless. They were busy calculating the alien's acceleration and the point of interception, using their own much greater acceleration. Within a few seconds all of the drones began to close on the doomed ship. Then, quite unexpectedly, the drones stopped. The alien ship proceeded to leave the field of the star map, unmolested by the lifeless drones.

"Impossible," Admiral Keel blurted. "There is no way that ship could have affected our drones like that."

"Well, Admiral," the Enforcement officer explained, "it didn't actually affect the drones. All it did was change its acceleration. The drones naturally stopped to recalculate an intercept point, which they were unable to do."

"Ship's drives can't change acceleration," the admiral said heavily. "Every drive has only one acceleration. It's either on or off—accelerating, decelerating, or coasting. Otherwise the drones couldn't calculate an intercept point in the first place."

"That's true," the Enforcement officer conceded, "for *our* drives. But not for the one you just saw. It's a ship with something—hell, a lot of things —that we can't match."

The officer paused to activate a large screen against the far wall. "That, gentlemen, is the *Mischenford.*" The words fell into an empty silence as the five men viewed the wreckage.

"It was the largest of our vessels engaged," the officer continued. "There were no survivors. But perhaps more important is the fact that not one of our other ships received the slightest damage. It was only when the *Mischenford*'s fire began to near-miss the *Ambol,* that it came under attack and its communications ceased. The *Ambol* or the personnel aboard her were apparently the Quaker's only interest."

A hush fell in the room at the mention of that name. It was almost a superstition—a myth that kept cropping up every fifty or sixty years. Always skirting the edges of civilization, ships and activities always involving destruction and death. The Quaker was a name, but behind it lay an organization of which the IXT knew little, except to fear. The organization was suspected of smuggling, of trading in forbidden alien commodities. But nothing could be proved, nothing could be found out, because the organization did not work for profit. It did not work for anything that could be clearly seen. It was this shadow motivation that more than anything fermented dread of contact and fear of too much discovery. Men died when they came too close. The IXT had gotten close in the past and they had lost men.

"Are you sure?" the admiral asked, his voice shaken. So many years.

He'd always hoped that time would somehow erase or remove the problem. "I almost wish it were some new and powerfully dangerous alien race. It would be something we could deal with then."

The Enforcement officer shook his head. "We've analyzed the tapes. The drives on those ships were hybrid. Part human, part something else. The dead man aboard the *Ambol*, Brodrick, has been suspected of connections like this. There's too much evidence that points to the Quaker."

A light came into the admiral's eyes. "The Quaker. And he wanted the *Ambol*. He wanted it badly enough to show himself after so many years. I think we've got something—something we'd better hold on to."

Jennings could see the implications, the sudden importance of *his* job. "The ship—and its cargo. Have you checked it?"

The Enforcement man nodded. "Nothing," he said. "It's got to be the passengers."

Admiral Keel stroked his chin. It wasn't often Enforcement had to ask favors from Justice and he was wondering how he could best take advantage of the situation. There were so many things Justice needed; more room, a better medical staff, and most of all more record-keeping time and memory on the IXT base's huge computer network.

"We'll do everything we can to co-operate," he said finally. "Commander Jennings here will begin the interrogation of his young prisoner immediately; and Captain Merrick, since his man Somack hasn't yet recovered, can begin a record search. I want to know every thing there is to know about the three passengers of the *Ambol*

Turning to the Enforcement officer, the admiral said, "Have you contacted Intelligence? We could use their help."

The room was silent for a moment. Everyone knew how delicate the question was. Intelligence, the public branch of the IXT, was shaky. There were more and more reports of agents resigning and worse yet, there were suspicions that some who had lost their dedication to the IXT had *not* resigned. Recruitment was falling off and there were signs that the Freedom League and all it stood for was gaining not only popular support but support from within the IXT itself. The League and its movement to reopen the frontiers of space was something the founders of the IXT had not foreseen and the organization was having trouble coping with the problem.

"Come now!" the admiral snapped. "Rumors are rumors and nothing more. Intelligence keeps all of the shipping and construction records and if we're going to get anywhere in backtracking the *Ambol* and her crew we are going to need their help."

The Enforcement man was shaking his head. The situation was too dangerous to let unreliable people into it. Combat was a constant reminder of the alien danger out there and Enforcement personnel needed no further convincing. They would do their duty and the public could go jump. Justice was even safer. In order to join its sparse ranks you had to be physicked out of Enforcement. Blown out would be a better word, and people who had lost a part of themselves didn't need much convincing that aliens could be nasty.

"It's your decision, Admiral," the man said finally. "I'm only here to coordinate your efforts with Enforcement. If you have to contact Intelligence, then you have to. We just want to see that the job gets done and done quickly."

"Very well," Admiral Keel said. "Let's stop talking and get to work."

The IXT Complex where Anna, Somack, and the *Ambol* were taken after their capture was close to one of the stars in the "Trap Cluster," as that close-bunched group was known. The Complex itself was a flying city; in its half-completed state it looked sort of like a cigar jammed with disastrous consequences into a good-sized rock. The rock part was just that—a rock, or rather, what was left of one. As for the cigar, that was the completed portion of the Complex. In between were the sections still under construction. It was in this area that asteroidal material was being converted into living space at a rate of two thousand tons per day, or about an extra six inches of cigar per week.

The Complex was no mean feat. For three hundred years (since the Hursk War) it had been growing at just about the same rate and was now well over a mile in length and a quarter mile across. If you looked closely, you could see the rings of age. No matter how hard the engineers tried they just couldn't make each bit of added length the same exact shade as the previous length. There were different impurities in each portion of rock they processed and that, coupled with advancing techniques, gave the Complex its rings. And they, in turn, were the Complex's only truly permanent color scheme. Everything else faded with time.

In the early days, when only the blunt-ended butt of the cigar existed and space inside the Complex was limited, all three departments of the

IXT had lived side by side; their offices mingled with each other in a helter-skelter jumble. Now things were more orderly. Each department occupied a separate wedge of the Complex and enjoyed more or less complete privacy from the other departments.

Justice, naturally, occupied the smallest of the three wedges and Enforcement the largest. This had once been a matter of some complaint but there was no arguing against the fact that Enforcement did indeed bear the greatest burden and had the majority of the personnel. It also had the ships and needed as much of the docking space at the butt end as it could get.

An example of Enforcement's problems was the present situation. All of its facilities were tied up with ships returning from the recent encounter, while Intelligence's docks were going completely unused and Justice had only one ship engaged: an old converted liner named *Matilda*, delivering much needed paper and microfilm stocks and taking on a load of documents for the archives back on Earth.

The *Ambol*, one of the many ships docked in the Enforcement area, was the target of considerable attention. Among the men looking her over was Captain James Merrick from Justice. It had cost him a few signed-off debts and considerable effort to get the co-operation he wanted, but he was finding the effort well spent. In fact, what he was learning aboard and about the *Ambol* would set into motion a series of events quite beyond what he could imagine at the moment. Had he known, he might have acted differently.

Merrick left the *Ambol* in high excitement. He had discovered something very interesting. There were indications that the *Ambol's* Encounter Program installation was of a younger, newer design than the ship itself. The system could have been updated in any number of places, but Merrick had an idea that the IXT had been responsible. It was possible that the *Ambol* had been involved in some other encounter at some time in the past.

There was one place he could check his hunch and Merrick made his way as quickly as possible to Intelligence's Datalibracom. He seated himself at one of the DLC's many consoles and thumbed the index scanner. It was some time before he found the file number he wanted; Previous Encounters —Disposition of Misc. Materials; flb #8483. Merrick punched in the code number and waited. A little light began to flash on his console and it sent a chill down his spine.

FILE IN USE, the light flashed, **NO DUP AVAILABLE...FILE IN USE...NO DUP—**

Merrick slapped his input demand off, but it was already too late. Whoever was using the file would already have seen the demand indicator on his console. Merrick punched in another file number at random and began to read up on spare parts orders for food-vac dispensers. His eyes wandered from the text occasionally as he tried to determine which, if any, of the people in the room had been after the same file he'd wanted. There were other console centers but it was possible the man he wanted was in the same room with him.

Who could have gotten ahead of him? Could Intelligence be conducting their own parallel investigation? He doubted it and if he was right, some unauthorized person was ahead of him.

He waited a quarter of an hour before shutting down his console and leaving. He made his way back into Justice territory as quickly as possible without appearing to be in a hurry. His precautions might be wasted effort. The coincidence could have been innocent. Could have been.

Merrick quickened his pace. There was another way he could check that file without using Intelligence's computer. Justice records were not as accessible, but they provided a check on the Intelligence files.

"I'm sorry, sir," the clerk said, "but our files only go back fifty years now. We've been shipping all the old ones back to the Archives. They take up too much space. Why don't you check the Datalibracom? They should have the information you're looking for."

"That's what I plan to do," Merrick said. "How long ago did you say these records were removed?"

"I didn't say," the clerk corrected. "It's strange that you should ask, though. The records were loaded aboard a freighter two days ago, along with a lot of other junk. It's the *Matilda,* I think—still docked as far as I know."

"Thanks," Merrick called over his shoulder as he left.

"I'm sorry, sir.

Merrick frowned. The sentence was becoming familiar. This time it was a guard at the dock. The guard was wearing an Intelligence uniform with a single private's stripe adorning each shoulder.

"What do you mean," Merrick snapped. "Let me by. I'm going aboard."

"I'm sorry, sir, but that's against orders."

"Whose orders," Merrick demanded.

"Standing orders," the private replied, unshaken. "Only Intelligence personnel allowed aboard civilian vessels, sir."

Merrick looked at the private's blank face and the hand resting on a late model needle-nose. He wasn't going to get anywhere with this man, not without some help. And it was beginning to look like he might not find that help. Not in time, anyway.

Two very long days later Captain Merrick sat at a small table in the rec room. He had discovered a good deal about the *Ambol* and the man Somack in that time, but at the moment his only interest was in warning his friend Jennings about the girl he was questioning and about something else—something that was going on at the Complex that shouldn't be. It was a warning he had to pass on without saying anything —without letting anyone else understand it was a message.

Merrick was so tired from his work of the past two days that he took advantage of the moments before his meeting to catch some rest. His head lay on folded forearms and a slight snoring noise came from his partially open mouth.

"Your coffee, sir," the waitress murmured, smiling maternally.

Merrick's head shot up. He smiled wearily at the familiar curves of the retreating figure. He shook his head. There were more pressing things to think about so he gripped the steaming cup with both hands and took a deep whiff. That woke him enough to feel dead tired instead of groggy. Even his right leg below the knee—the part he'd lost—was aching, and that was a sign of fatigue he seldom ignored. But he had to stay awake for just a few hours longer. He sipped at the coffee, burning his lips and the tip of his tongue in the process. This, plus a loud laugh from behind, brought him back to life.

"Did you really call me here for a game of chess?" Jennings asked, still laughing. "It looks like you're more in need of sleep than a game of skill."

Merrick grinned weakly, fumbled with the pieces his unscheduled sleep had disrupted.

"There are things about this whole business," Merrick muttered, opening the play with a king's knight to rook three. "Things that are bothering me."

"I see," Jennings said, still smiling. He was looking hard at his friend's first move. It stirred old memories. Memories of a time when both of them had been whole, young, and eager to learn. He could still see their Professor, Captain H. B. Dick, giving the pair sour looks and wondering how they "survived" situations that no one else could. The class had been Message Delivery Systems and the two of them had emerged as the top team. But neither of them had gone further in Intelligence work. They had both opted for the excitement of Enforcement instead and Merrick's use of one of the old tricks was puzzling. King's knight to rook three meant "contact under observation" in one of their private little codes—they were being watched.

"Isn't that opening a little wild?" he asked, wanting to confirm his suspicion.

"No," Merrick answered seriously, "Appropriate would be a better word."

Jennings looked at his friend's bloodshot eyes and the rings of fatigue beneath. No, he wasn't playing this game for the fun of it.

"O.K.," Jennings answered. He would watch and listen if that was what Merrick wanted him to do.

"How is your interrogation going?" Merrick asked with a casual wave of his hand.

"Fairly well, considering," Jennings answered. He was watching the play carefully. "She's not co-operating, but then we are still taking it easy right now."

Merrick grinned and moved a pawn to king's knight three.

Take special care the move said. Jennings frowned. Did that mean that the girl was more than she appeared? How would Merrick know that if he was working on the *Ambol* and Somack end of this thing?

"Keep playing like this," he commented lightly, glancing around the near empty room, "and you may lose the game."

"Better be careful yourself," Merrick returned with a good-humored contempt for his friend's playing ability. And as he spoke he castled his king on the queen side.

Friends are enemies. The game was getting suddenly serious and Jennings found it difficult to maintain an expression of cheer. Just what was Merrick driving at? Was there someone within the IXT working to destroy their leads on the Quaker, or was it something else?

"Has Intelligence been giving you trouble?" Jennings probed, and Merrick answered with a rook move. *Yes.*

Aloud Merrick said, "No. They've been co-operating better than usual."

There *was* something rotten in Intelligence then.

"Has good old Admiral Keel been breathing down your neck too?" Jennings probed, and Merrick answered with a bishop move. *No.* The admiral wasn't involved.

"I was just going in to see him," Merrick said, and Jennings could feel the tension in the words. He was giving Jennings this warning in case something went wrong, in case he wasn't able to contact the admiral, or any one else, in the next few hours. He might die trying, or he might be wrong about his suspicions and nothing at all would happen.

The two men finished the game in silence. Merrick left and Jennings sat for a moment thinking. There had been so few words said and yet now he was warned. He would go through the rest of the day alert. And if nothing happened *he* would take action. He would find out what was happening and what Merrick was into.

———

The interrogation room where Jennings presided was larger than the trial room. There was one table located at the center, and a chair was provided for the subject of the interrogation. Any other furniture present was of a merely transient nature, to be changed with changing circumstances. The ceiling and walls were provided with an extensive lighting system. Illumination in the room also varied with circumstances.

At the moment the lighting was normal, with just the overhead fluorescent grid on, giving the room a clean hospital look. The subject was already present and seated, as were the two duty interrogators: An officer named Black from Enforcement and a female officer from Intelligence. It was the Intelligence officer's first morning on the job and she was doing most of the questioning at the moment.

A matron stood a short distance behind the subject. It was the same matron who had accompanied Anna to her trial and there was a faint frown showing on her scarred face. She was displaying an uneasiness which came from being the only representative of Justice present at the moment. The Intelligence officer was especially hard for the matron to take. The furtive glances by that young lady at the scars on her face and the veiled expressions of disgust were far worse than Black's averted eyes and pretended indifference. If anything, the matron's sympathies lay with the prisoner. How little that poor creature knew of what she would face if co-operation didn't come voluntarily. There were ways of questioning, and the matron had seen some who had never recovered from them.

Commander Jennings entered the room late, as was his usual fashion. The moment he stepped into the room the whole atmosphere changed. The matron relaxed and the prisoner looked up from the floor she seemed to find so fascinating.

The Enforcement and Intelligence officers discontinued their questioning and looked around. "Late again," was Black's dry comment.

But Jennings wasn't even aware that Black had spoken. His whole attention was focused on the Intelligence officer; a mature and good-looking woman whose light blue uniform did nothing to detract from the over-all effect of her presence.

"What, may I ask, is Intelligence doing here?" he asked, and it came out as more of a snarl than a question.

Black was smiling now as he watched the two old friends stare at each other. "I take it," he said, "that you two already know one another."

"Commander Jennings and I have met," the blonde said with an unreadable smile. Then, as she spoke to Jennings, she was all business again. "I was instructed to sit in on this session as the deciding vote."

"Deciding vote on what?" Jennings growled.

This retort evoked raised eyebrows. "Come now. Surely you know that Black has been pressing for more drastic measures on this interrogation. He says you're going by the book, wasting time that we can ill afford to lose."

"That's the first time I've heard anyone complain about me going by the book. If Black or his Enforcement superiors have complaints they should have been made to me first."

Black coughed. "Captain Stevens is here at Enforcement request. As an expert."

"She's that," Jennings snapped, "and I'll be filing objections to this procedure."

"All that as it may be," Stevens interrupted, "I am here now, none the less. You may proceed with the questioning and I will inform you when I have made my decision."

Jennings closed his mouth and swallowed hard. There couldn't have been a worse time for this to happen. When he needed to think straight, when everything depended on him doing just that, she had to show up. Three years was a long time and he could see that Margy was over it, probably had been for a long time. That was easy to explain, since he wasn't the man he used to be. But she hadn't changed that much and he had a hard time not noticing the fine lines of her face, and the way she sat turned toward him like that. He tore his eyes away and looked instead at the prisoner.

It was then, in that one glance, that he caught his prisoner looking at him. She looked down again immediately, but there was no mistaking the expression on her face. Sympathy! She felt sorry for him! The steel prongs on Jennings' hand clenched convulsively and he took one quick step forward. But then his blind rage drained away and he stood quite still. He watched the girl, puzzled. Had her shoulders cringed just as he was about to strike? And then, as he regained control again, had they relaxed? Yes, he was sure of it.

She looked up at him and he could see the fear in her at the realization in his mind.

"Is something wrong?" Black asked.

"No," Jennings answered, taking his seat hurriedly. "Why don't you continue where you left off."

The room and the drone of Black's voice asking questions, even Margy's disturbing presence, faded from his mind. He had an answer, or at least a partial answer to this girl's importance. There were telepaths, everyone knew that—but so rare, so terribly rare. How had Merrick known about it —or had he? Was there something else to make her important?

"That's enough, Black," Margy Stevens ordered. She was senior officer present, and despite belonging to Intelligence and being out of place, her voice sounded with authority.

Jennings looked up at the sound of command and he studied the badges of rank on his fellow officer's shoulders. She had risen three full ranks in only three years. It was a feat possible only in Intelligence. He stood alone now; outranked, outnumbered, and about to be outmaneuvered if he didn't do something fast.

"Is there something wrong, Captain Stevens?" he asked evenly.

"This questioning is useless," she answered, frowning slightly. "The prisoner doesn't even answer the questions, and you," she added, "aren't even paying attention."

Jennings smiled as calmly as he could. "I'm sure that you're as much aware of the theories as I am, Captain. I'm not the one who matters here. As long as the prisoner hears and thinks about the questions over the specified three-day period we are accomplishing something. Any shortening of this period might result in damage to the prisoner during the forced extraction, if that process should become necessary."

The captain colored at this unexpected comeback. "Don't preach theories to me, Commander," she said, with special emphasis on the last word. "I've helped to develop some of them."

"I'm sure you did." He was surprised at the ease with which he could say something like that to Margy and make it come out sounding the way it did. There must have been some trace left, somewhere deep inside, because she looked at him now and he could tell that last line had hurt, especially coming from him. But there was no turning back now. He had plunged the dagger in and was about to give it a twist when Black interrupted.

"I don't think you realize what you're saying, Jennings. Captain Stevens and I have been instructed to terminate this interrogation today if nothing is forthcoming—not speed it up."

"What?" Jennings could scarcely hide his disbelief.

"That's right, Commander," Black continued. "There are other ways in which we can make use of our subject here. She or something she knows is going to give us the key we want to our friend out there, the Quaker. If she won't talk today, she can be scraped for what she knows. There are better ways to make use of her body than letting it sit around here doing nothing. We've got to move quickly on this thing."

"She'll not be scraped ahead of schedule—not while she's still under Justice's jurisdiction," Jennings insisted.

Black looked up at the ceiling as if appealing to some higher power, then shrugged. "There isn't that much time left for argument. Your admiral Keel is meeting with Admirals Dillon and Brynt right now in A Section. They've personally instructed Captain Stevens to bring the prisoner there if she thinks the questioning isn't going well enough here."

"Is that right?" Jennings asked, and Margy looked at him with a hardened expression.

"That' s right," she answered with a tone of finality.

"Very well," Jennings said, acquiescing unexpectedly, "let's go."

He was on his feet before either of them could make a response, gesturing for the matron to follow with the prisoner.

"But . . ." Black started, but the rest of his protest died unspoken. Jennings had already left the room. Black and Miss Stevens followed quickly. So long as they were in Justice, no matter what ranks were involved, Jennings was in technical command. He might regret his impertinence later, but right now he could give the orders.

It was a long walk to A Section and Jennings set a fast pace. The strange procession marched past door after door and drew the curious attention of all as they passed. Much of this, of course, was focused on Captain Stevens and the seldom-seen blue of Intelligence; although there were many who were not all that interested in the uniform so much as what lay beneath it.

Jennings was grinning just a little bit. It was like walking through a strange zoo, for Justice was a fine collection of survivors; only here they were the normal ones and Margy was the attraction. Her cheeks burned at the concentrated attention. Perhaps he should have gone the right way, through the prison warrens. Perhaps he was throwing his two fellow officers off balance for no purpose. But he thought not. He was calling their bluff and he expected A Section to be as empty of admirals as it should be. A loading dock conference room just wasn't a place admirals usually met to discuss matters of this importance.

The A Section executive conference room door was closed. Jennings burst through without knocking. The still life he caught in that brief second of surprise was something he would never forget.

There were three admirals seated around the conference table. Two, the Enforcement and Intelligence men, were seated facing the opposite wall; facing the door from the prison section and the door he should have been entering by. Facing him, with a startled expression on his face was a man dressed in a uniform closely resembling Admiral Keel's. This man was facing Jennings and had his back to the door through which Jennings should have come. In addition to the seated men, there were two burly types dressed in Intelligence blue standing by that door he should have come through.

For a startled second Jennings stared at them and they stared right back at him, surprise and then anger crossing their faces. Then Jennings acted. It was quickly, with a trapped animal ferocity.

Two quick steps and he planted his right foot in the small of the phony Intelligence admiral's back and felt it give. The Enforcement admiral's head turned toward him. The man's mouth was open, shouting something, as his hand was reaching for a sidearm. Jennings swung hard sideways and the face dissolved under the impact of his metal, clawlike fist. He never did hear what that man had been trying to say.

Sound exploded everywhere at once. The two men against the opposite wall surged toward him. Since they were apparently unarmed, Jennings ignored them. Instead, he reached across the table and gripped "Admiral Keel's" uniform and tie, pulling it toward him. The uniform gave way, but the tie held together and the phony admiral followed it, choking for breath.

That was the last thing Jennings remembered clearly, because something hard hit him in the back of the head. He staggered and fell, scarring the table permanently as his hand clenched and scraped on it as he slid down. So, there had been men waiting at both doors, he thought vaguely just before hitting the floor. He could see one of them bending over him and grinning, holding something dark and rubbery-looking in his hand. Jennings willed his mechanical hand to move and erase that smile, but it wouldn't.

Quite unexpectedly the man's grin faded anyway. He stiffened, then toppled to one side. With his view no longer obstructed, Jennings could see the door through which he had come only seconds before. Standing in that entrance, like a troll at the mouth of a cave, was matron MacGee. She held Anna's arm in one hand and a tranquilizer gun in the other. Unfortunately, the tranquilizer gun had only two charges and MacGee used its second one on her prisoner—as regulations dictated. Anna slipped to the floor, into a little heap which was promptly ignored.

A man charged forward, apparently with the intent of engaging the matron in hand-to-hand combat. She brought down her meaty fist on the man's head, shattering the empty tranquilizer gun with the impact. Something else shattered also and the man sank away with a sickening groan.

The two remaining men hesitated, looking at each other uncertainly. MacGee stepped toward them, grinning widely. But then she staggered, clutching at her side.

The half choked man, his neck bent at an odd angle, lay sprawled on the table where Jennings had dropped him, but in his hand he held a deadly needle-nose laser. He fired at the falling, staggering matron four more times. Only when she finally hit the ground did he turn the gun on Jennings. But then, with a crooked smile, he changed his mind.

With that decision not to fire a certain order returned.

"Miller!" the man on the table called, "get those doors closed and stand outside. The prisoner tried to escape if anyone asks."

"Yes, sir, Mr. Devlon," the man called back.

"Debbs," the man on the table continued, "get this place cleaned up. And I mean clean!" He groaned and shifted position slightly, bringing his weapon to bear on Black and Margy Stevens.

"What happened?" Black muttered, looking around the room. "How did he know? Why did he react so quickly?" Then Black looked up and saw that he was on the business end of a needle-nose. His mouth snapped shut.

"Those are just the questions I was going to ask you two," the man on the table said, giving them the same crooked grin he'd given Jennings. "I thought everything was perfectly planned. There were going to be no problems."

No answers were immediately forthcoming. Black simply stared without comprehension while Margy Stevens reacted with a flash of indignation.

"What do you think you are doing, Devlon?" she snapped, her eyes burning.

"Using caution, my dear, simple caution," the man replied. "At least one of you cannot be trusted. Jennings came in here expecting something."

Margy sputtered, but before she could find the right words two men burst into the room through its third set of doors—the doors leading directly to the docking area.

"What happened?" they asked in unison. They were both wearing civilian clothing and they looked to Devlon for direction.

"Never mind what happened," Devlon groaned. "Get those document crates in here. Get these people and everything else in here loaded aboard the *Matilda* before anything else goes wrong."

Within a few minutes the battered freighter *Matilda* backed away from its berth a few hundred feet from the A Section of Justice's part of the huge IXT Complex. In seconds it was in drive and gone, but its departure did not go unnoticed. Nor was the IXT as incompetent as it might appear. It was aware of the *Matilda's* new cargo and had made preparations. A number of alterations had been made on the *Matilda's* detection system. The ship would continue to function normally except for one small detail; she could no longer see a certain IXT variety of drive. This alteration in the *Matilda's* detection system made her very easy to follow and an IXT Enforcement ship was doing that very thing.

Merrick was among those who watched the departure of the *Matilda* and her shadowing IXT ship. He was puzzled by the necessity of giving up so important a prisoner and the sacrifice of his friend Jennings.

"Why?" he asked. "Why did we do it?"

Admiral Keel answered as best he could. "We did it to clean ourselves out. The Freedom League has been converting our Intelligence personnel faster than we like to admit. This way we not only exposed a lot of these people, but we've made the Freedom League do something it will regret. Devlon's through as their leader—a dead man. And the girl—she may still lead us to the Quaker—a lot quicker this way than if she were our prisoner. They've killed IXT personnel now—we can deal with those Freedom Leaguers any way we want to now, and be perfectly legal."

Merrick shook his head. It had only taken the sacrifice of his one real friend.

CHAPTER 5. MAN WITH A
CROOKED SMILE

The room was dark and smelled of recycled air. When Anna opened her eyes there was nothing to see but she could feel and hear the throb and low rumble of the ship's drive. She could feel herself surrounded by soft and comfortable fabric. It was a sharp contrast to her last memories of IXT prison walls and hard cots. As she lay awake even more recent memories returned; those of confusion and violence, death and dying. She shivered and seeing it all again pulled the blankets tighter. It was better just to lie quietly and sleep again.

This was not allowed however. A crackle sounded from above, followed by a sweet feminine voice. It spoke soothingly, "Good morning, Miss Bey. We hope you have enjoyed a relaxing sleep. Mr. Devlon sends you his compliments and requests your presence for luncheon in the captain's quarters. You will find a wide variety of clothing from which to choose. Please make your any wish known to me and the need will be filled. You will find my sensors located at convenient intervals throughout the ship. Please feel free to make use of them at any time. Thank you for your co-operation and kind attention."

Lights came on in the room and Anna was stirred into reluctant activity. There was indeed an extravagant collection of apparel from which to choose. It ranged from the wildest flights of the most recent and not-so-recent fancy to modest and almost puritan dress. She stood and marveled. Here was freedom again, even if only in such a small thing, and for a time helplessness and worry were forgotten.

She chose a modest, peasant-like dress. It felt so soft and close she smiled with pleasure. Its fabric flowed down and fell almost to the floor with a luxurious fullness. For her feet she chose warm and snugly fitted slippers. The cold steel deck could not penetrate them and she stood combing her hair and thinking.

Perhaps she was prone to sentiment and perhaps she was liable to feel for people because she came to know them better. It was something she lived with; and because so few of them felt back, the ones who did affected her. If she chose to remember Somack—that was her business, and if she chose to do more than remember—that was also her business.

A hesitant knock at the door interrupted her. It opened slowly and a mousy-looking man stood there, his head drooping. He was fingering the rim of his cap nervously. "The captain's compliments, ma'am. I'm to show you to his quarters."

The walk was a long one and Anna began to appreciate the size of the ship she was on. Room after room on level after level stood open; filled now with bulk cargo instead of people. Such was the fate allotted to old liners, ships whose usefulness was nearing an end. In another day and time these rooms might have been filled by the rich and respected citizens of many worlds. Now, they were merely space to store things in. Finally, at the end of one last corridor, they came to the captain's cabin. It bore a faded plaque with the inscription: **CPTN M. EYEADA, COMMANDING**, and it stood slightly ajar. The little man, his hat once more clasped in nervous hands, approached and knocked lightly.

A voice from within acknowledged the knock with a gruff question. "Did you bring her?"

"Yes, sir."

"Well then, send her in," the voice said testily. "And close the door," it called irritably after the little man had urged her inside.

The captain sat behind a large table set for dinner. He was dressed in the full uniform of a civilian master-pilot and by his uneasy manner it was obviously not his normal dress. He wore a sour look which changed into a frown as he inspected Anna with his deeply shadowed eyes. He rapped impatiently on the intercom at his elbow.

"Get that food in here!" he barked.

"Yes, sir," the ship answered, unperturbed. An ancient and rickety service robot tottered out from an opening in the wall. It was an anachronism and showed its age with jerky motions as it served the food. One bowl of soup saw a little wastage before the robot finished.

"Get that thing fixed, damn it!" the captain growled into his intercom.

"I'm sorry, sir. As I informed you twenty-three days ago, spare parts are no longer available and replacement material must be supplied me before I can make the repairs myself."

"Go to hell," the captain said amiably.

"Yes, sir," the ship's sweet voice answered. Then after a pause, "Co-ordinates are not available."

"Belay that order and get this piece of junk out of here."

"Yes, sir." The robo-server tottered back into the far wall. Throughout the exchange Anna stood quietly by the door. The captain finally noticed this.

"Have a seat, young lady. You'll have to excuse our arrangements here. *Matilda* just isn't the ship she used to be."

Anna sat down gingerly, carefully folding her hands in her lap.

"Mr. Devlon," the captain continued, "will be here shortly. My name is Eyeada—as you could see if you read the name plate."

"A pleasure," she murmured. The food was steaming away right in front of her and she found it hard to keep her thoughts on more important things.

"Help yourself," Eyeada said, and immediately followed his own advice.

The door opened and Devlon stepped in. He was smiling, either in pain or at some private joke, and his neck was awkwardly encased in a bulky brace.

"Excuse the delay, Captain," Devlon said, still smiling. "And the appearance," he added, tapping his neck brace with a finger and looking directly at Anna. "Well, well. Our guest looks much better in clothes befitting a lady. Don't you think so, Captain?"

"Quite," Eyeada answered. He did not look up from his food.

"You'll have to excuse the captain," Devlon apologized. "Nothing stands in his way where food is concerned."

The captain slurped and nearly choked on this. He was clearly amused at Devlon's display of distaste. Anna herself was eating now, but without the relish of her host. In fact, even sitting quietly with her eyes averted, she was beginning to lose her appetite.

Devlon, not knowing he was the cause, seated himself and leaned forward, patting her hand gently. "I hope the food is to your liking. Much better, I hope, than what you've been used to lately?"

"Yes, thank you," Anna answered, swallowing hard. Somehow she managed not to shiver or snatch her hand away. There were times when seeing into a mind had its drawbacks.

"We are going to ask your help in something, Miss Bey, or Anna—if you don't mind the familiarity. Perhaps," Devlon continued, "in return for what we have done for you—setting you free from the IXT and all—you will help us."

"And how can I help?" she asked, turning her eyes toward the captain. She did not feel up to commenting on Devlon's use of her first name.

'You were questioned, were you not, while kept in captivity by the IXT?"

"Yes," Anna answered, looking confused by the direction of the conversation. "But I would rather not talk about it."

"Yes. We understand completely," Devlon said, oozing sympathy. "But such matters are best brought out into the open. "You didn't answer any of their questions, did you?"

"No," she said, and the puzzlement was evident in her voice. "I couldn't understand what they wanted. They kept asking me about spaceships and aliens and things I didn't know about."

"I see," Devlon said eagerly, leaning forward as far as his neck brace would allow. "And you didn't tell them anything?"

"Just a little, maybe. But I don't remember too well; they gave me things and did things."

"Ah," Devlon said with some relief, perceiving at last a reason for the girl's stupidity. "Now I understand. There's just one more thing you can do for us. Can you tell me if any of the questioners—there were three— you do remember three, don't you?"

"I—" and Anna paused, looking confused. "I don't know. I think there were three."

"Yes, good. Now, could you tell us which of them were with you when they did things to you?"

"I think so. Two of them did."

"Which two?" Devlon pounced.

"The woman," Anna blurted, startled by the question. "The woman and a man."

"Which man?" Devlon asked, showing signs of disgust. "Can't you remember better!"

No answer was forthcoming.

"I think the lady needs some more rest," the captain said, cutting in before Devlon could repeat his question. He tapped the intercom with his knuckle. "Get Bling in here," he snapped.

Almost instantly there was a light knock at the door. It opened a crack, allowing a bald head to peer through. "You called, sir?"

"Escort our guest back to her quarters," Eyeada rasped. "She needs more rest."

Anna hurriedly ate the last bit of food on her plate and looked at the captain in timid bewilderment.

"You may go," Eyeada grumbled, not even trying to smile reassurance.

The moment the door closed behind her Devlon began tapping his fingers on the table in irritation. "What do you think?" he asked, "Did they put her under and have her scraped? And if they did, which of them got the information?"

Eyeada did not answer. The dark eyes under his heavy brows were deep in thought. He was very much aware of something. The young lady who had just departed was dangerous, far more dangerous than a man like Devlon could believe possible. "We will play it both ways," he answered at last.

"You mean you want me to go easy on them all?" Devlon accused, his brows coming together.

"Exactly," Eyeada said, coming to his feet. "You can have what you want *after* we've got the information. Until then leave the girl alone. You can do what you want with the other three, just so long as you keep them alive. Understand?"

Devlon rose slowly. He was burning mad. "Someday, Captain, you'll know what it means to be the follower in a movement."

"You lead your movement, Devlon—but I run this ship, and so long as you care to remain aboard you and your men will do as I say."

"The Freedom Movement doesn't mean a thing to you then? Countless innocent aliens trapped and killed under the IXT gun and human culture is strangled into stagnation when an ocean of vital thought lies just over the horizon—and you don't care!" The veins in Devlon's forehead were standing out now and his face was flushed. His fiery indignation was building—a quality which brought more of the population into the movement every time he spoke. "We can't live forever hemmed in by outmoded ideas passed down from a generation of paranoid ancestors!"

"I think you had better go," Eyeada said very gently. "We both have important work to do."

O n the long walk back to her cabin Anna was thinking furiously. There was an empty cold lump eating at the pit of her stomach, an uncontrolled fear she was fighting desperately to confine. She had seen brutal men in her life, seen them as other people could not, but never had she come across anyone like Devlon. He'd seen her and from that moment on . . . She had to do something. It was as simple as that.

"Bling," she said meekly as they approached the door of her compartment, "could you do something for me?"

"Why, yes." He smiled uncertainly. "As long as it doesn't break any rules."

"Oh, I'm sure it doesn't—all I want you to do is give the captain a message for me."

Bling did not comprehend this. "But all you have to do is tell *Matilda*, and she'll pass it on to the capt'n."

"*Matilda?*"

"The ship, miss. *Matilda* is the ship. The very best there is." The little man seemed to straighten up a bit with the secondhand pride which came from serving on the "very best there is."

"But you don't understand," Anna pleaded, "I don't want him to get the message right away. I want you to give it to him three hours from now."

"What kind of message is this?" Bling asked with the beginnings of suspicion.

"I just want you to tell him that I'm a Friend of Man, a friend with a capital F."

"You want me to tell him that you're a friend?" The little man was beginning to comprehend a little now and a slow smile spread across his face. "And you want three hours to get ready?" He was looking at her with interest now.

"That's right," she replied, hopefully, blushing at the thoughts she could see going through his mind. "A friend with a capital F."

"Capital F." He laughed, shaking his head. "That's a new one on me. But I guess it's safe enough to give him that message." He turned away, chuckling under his breath. It had been a long time since he had had a chance to do something Captain Eyeada would thank him for. It almost, but not quite, made him happy to think about seeing his commander again.

When the door closed behind Anna she was not surprised to hear it lock. Nor did she look ahead now without hope. So long as Bling delivered her message on time there was a chance.

Devlon looked over his three IXT prisoners without a trace of pity for their likely fates. He himself, personally, would deliver those fates to them.

"Now, Commander Jennings," he began. "Let's be reasonable. Just tell me which one of these two let you in on our little escape plan."

"You fool!" Black snapped, straining uselessly at his bonds. "Can't you see that neither of us told him a thing. Do you think we could have gotten away at all, if the base had been alerted. Don't be an idiot."

"Mustn't interrupt," Devlon scolded. He depressed a button and the steel hands on Black's wrists tightened. Black winced in pain.

"Now, Commander," Devlon said, turning back to Jennings, "you don't owe either one of these traitors a thing. They're traitors to the IXT and to me and the Freedom League as well. Don't make me use methods I'd rather not employ."

Jennings smiled slightly. He was looking down at his left arm. They had removed his steel fingers but had not tampered with the delicate power unit and connecting mechanism. Perhaps they'd left him something to lose, something he would be willing to talk for.

"I know what is going to happen to me," he said bluntly. "If you want me to talk, you're going to have to satisfy my curiosity on a few points."

Devlon fingered the brace on his neck. "What makes you so pessimistic? Certainly it isn't this little injury you gave me? Why, I don't hold a grudge. On the contrary, I admire a man who is good at doing his duty."

"Bunk," Jennings said tiredly. "I'm not a fool and neither are you."

Devlon's crooked smile disappeared. "You are quite right. Now, exactly what useless information would you like to take to your grave with you?"

"Just how badly riddled is the IXT? How did you get in?"

"The IXT is dying!" Devlon sneered, leaning forward as best he could.

"Intelligence *and* Enforcement are so shot full of holes that we can sail this junk heap *Matilda* right in whenever we want. Enforcement controllers have us down as a licensed supply ship and Intelligence cleared our credentials. Does that give you an idea of just how far gone the good old IXT is?"

"And Justice?" Jennings asked quietly.

"Justice!" Devlon laughed. "You have to be a freak to get into Justice, and once you're in—why the IXT is the only thing left to live for. No, your precious Justice is safe from us. But it's done us some good, at times, anyway."

"How is that?" Jennings asked, and out of the corner of his eye he saw that Margy was looking at him.

"Why it helps us with recruiting," Devlon answered, smiling maliciously. "How do you think we get people like Miss Stevens here. Not with money, certainly. Why don't you tell Commander Jennings why you joined the Freedom League, Margy. I'm sure he'd be interested."

She was looking straight ahead now and her face was neutral, but the blotches of red on her neck and cheeks showed how much the question affected her. "The IXT's purpose is no longer consistent with the goals of mankind," she said, almost quoting from the League's handbook. "Instead of preventing contact with other intelligent races we should be searching them out, trading with them and learning; not attacking and destroying them whenever they stumble across us."

"Commendable words!" Devlon leered, "but not the answer to my question. You came to us three years ago, didn't you?"

There was no answer.

"Just after a certain incident?" Devlon pressed.

Her lips were trembling now and her eyes were closed, slow tears running down her cheeks in perfect unison. Jennings watched with a sinking comprehension.

"It was just after a friend of yours, an Enforcement officer at the time, I believe, was reduced from a man to a handless freak and transferred to the trash bin of Justice. Isn't that right?" Devlon was laughing now, quite aware of the effect he was producing on two of his prisoners.

"So you see, Jennings," he continued, "Justice serves us too. No one worked harder for us than Miss Stevens here. Righting the wrongs of an unjust system and helping to reduce the IXT to the impotence it deserves. She has advanced herself in rank and position to help us the better. Unfortunately, her usefulness is now in question. Only you can clear this question up, Jennings. All you have to do is tell us which one, or if both of them have turned their backs on humanity and returned to the safe haven of the IXT."

Jennings was looking at Devlon; trying to decide just how he would finish the neck-twisting job he had begun, if given the chance again. He was also considering just how to answer the question Devlon wanted answered. In the end he decided that the truth would probably work the best.

"Neither of them told me a thing."

Devlon smiled tolerantly. "I'm a patient man, Jennings. The longer you hold out, the more pain you, and your friends, will go through. Perhaps you will understand this better after another day in the hands of my gentle machines here. They will not hurt you. It will only feel that way. Now if you will excuse me, I have other business to attend to."

The knock, when it came, was earlier than Anna expected; almost half an hour early. She sat on the edge of her bed, dressed as she had been for lunch.

"Who is it?" she called quietly, knowing quite well who it was.

The door opened without a sound and Devlon stepped in. "I hope I'm not disturbing you, Miss Bey," he said sincerely, "but there are a few more questions I would like to ask you."

"Yes?" she said expectantly as he crossed to the far side of the room and fiddled with some knobs on the wall.

"There," he said, with some relief, "now we can talk in private. I wouldn't want that brute of a captain to interrupt anything important you might have to say. You wouldn't want that, now would you?" As he was talking Devlon moved about the room, looking in corners and behind anything big enough to conceal a microphone or hidden pickup. The search took him a few minutes and he chatted amiably throughout, mainly about how important it was that she remember what she could about the strange ships which had followed the *Ambol* and what had made her use the Manual Trigger. "You can't imagine the importance of this to mankind," he said. "Here is a ship, and a man—the Quaker—who have obviously been in contact with numerous races unknown to the rest of us; and look how much they were able to do for him. His ship could resist, without damage, many times its number of our own ships. You understand now how important everything, and I mean everything, you can remember about this man is."

"Yes," she answered, looking up at him with her eyes rounded in admiration.

"Well then," he said reassuringly, sitting down on the bed next to her, "try hard to remember."

There was nothing farther from her mind. She was trying with all her might not to lose control. Holding on to the hope that Bling would deliver the message she had given him on time.

"I'm trying," she said, closing her eyes in mock concentration.

"Good," he said, and patted her on the shoulder encouragingly. His hand lingered there, cold to the touch.

She opened her eyes and looked into his. The hand on her shoulder became a grip, sliding beneath the cloth and moving outward.

"Excuse me, Mr. Devlon, but . . ." She spoke timidly and glanced at the room's tiny closet toilet.

"What?" he said, dumfounded. Then he looked disgusted. This girl really was an idiot.

He did not try to stop her when she rose and crossed to the small room. She slid the flimsy partition closed behind her and had an almost irresistible urge to gag. How long would be be content to wait out there? Not very long. Oh, why did everything have to go wrong?

She searched the tiny room for something, anything she could use as a weapon. But the tiny closet was just like the rest of her compartment. It was designed for the protection and comfort of its passengers, not for supplying weapons.

"WHO is it?" Eyeada barked when the knock sounded on his door. "Damn it, Bling!" he growled when no answer was forthcoming. "Get in here before I come out and drag you in—and it better be good. You know better than to interrupt me while I'm plotting." He pushed the complex instrumentation away from him and dropped his calculator into its slot. He swiveled in his chair, ripping the remnants of his dress tie off and tossing it toward the corner where it joined his dress coat. His shirt was stained with perspiration and he did not look at all in the mood for interruption.

Bling worried at the edge of his cap and kept his head down while he spoke. "A message, Capt'n," he mumbled.

"Speak up, you dunderhead!"

"It's the girl, sir," Bling quavered. "She sends you her compliments and says that she's your friend, sir."

"Friend? What kind of nonsense is this? Are you trying to get yourself spaced?"

"No, sir!" Bling squealed. "She said friend, friend with a capital F. I thought you'd be . . ."

"Shut up!" The captain's eyes were burning now. "Get out," he said absently as he turned to the communicator and gave it a sharp crack. "Get me Miss Bey's room!" he growled. "Immediately."

"I'm sorry," the ship answered, "but communications with room D-86 have been interrupted at the occupant's request."

"What?" the captain shouted. He was already halfway to the door when the computer attempted to answer his question.

"Please repeat your request in more detail," it murmured as the door slammed.

Anna slid the partition open just as Devlon was making up his mind to do it for her. She smiled at him uncertainly and walked back toward the bed where he was waiting. "I remember something," she said, in one last play for time.

"Never mind that now," he said, gripping her arm roughly.

She stumbled awkwardly and fell, desperately flinging out her free arm for support. It was just by chance that her hand caught on the lip of his neck brace. He followed her to the floor, crying out in anguish at the pain in his neck.

"Damn you," he grunted painfully, struggling for a better hold.

"No, Devlon," Eyeada's voice growled, "it's you who's to be damned."

The silence which followed was so deep that the sound of running feet could be heard in the corridor outside. Devlon was constrained by his awkward position and neck brace into looking up very slowly. He saw Eyeada's tarnished belt buckle and an inch higher he found his right eyeball looking down several inches of polished steel bore. The first inch or so of the rifling was quite clear, beyond that there was only darkness.

The room was filled with a crystal quiet—ready to shatter in a fatal way. For a moment, just one short second, Devlon's life dangled by the thinnest of threads. He was looking death in the face and had the sense to know it. His high political rank and pull meant nothing in the here and now. He made no move to protest the captain's highhandedness. Had he done so his life would have ended. In remaining perfectly still, ignoring the pain in his neck and the awkwardness of his position, he found the way to save himself. The moment passed.

"Perhaps you failed to understand me," Eyeada said softly. "When I said we would entertain every possibility, especially where our young guest here is concerned, I meant it."

Devlon rose to his feet slowly, carefully keeping his hands at his side and his face blank of the thoughts going through his mind. "Perhaps I was hasty in my judgment," he admitted.

Eyeada eased the locked hammer back and then forward into a safe position. Without a word of apology he slid the black metallic pistol back under his belt.

The door behind Eyeada pushed open and a pair of anxious faces peered in. "Is anything wrong, sir?" the foremost asked, panting and looking around uncertainly. "I thought you might need—"

"Hardly," the captain interrupted, an icy edge in his voice. "Mr. Devlon and I were merely discussing details of the trip."

The crewman looked at his captain's black scowl, at Anna seated on the cabin floor, her hair tousled and livid finger marks still visible on her arm, and at Devlon's pale, press-lipped face. "Aye, sir," he sputtered, backing and elbowing his way into those behind. The door closed quickly and there was a flurry of sound as the crewmen scattered back to their stations.

"You had better go too, Devlon. Before I change my mind."

Devlon left.

Eyeada began to pace and as he paced he shot dark glances in Anna's direction. She was still seated on the cold deck, long black hair covering downcast eyes and hunched shoulders. He paused at the far side of the room and stroked his chin.

"It's all your fault, you know," he said, not unkindly. "Play-acting is a dangerous game where Devlon is concerned. He is far too likely to take a person at face value."

Her head came up at this, eyes glistening, but she did not cry. Instead she smiled at him wistfully and looked back at the steel deck. She began to trace designs in the scratches and gouges time had left there.

"Now," Eyeada said gruffly, lifting her to her feet, "why don't you tell me what your little message meant."

Anna, brushing the hair from her face was very serious. "The Quaker has Friends. You and I are among them."

All expression left Eyeada's eyes. He searched Anna's face closely, then standing back, looked her over as a whole. He was trying to decide something.

"I—" she began, but he held up his hand.

"I think you've said and done quite enough for the moment, young lady."

There was a note of finality in the statement and she could hardly help but notice his hand resting on the worn pistol butt.

"You've yet to be given a tour of the ship," he said, nodding toward the door. "I think now is the time."

Matilda was large. Her engine spaces were enormous; a testimony to the age and the reliability of her outmoded drive. Eyeada took Anna down into the maze of her service ways and maintenance stations; down into his own private retreat. All of the time, as he talked and explained, his right hand never strayed far from the buckle in his belt. Nor did his eyes leave the diminutive figure of a girl who knew things no one was supposed to know.

"This," he said at last, pointing to a small hatch poorly lit at the end of a long corridor, "is an emergency exit. Beyond it and another air-tight door lie nothing." He gave the hatch a spin and a tug. It opened slowly, swinging with the steady speed of a massive object.

"Get in."

Anna stood still in the dim light. She looked from Eyeada's deep-set, perfectly calm eyes, to the gun he now held in his hand. She did as he said, ducking her head and stepping into the small polished chamber. The air was stale and smelled of steel, grease, and age.

Eyeada remained outside. Squatting down, he rested the gun on one knee but its aim remained true. The hammer clicked four times as he brought it back.

"Now," he spoke in a near whisper. "Explain."

"Would you really?" she asked softly, knowing the answer even as she spoke.

He said nothing. He merely remained quiet, waiting for her to explain if she could.

"I can read your mind," she said quietly, and stood with as much dignity as she could, feeling the closeness of the end. "This is how I know you work for the Quaker," she continued. "It is also the reason—and the proof—that I work for him."

A long silence followed this.

"You wanted me to kill him," Eyeada said. "You wanted Devlon dead —and you planned it—you tried to use me to do it." Anna knew it was a question. She could not see how he wanted it answered—she could only feel her heart tighten as she spoke. "Yes," she breathed. "Yes. I wanted him to be dead."

Eyeada looked into her eyes. There was something there—something that made her alive, and made him want her to stay.

"Very well," he said at last. "You will live. Not because I believe you work for the Quaker. Not even because I believe you can read my mind— and I know what the Quaker would do if I let such an asset slip away. You're going to live because you're too much alive and I can't kill you when you're like that. When you tell the truth."

He stood up and motioned her out of the small chamber. "I hope you understand how much of a problem you represent. How much your life depends on how you act. Don't do what you did before. Don't try to use me like that again."

PART II

TANGLED WEB

CHAPTER 6. SWEET
DREAMS

S omack tossed in his sleep. A monitoring device began to register an increased alpha activity. An IXT medical attendant glanced at his displays. He spoke to the officer seated next to him.

"He's having another dream."

He pointed out the characteristic patterns forming on the tape.

"Is that an encouraging sign?" the officer asked.

"He's recovering," the attendant confirmed. "That much we know for sure. But these dreams—why they keep repeating the same pattern—that's what we're worried about."

Merrick considered what the medical attendant had told him and what he had learned about Somack on his own. "Is there some way we can look in on what he is seeing and dreaming about?"

The medical man frowned. "It's possible—if you had a powerful telepath perhaps. It would be difficult though; these are not surface thoughts. I've never seen a similar phenomenon. It's almost as if they'd been put there by some outside agency. I wouldn't be surprised if the man himself has some difficulty in seeing them or comprehending them—consciously that is."

"And mechanically?" Merrick asked. "Is there any way we can get at them with the instruments at our disposal?"

The medic shook his head. "I doubt it. You could try, but it would probably result in the death of the patient without any sure results. I would try some indirect means if I were you."

Merrick nodded agreement. "We're going to be moving him back aboard his ship. When he wakes up aboard the *Ambol* he won't remember anything about the IXT, will he?"

"How can he?" the medical attendant answered, slightly irritated. "He's been under since the ship came in. His memories will be the same as they were before he went into coma."

"Good," Merrick said, wetting his lips. "Very good."

S omack was placed aboard the *Ambol* and he and the ship were returned to the double-star system where Somack had been injured. The *Ambol's* log made this possible and the IXT did everything possible to return the ship to the location he would last remember. They would watch him as he woke up—and they had prepared things. By his reactions perhaps they could learn something about what he carried in his mind.

Merrick and the giant IXT ship *Exeter* remained close to the *Ambol.*

From aboard her they could watch Somack as he endured a final time the dream which stayed with him so.

He fled from chaos. Behind him darkness grew, spreading like a cancer across the face of the universe. Where it spread life ceased. He wept as his people disappeared into the swirling edge of nothing. They were gone, but he remained; fleeing across the ruins of a galaxy. Chaos crept after him—engulfing everything.

Soon only he remained. He and his cargo. It was the repository of hope. From it his people would be once more.

But the chaos was not through. It crept on: slow, timeless, persistent. He ran until there remained no more energy, nor a place to run. It was a millennium catching him and he watched it come, powerless to turn it back.

He resisted. Oh, how hard he fought. It came on, endlessly battering against him. He would not, could not die. But his cargo—his ever precious cargo—slowly ebbed. The time of battle passed. He had won. Motionless—without energy—a cargo of dust—and yet he was the victor. By his very remaining he had won.

Time passed. He drifted with infinite patience through empty space. Slowly the stars returned, blossoming and lighting the blackness all around. Joy and life sprang up about him. It was not his life, not the life he had fought to save, but it was life none the less. It was lowly and it waxed in bursts and fits. He drifted by, powerless to help or hinder. But it prospered and he was serene in the knowledge that when the time came he would do his part. He would warn of the chaos. He would not let it come a second time.

Somack opened his eyes. The dream faded. As always, it left him with a sense of loneliness; a sense of loneliness overshadowed only by the importance of the task before him.

It was out there somewhere, waiting for him. He knew, even as he strove toward it, that if he failed to come it would continue to wait. Someday he, or someone like him, would find it again. The wait might be long, for it would give its message to only a few. He was one of those few, just as the man who had died giving it to him had been. And should he falter, it was his duty to pass the dream on, just as it had been passed on to him.

He thought of this now, with death so close, and he wanted to pass his message along; to share the burden so long borne alone. But there was something terribly wrong—there was no one here. He could feel only emptiness about him where there should be life. And the pain; it was gone. The *Ambol* hummed in the background, but there was nothing else. He could feel that. Only moments before Anna had been kneeling down beside him, hair streaming. Now she was gone.

He struggled to sit up, only to drop back in a blur. His vision cleared slowly and he was more careful in his motions. Next to him was a table and on it a glass of pale liquid. Propped against the glass was a note.

"Drink this," the note read in what could have been a feminine hand, "and don't worry." The note was signed simply, "Anna."

He drank. The liquid was thick and syrupy but left no aftertaste. It made him feel heavy and tired. He sank back and before long he was sleeping. A natural sleep—and the first such in a long time.

Aboard the IXT ship *Exeter,* Merrick stood behind the monitor on watch.

"How is it going'?" he asked the monitor.

"He was awake for a few moments awhile back, but he's sleeping now."

Merrick nodded. "Notify me when he wakes up again." Leaning over, he removed the recordings from the previous watch. "I'm taking these to my quarters," he said, signing the ledger. "Don't forget to let your replacement know that I want to be notified the instant anything unusual happens."

"Aye, sir," the monitor answered.

Somack was up and about after his sleep. The first thing he did was search the ship. He found another note, written in the same feminine hand.

"Have departed with friends. They assure me you will be cared for—and will recover."

Again it was signed, "Anna."

Somack was unsatisfied. Why had Anna gone off suddenly with "friends," after staying so long to help him? He continued to search the ship, fuming. The ship itself was strangely unresponsive, answering his inquiries with a blunt disavowal of any knowledge.

Outside, on the screens, everything was the same. The *Ambol* drifted quietly next to the same chunk of rock he had last seen when Anna and Brodrick had gone prospecting. Beyond that was the same beautiful and frightening array of planetary debris.

Somack refused to believe his eyes or the notes or the ship. He began to search again. Only this time, he made the search count. He began to notice small scratches and dents in the ship's plates; scratches and dents that hadn't been there before.

"What's he doing now?" Merrick asked anxiously.

The monitor on duty shrugged irritably. "Still the same old

thing, wandering around the ship. He seems to be inspecting the bulkheads."

"Damn it," Merrick muttered. "Well, even if he does suspect what is going on, there's nothing he can do. Those devices on the *Ambol* are tamperproof."

"He's headed back toward her control room now," the monitor said. "He's sitting in the command chair."

"What's he doing?"

"Nothing," the monitor grumbled. "Just sitting there, not doing a thing . . . Wait a minute, something is wrong. I'm losing resolution." His monitor's voice rose an octave. "There's something going on. Pickups are failing. We're losing"—and he grimaced—"we're losing control of the *Ambol*—can feel her slipping away."

Somack didn't know what to do, so he just sat; sat and thought. Someone had fiddled with the *Ambol*—*that* much was clear. But what to do about it was not so clear. The ship might not even function in its present condition.

As if to confirm his doubts the *Ambol* began to act up. The screens went blank and console failed to respond. Then, slowly, very slowly, function began to return.

HOLDING, the console flashed.

INTERRUPT ON . . . PROCEED.

HOLDING . . . HOLDING . . . INTERNAL DISRUPTION.

CONTINUE INTERRUPT.

OPERATIONAL OVERRIDE . . . PARTIAL RESPONSE.

RESTORE . . . HOLDING INTERRUPT.

Somack watched in fascination. It was like nothing he had ever seen. A ship talking to itself.

CONTINUE DAMPER REMOVAL.

SUPPRESS OVERLOAD . . .

COMPLETE . . . INTEGRITY RETENTION.

ALTERATION REMOVAL COMPLETE.

The console dimmed. In seconds power returned to the screens and they flashed back into being.

"What," Somack asked, arms folded, "what exactly was all that?"

SELF-RESTORATION IS NOW COMPLETE.

Somack leaned forward, fully intent. "Self-restoration? You mean restoration of damaged components?"

AFFIRMATIVE, the ship responded and Somack relaxed, only to stiffen again as it continued, **PARTS TAMPERED WITH DURING YOUR ABSENCE HAVE BEEN REPLACED. OVERLAY PROGRAMMING AND ATTEMPTED ALTERATIONS OF BASIC DIRECTIVES HAVE BEEN DISAVOWED AND PURGED. FUNCTION IS COMPLETELY RESTORED. AWAITING PROPER INSTRUCTION.**

Somack sat back in his chair. "Just how—"

VESSEL IS APPROACHING, the *Ambol* interrupted.

He turned slowly and froze when he saw it. The ship was not merely approaching, it was literally looming up around them. It was a massive warship bearing the black emblem of the IXT: A shield being transfixed by a double-edged sword, and behind the shield, a mailed fist holding and crushing the broken-off tip of the sword. The emblem was sinister enough, but framed as it was by jutting turrets and inscribed in figures the size of the *Ambol,* it was something else again. Somack swallowed and found it hard to watch as the monster ship rushed on its collision course with them. The *Ambol* made no attempt to avoid the disaster.

The big IXT ship was impossible to maneuver around and there wasn't time to warm up for a jump into main drive. A shadow fell across the *Ambol* as the hulking giant approached. The charcoal-red letters *Exeter* glowed from beneath the fist-and-shield emblem. The sun and stars were blotted out by the ship's fast-approaching size. Then something happened.

A crack and then a hole appeared in the huge ship's plating, a dilating opening just the size of the *Ambol.*

They were inside. The opening in the *Exeter's* plates closed behind them, shutting out the light completely. The darkness did not last long. Lights blazed all around and two people moved along a catwalk toward the *Ambol's* control room hatch.

"Strange," Somack muttered. He was taking a careful look at the catwalk and its position with respect to the *Ambol.* "I guess we had better let them in. But"—and he made the word emphatic—"first I think *we* ought to discuss certain things."

The *Ambol* did not respond at first, nor should it have. Ships are not supposed to have personalities and they are not supposed to do things they have not been programmed or ordered to do. **WHAT THINGS?** the console flashed at last.

"Your design for one," Somack said, stroking his chin and smiling slightly at the ship's discomfiture.

MY DESIGN IS: STANDARD LONG HAUL PACKET; #856-CX49.

"That's what your papers say," Somack conceded. "I wonder, do all 'Standard Long Haul Packets' carry weapons systems, repair themselves extensively, and select their own programming—let alone concealing things from their owners? Is that correct?" There was a note of sarcasm in his voice.

CERTAIN ALTERATIONS HAVE BEEN MADE IN THE BASIC DESIGN.

"And just who made these alterations?"

OFFICIALS ARE BECOMING IMPATIENT AT THE CONTROL ROOM HATCH, the *Ambol* answered, deftly changing the subject.

"Let them wait," Somack replied calmly. He didn't even glance in that direction. "Just answer the question."

I AM NOT AT LIBERTY TO DISCLOSE THAT INFORMATION UNDER THE PRESENT CIRCUMSTANCES. YOU MAY AS YET BE FORCED TO REVEAL IT TO UNAUTHORIZED PERSONNEL.

Somack glanced at the screen and at the two officials standing there. They had given up trying to communicate their desire to enter and were now directing the setting up of heavy cutting equipment. They must be the "unauthorized personnel" referred to by the ship. Ships who considered the IXT "unauthorized" were strange indeed. Somack opened his mouth to ask the ship one more question, but he was too late.

The console lights faded and the screens darkened. The ship, it seemed, was going into hiding.

The control room hatches opened, admitting two rather flustered IXT officers. A number of technicians, non-coms, and other assorted people hovered uncertainly just outside the hatch.

"Come in, come in," Somack smiled, gesturing the two hesitant officers forward. "Don't be bashful. You're just the people I want to see."

The officers exchanged glances.

"Certainly you're not as confused about everything as I am?" Somack asked in mock astonishment. "Surely you can answer all the questions I'm dying to ask?"

"Before you say anything more," one officer interrupted, "let me make it clear that we will do the asking, not you."

"Ask away," Somack acquiesced eagerly. "But I'm afraid my answers will not do you much good."

The officers conferred quietly. Clearly neither had been expecting nor prepared to deal with anyone so co-operative. They finally decided that the situation called for smoothly passing responsibility along to someone with more rank.

"Come with us."

Somack followed, still smiling. He did not even protest as the technicians, etc., crowded into the *Ambol*. He did, however, pause at the edge of the outer hatch and glance down at the catwalk. It was snug against the *Ambol's* side and as he ran his foot across the area he found it perfectly flush. A perfect fit without needing adjustment. Somack smiled at the simple mistake which told him the *Ambol* had been in this slot before.

"Come along," one of the officers urged irritably.

Somack came.

Т he interview was a complete disaster. At least from the IXT's point of view it was. Somack continued to co-operate fully and did it in a way which seemed to irritate the interviewing officers. A typical piece of dialogue went:

Q UESTION (Lt. J. B. Hadely): And when you woke up after this mysterious interval, about which you can remember nothing, what did you do?

ANSWER (W. Somack): Well, there was a glass of something (illustrates shape of glass with hands)—you know, the glass you people left there for me to drink . . .

INTERRUPTION (Lt. F. Bailey): We didn't—

PRESIDING OFFICER: Let the subject answer in his own words, please. You may proceed, Mr. Somack.

ANSWER (W. Somack): . . . (long pause) . . . the drink, it was sort of pink. I wasn't going to drink it at first, but I read the note you left.

PRESIDING OFFICER: You are referring to the shorter of the two notes signed "Anna."

(subject nods in the affirmative)

PRESIDING OFFICER: Let the record so state.

INTERRUPTION (Lt. F. Bailey): This is a farce.

PRESIDING OFFICER: Five-minute recess. Mr. Bailey, I will see you outside.

OBJECTION (Lt. J. B. Hadely): What about my question?

PRESIDING OFFICER: We will come to that later.

A nd so it went for several hours until all patience was lost and the presiding officer—who also happened to be the *Exeter*'s commanding officer—called a halt. He had just received word from the crew examining the *Ambol* that all the instruments implanted there were still seemingly intact. The only thing wrong was that they just didn't seem to work any more.

Abe Kane had served long and hard in the IXT and now, as commander of the *Exeter,* he was witnessing the worst botch-up he'd seen in all those years—and he'd seen a few good ones. Being on extended duty most of the time, and therefore away from the IXT's bureaucracy, he had become intolerant. After he concluded the futile interview he had only one thing to say.

"I want the fool responsible for all of this in my office in five minutes!"

Shortly there were two men in Kane's office waiting for him to explode. One was a liaison staff officer representing the IXT's over-all command posture toward the *Ambol* incident. The other man was Merrick, representing Justice's special interest in Somack.

Kane stood looking down on the liaison staff officer. And that officer didn't even seem to know what the problem was. Kane started off calmly; an ominous sign.

"You know what I think—I think you people back at the Complex have got rocks in your heads. You have been after the wrong thing all along. You've been trying to get your hands on the Quaker. And to do this, you have given away what could be much more important. What was the Quaker after in the first place? Perhaps *he* knew what was important after all. He certainly risked enough by chasing the *Ambol* into our alien reception center."

"We haven't given anything away," the liaison man snapped defensively. 'We still have Somack and the *Ambol* right here with us."

"And the girl?"

The liaison man flushed. "She was considered expendable. She was extremely useful in exposing certain weaknesses in our organization. We have the *Matilda* under observation and the girl may still be alive."

"Doubtful," Kane huffed. "The Freedom League isn't known for its gentleness in certain matters. If she knew anything useful—and she probably did—then they know it now and she is probably dead as a result. No. I'm afraid I'll have to agree with Justice on this one. You people acted in too much haste. In order to clean house in Intelligence, you have risked a greater loss."

The liaison officer turned a darker shade of red. "I can't see how you— of all people—can complain about what we did. You know what it is like trying to stop this illicit trade with aliens and smuggling. As long as the Freedom League is able to get information from its spies in Intelligence whenever it wants to, we are never going to put a halt to it. I am surprised that you should be critical of the priorities established at the Complex."

Kane tapped his fingers on the desk. He was restraining himself with an effort. "Smuggling is petty, compared with the problem we are faced with here. I have seen films of what the Quaker's ship did to us."

"Exactly!" the liaison man said, grasping a chance to justify his position. "The *Ambol's* navigation tape showed us where it first encountered the Quakers ship—and that was right here in this debris-strewn system. We brought the *Ambol* back as bait—"

"Bait! Staff officers seem to have bait on the brain. Can't you realize that *your bait may be more important than your catch.*"

The liaison officer was dumfounded. The thought had never occurred to him. "I . . . I—" he stammered.

"Shut up," Kane snapped. He was disgusted. "Get out."

The liaison man did not protest the order. He left quickly. When he was gone Merrick rose from his corner of the room.

"I am glad you have decided to trust me," Merrick said quietly.

"It isn't so much a matter of trust," Kane said. "It's a matter of facts, and you have them. When you first came aboard you were suffering from lack of sleep and I was surprised that Justice would allow a man in such groggy condition to hold a position of responsibility. You were technically in charge of Somack's disposition, but staff liaison made it clear that they had priority. It is not unusual in cases of this importance to overrule Justice, and when you came to me with your theory, all you had to support it were a few dusty data files."

"You agree then—that the *Ambol* is the same ship."

Kane nodded. "I don't think there can be much doubt about it now, not after the way it's been acting up. But I still can't understand how Somack managed to find it."

"I don't think that is too hard to explain. According to our records, we sold the *Ambol* for scrap nearly forty years ago—after its owner originally was sentenced to life at hard labor for failing to co-operate in the investigation of an encounter.

"It's that—the *Ambol's* first encounter with something forty years ago. That's the missing link," Merrick concluded.

"You mean the *Ambol* and her previous owner found something? What?" Kane asked.

"That's the whole point. *We don't know.* There was a group of people involved in freeing the *Ambol's* original owner before he could be questioned properly. It was quite an operation—and the *only* successful escape from Justice in our three-hundred-year history. There was a connection, I think, between this group and the Quaker. They did a heavy job of interrogating the original owner of the *Ambol* before we could locate them and break them up. It was during our raid, in the confusion —this owner fellow escaped again—briefly, and stumbled into a nearby house where he died from the effects of his interrogation."

"Then no one knows what he and the *Ambol* found?" Kane asked. He was suddenly beginning to appreciate the extensive nature of the operation confronting him.

"Maybe," Merrick answered, smiling. "You see, the house our dying fugitive stumbled into was the same one where Somack was born and raised. He was five years old at the time of the incident."

Kane raised an eyebrow. "An interesting connection. I can see now why you think Somack and the *Ambol* are not *accidentally* together."

Merrick agreed. "I think Somack has some of the same information that the previous owner of the *Ambol* had. I don't see how you can explain in any other way his saving for so many years to purchase the *Ambol*. Not just any ship, but the *Ambol*. He gave up a good position as pilot on a major passenger line and traded it in for a shabby living on the *Ambol*. He didn't do it by chance. And he must be expecting something mighty big in return for the sacrifices he's been making all his life."

Kane looked puzzled. "And the Quaker? What's he after?"

"I think he's after the same thing Somack is!" Merrick said emphatically. "He's known to deal in alien things. His ship shows that.

"And there's something else," Merrick added. "I've discovered it was no accident that Miss Bey and Mr. Brodrick were the only people to answer Somack's advertising for passengers. Intimidation was used to keep anyone else from inadvertently interfering. I feel they are connected to the Quaker and it was their job to get information from Somack. And they must have failed, otherwise Brodrick wouldn't have been killed and the girl wouldn't have tried escaping with the Manual Trigger the way she did."

Kane looked relieved. "It's a shame that your superiors back on the Complex didn't give this information the hearing it deserved. They wouldn't be playing these foolish games if they had. The Quaker has an organization we can't penetrate and a ship we can't catch. What do they expect to gain by risking our only trump?"

"Exactly," Merrick agreed. 'We have what he wants, and he wants Somack. If we're wise we'll pay more attention to Mr. Somack and less to the Quaker."

"Very well," Kane agreed. "I can see the possibilities. You do what you think is best and I will back you to the hilt."

"Thank you, sir."

"Mr. William Somack?" Merrick asked, looking down on a sheaf of papers.

"Yes."

Merrick pushed the papers away. "Tell me, Mr. Somack, why did you purchase the *R. B. Ambol?*"

"I wanted to travel." Somack answered with the simple truth.

"You didn't get far in your travels, did you?"

"You've seen the ship's log," Somack smiled, "and no doubt a good deal more. Why don't *you* tell *me?*"

It was Merrick's turn to smile. "I don't think you understand the situation, Mr. Somack. I am not trying to trap you into anything. That is the last thing I am interested in doing. In fact, just the opposite. I want to help you. Your wish is our command."

"Then, maybe you will explain what is going on."

Merrick's smile became a bit strained. "Now that is not an easy thing to do. You see, we aren't really sure ourselves what is going on. But as far as we can tell, this is everything that has happened to you, your passengers, and ship since your near-fatal injury."

Somack examined the piece of paper Merrick passed to him and frowned. He read it through slowly, and then again a second time. He looked up at last and said, "So you were using us all to bait a trap."

"Two different traps, really," Merrick corrected. "It was a mistake. We realize that now, and we want to rectify that mistake. In order to do that we have got to know what it is that you know. We need to know what you are looking for—and the location."

Somack glanced back at the piece of paper. "Where is Anna?"

"Well, she's still aboard the *Matilda* right now. We have that ship under observation."

"You mean she is still being used as bait, don't you?"

"Regrettably so," Merrick answered, shuffling his papers uneasily. "There is nothing we can do to stop the *Matilda*—not while she's still in drive. But that shouldn't make it impossible for us to co-operate."

"I am afraid that it does," was the tired answer. "How do you know she is still alive? How can you tell what the Freedom League will do— especially since you've made them kill some of your own people?"

"I can only assure you that we are doing our best. But we can't do anything until we hear from our observation ship—and that won't happen until the *Matilda* stops."

Somack stood slowly. "When that happens, you let me know." He turned and left the room.

"We will," Merrick said in parting. He could tell that it was going to be more difficult to get co-operation than he had planned. Somack's concern for the girl was something he hadn't foreseen. Still it would be worth the patience. If the IXT could discover what the Quaker wanted so much, perhaps they could use it to counteract what the Quaker already had.

Somack was surprised to find that he could return to the *Ambol*. She was still nestled in the *Exeter's* docking cavity. Somack marveled at being aboard a ship so large it could consider the *Ambol* as a launch. This reminded him a little of the odds he faced—of what could happen if he did something wrong.

When Somack boarded the *Ambol* he found her empty of IXT personnel. They had left no trace of the extensive searching and probing which had been done while he was away. He sat in the command chair and thought long and hard. Nothing looked very bright to him at the moment. Even the IXT's offer to help, instead of hinder, was tinged with self-interest. They were 95 per cent to blame for the mess everything was in, and it looked like he might end up helping them whether he liked it or not.

The *Ambol,* quiet at first, slowly came to life around him. It was patient and waited for him to make the first move.

"Welcome back," he said without much enthusiasm.

NO ALTERATIONS WERE MADE DURING YOUR ABSENCE. ALL DEVICES PLANTED EARLIER WERE REMOVED.

Somack looked at the *Ambol's* console for a long time. "Can you tell me now," he said finally, "what makes you more than what your papers say you are?"

The *Ambol* did not answer immediately. It considered first the numerous aspects of what it could and what it could not say. Programming priorities of conflicting natures made it difficult to arrive at a suitable response.

MY BASIC DESIGN IS AS STATED IN MY PAPERS. IT HAS BEEN ALTERED TWICE. ONCE BY HUMAN AGENCIES ABOUT WHICH I CANNOT SPEAK. THE MOST RECENT ALTERATION IN MY DESIGN WAS CARRIED OUT BY AN AGENCY OF A FOREIGN NATURE. YOU KNOW SOMETHING OF THIS, AS YOU HAVE BEEN ALTERED ALSO. YOUR MIND HAS ACQUIRED ADDITIONAL MEMORIES. A DREAM. IT IS MY DUTY TO PRESERVE THOSE WHO HAVE ACQUIRED THESE MEMORIES. IS THIS STATEMENT SUFFICIENT?

Somack was slow in replying. "Yes," he said, "I understand." And he did understand what the ship was saying, but the knowledge did not bring with it the joy it might once have brought. He knew now that he was going to find what he had been searching for, for so long. But he realized that there was something else he wanted to do first. There was someone else he wanted to take and have with him.

CHAPTER 7. HOME AGAIN

"This," Eyeada pointed out, "is the *Matilda's* main coil. You know what a main coil is for?"

Anna looked from the black mass in front of her to the man at her side. He was giving her a real tour of the ship this time, and enjoying every minute of it. "Not so well as you could explain it," she answered lightly, feeling and reveling in the relative security of her present position.

"Very discreet," Eyeada smiled, "I like that. Never boast about your assets—it's a good policy." He turned back to the main coil. "It is the secret of the drive, of course," he said, patting the thing and dislodging small flecks of black paint. "She stores her power here; stores it and releases it all at once to boost herself into drive. Once you're there, of course, it's no trouble —but the coil here, it is what puts you there. It is the only thing that wears out very often on a ship. That's why you've got to have a backup." He pointed to a much smaller coil, dwarfed next to the main one. "There it is. A one-shot job. You've got to replace that little one every time, but the one shot it carries has brought this old ship home many a time."

"Do all ships carry those little ones?" Anna asked, genuinely interested. "Oh no." Eyeada laughed. "No, I have trouble these days even finding replacements for the thing. Most ships just carry two main coils. Much easier—and safer. It is a long way to anywhere on secondary."

Eyeada glanced at his watch. "Well, I think that's enough for now. I'd better be getting back to work—and getting you back where I can safely keep an eye on you."

"Why did you do it?" Anna asked. "Show me all of this?"

Eyeada looked down at her and thought all the thoughts he'd been trying not to think. "It's been a long time, miss, since I've met someone whose company I have enjoyed. I think you know, more than anything else, that is why you are still alive."

Anna looked down at the ground, ashamed of the knowledge she obtained from people so cheaply.

"A vendetta is a lonely thing," the captain continued, "and that's what my life has been. It's many a year I've had only the *Matilda* and a company of fools as companions. Does that answer your question?"

"Yes," she whispered.

Eyeada smiled a little bit. "Now you've gone and done it."

"What?"

"You've made me curious. Not only that, you've started the question game and I am at a disadvantage. You not only get my answers, you get to know if I'm a liar as well. Distinctly unfair."

Anna bit her lip. What he said was very close to the truth. She had been watching, trying to determine what his intentions were. He was not so easy though; not like Devlon. There was more to the captain than met the eye and more than lay on the surface of his mind. Like the vendetta he mentioned. Its meaning eluded her. There was something deep down she could not see and he seemed to be watching and waiting, wondering if she could find what he was hiding so well.

"So intense," Eyeada said, breaking her concentration. "If you keep this up I may come to believe you yet."

"In what way?" Anna asked. She was shaken by the note of mockery in his voice and by the intimate and almost instinctive way he caught her when she was really trying to dig beneath the surface of his mind.

"You are awfully young, little Miss Bey, to be playing in a league where death is the casual by-product of a mistake. Tell me—if you can— how it came about."

"The Quaker asked me," Anna answered. She knew he was testing her. He wanted to know how much she knew; if she was simply a good liar, or if she really did work for the Quaker. She explained how the Quaker had come to her when she was very young and how he had nearly raised her. The Quaker had been the only man to notice that she was different—and he had liked her for it and encouraged her when she was alone in the world. He was different too, from other people, and it had made her like him. She worked for him now because it was something he wanted and it was something that had to be done. The Quaker was protecting people from aliens—like the aliens who had hurt him so much.

"Humf," Eyeada snorted. He frowned. Everything the girl said smacked of the truth. He was surprised she knew something of the Quaker's past. Very few did.

"You like it then," he said gruffly, "peeping and scratching around where you aren't wanted. Must make you feel powerful."

Anna was startled by his reaction. It was almost as if he would have preferred her to be a liar, preferred it to the truth. His mind was all milky and unclear. Suddenly she was scared again. What had she done to make him angry? "I don't understand," she said. It was the only thing she could think of saying.

"No. Of course you don't." Eyeada was grinning again and some of the clouding was gone from his mind. "Don't let it bother you. I sometimes forget where I am and who I am talking to. It's not your fault that the Quaker found you and can use your talents."

"What do you mean?"

"Nothing," the captain said. "We had better start back now. There are a number of things I have to take care of before the watch is up." He turned and she followed quietly, no longer sure of herself or the man she stepped behind. He was strange and different to the point where he could speak and think about the Quaker without fear. It was something she had never encountered before in someone who knew the big man and knew the power he could wield.

The climb out of the *Matilda's* hold was a long one, unaided by the lift, which saw service only when there was heavy cargo to be moved. Dusty staterooms displaced machinery as they approached the end of their walk.

"I am going to have the lock on your door changed," Eyeada mentioned as the last turn loomed ahead. "You will be able to lock it from the inside and leave it whenever you want. I advise against the latter, though. There is only so much time that I can devote to watching Devlon."

Anna did not answer. She was feeling a sudden emptiness—a nameless apprehension. They turned the last corner and down the long corridor she could see someone standing in the open door of her room. She reached for the captain's elbow and started to speak, but he was already moving, bringing his pistol out to cover the man in the doorway.

"No, behind—"

They were the only two words Anna could get out and they were almost enough. Eyeada swiveled, crouching in the same instant. Noiselessly a streak of blood appeared along his cheek and ear. Eyeada fired once and a man far down the corridor fell back into the room from which he had emerged. The sound of that first shot was still reverberating as Eyeada turned to face the man in the doorway again. This man, like his partner, was armed with a needle-nose and it was aimed directly at Anna.

Seeing this, Eyeada smacked her and shoved her aside. The man fired and missed. It took only a split second for a needle-nose to rebuild its firing charge, a split second which was not long enough for Eyeada. Both men had to shift aim, but the man in the doorway only a few inches. He fired first and a tiny spot appeared in the fabric of the captain's uniform. The wound was fatal, and though Eyeada could feel this he did not blink. He simply carried through with what he was doing; aiming carefully and firing. The man he shot flew backward at the impact, spinning off the wall and sliding several yards down the corridor. Eyeada smiled. If the man had been using a relic, instead of the needle-nose, he would still be alive. (The impact of a bullet spoils your aim, while a laser burn does not.)

Looking down, Eyeada dabbed at the small hole in his shirt. Blood came away on his finger and he could feel his heart beginning to falter. He took a step backward and the shock hit him, loosening his knees.

Anna watched in horror as he leaned back against the opposite wall and slid quietly to the ground, his back leaving just a trace of blood on the wall as he went down. He was still smiling, ironically it seemed as he looked at her. He opened his mouth to speak, but nothing happened.

He smiled again, sadly, and pushed his black pistol toward her. His eyes closed and his head began to sag, but he brought it back up again with an effort and the cloud of his thought cleared for just a moment.

"Tell Matilda I'll be coming home on the five-oh-five, five-oh-five. She'll meet me there, when I come. Tell Matilda . . . Oh God, take me home again . . ."

Anna couldn't move. She sat quietly, her cheek pressed against the coolly solid wall. But she couldn't move.

It was the sound of the shots, shots that should never have been fired, that brought the crew. They approached the scene cautiously, not knowing for sure if it was safe. Finally a young man appeared. He was the first officer—an office which meant little under Eyeada. But now he was suddenly in charge. He glanced at Anna, then stooped by the captain's slumped body and lifted a limp eyelid.

"He's dead," the young officer said, hardly able to believe the evidence before his eyes.

He rose slowly and went to examine the other two men. This he did carefully, not because they needed help—they didn't—but because he wanted to make sure of their identities.

"Two of Devlon's men," he said to the gathering crew. "They are going to pay for this." He motioned at Anna. "Bring her to the captain's cabin. Maybe she can tell us what happened."

"Can't you see she's in shock?" another countered. "We know what happened. Let's take care of those damn Freedom Leaguers before they take care of us."

"Maybe you're right," the young first officer said, hesitant at the responsibility of command. He switched the intercom on. "Call the crew to emergency stations, seal off the golden-suite section."

Nothing happened.

"Damn it," the first officer lamented. "It's still voice-coded, of course. We're ruined. The *Matilda* won't take orders from anyone but a dead man."

"He must have a key for removing the voice code," the other voice insisted. "Look for it!"

Paper and charts were scattered from the captain's desk. "There's nothing here," the first officer cried. 'What are we going to do? The ship will take us right into the Freedom League's headquarters. Those were Eyeada's last orders. Even if we wipe out Devlon and the men he has with him, they'll still get us in the end."

"Maybe the girl knows something."

"Listen," the first officer said, peering into Anna's eyes while shaking her. "Did the captain say anything—anything at all before he died?"

She looked at the young man and at the other man in the background. How could they know what Eyeada's words meant—how could they feel the impact of all those years of waiting, as she had? They couldn't. But she could see Devlon, vicious, and waiting for her. It cleared her mind.

"Yes," she said slowly, "Captain Eyeada did say something. 'Tell Matilda I'll be coming home on the five-oh-five, five-oh-five. She'll meet me there, when I come.'"

"Was that all he said?" the young first officer demanded in frustration.

"No, he said, 'Tell Matilda . . . Oh God, take me home again . . .'"

The young man threw up his hands in a hopeless gesture, only to hold them there in sheer horror as the ship shook. It was a single bone-jarring shudder which died away slowly, leaving a shaken silence in its wake.

"What the hell—"

But the sentence was interrupted by a voice from the intercom, a panicked voice from the control room by a man who didn't know about the murder. "We are changing course, Captain Eyeada—did you order a change in course?"

———

Anna left the room quietly. They did not notice her leaving, nor did they care. The *Matilda* was out of their control and it was all they could do to keep their mind on this problem. So she left them to their bickering, arguing, and futile suggestions. The long grey corridors seemed greyer now, somehow reflecting in their weathered age the beaten void she was feeling. For a few minutes, down among the ship's machinery, she'd almost been happy—free from loneliness—and she knew the captain had felt the same thing, only more so. Now he was gone.

She wandered back to the corridor where it happened. Only one crew member remained, the little man Bling. He stood in the empty corridor looking down on the captain's black pistol, his face a mask of bewilderment.

"They say he is dead," the little man muttered as she approached.

Anna averted her eyes from the dead League man, stepping around his body. "Where is he?" she asked of Bling, looking at the bloodstained but otherwise empty floor where he had lain.

"*Matilda*, they said one of her robots came for him, took him away before I got here. Took him down below," the little man added ominously.

Anna bent down and picked up the pistol, left there out of contempt or superstition by the crew. "Show me," she directed.

The little man shrugged. He led her down and proved to her what he had known would be. All the hatches leading below were sealed.

"They didn't know him like I did," Bling commented, meaning the rest of the crew. "He always signed them on new, and let them go at the end of a cruise; all except me. He weren't no saint, ma'am, but he wasn't as bad as he seemed. He used to go down below more often when I was young—lock all the hatches just like now—wouldn't see him again for days. But he didn't do that so much of late, not since we fell in with these League fellows."

Anna listened as they climbed back up, and for Bling—to whom nobody listened—this was a real treat.

"He was a strange man, ma'am." And lowering his voice significantly, he added, "Didn't grow a day older in all the time I served him. Over fifty years since I signed on as his cabin boy, and not a day older."

"I know," Anna said softly, and the little man looked at her, startled, with something like terror in his eyes. "I know," she repeated, but Bling was already gone.

The area of the *Matilda* occupied by the Freedom League, called the "golden suite" from its days as the ship's highest-class section, no longer bore the slightest resemblance to its former construction. Its exterior walls had been extensively reinforced and many of its interior walls removed altogether. It was Devlon's home away from home, so to speak, and when he traveled aboard the *Matilda* he seldom left its secure confines. For reasons of security there was only one entrance into the "golden suite," and that was a fact which at the moment brought Devlon very little satisfaction.

He was not at all satisfied with the result of his recent initiative. He'd sent two men to do a job that should have taken only one, and when neither had returned, he'd sent a third to discover why. This third man had just returned to him in a gravely wounded state with the news that there were now armed crewmen just outside the League's little fortress and they tended to fire rather indiscriminately on anyone trying to leave.

It took very little thought to deduce the reason for this animosity; something had gone wrong. Either Eyeada was still alive, hardly likely—but still possible—or the *Matilda's* crew was simply playing it safe.

In the end it mattered very little which. Another day would see them safely back at the League's stronghold on Blake's World. All he had to do was wait patiently and things would take care of themselves, just as they always did when it was a matter of humanity's ultimate good. The crew would either see the light of reason, or they would have to be put out of the way.

In the meantime, Devlon had more important matters to tend to. He had three prisoners, one or more of whom knew the nature, and perhaps the location of, a new alien race. No other knowledge would so upset the IXT and it was the League's duty to obtain it and use it for the good of all. Otherwise, the IXT would cover it up and the only people to benefit would be smugglers of Eyeada's ilk. The sooner he freed humanity from the strait jacket imposed on it by the IXT for so long, the sooner would his own destiny he fulfilled.

Here—standing between him and the wide-open universe—were three people. He was tired. He would brook no more opposition, from anyone.

"Are you ready to talk?" he began, retaining his calm with herculean effort.

They just looked at him, like three dumb horses—raising their heads from a bin full of fodder. Now Black, there; he looked like he was just about ready to talk. Just a little more pain would do it. The poor man writhed under the increased stimulus. Blood trickled from his open mouth, but no sound came. Just a bit more pain ought to do it.

Lieutenant Commander Eric Black died. He did it quietly, without changing expression. Only the indicators on Devlon's machine showed that he was dead. It had not been a particularly brave death. He would have spoken, gladly, if only he'd had the strength and breath to do so.

Several moments passed before Devlon glanced at his machine's dials and discovered that he could learn no more from Commander Black. It dawned on him finally why the poor man had not unloaded his conscience before departing this world. The knowledge did nothing to improve Devlon's temper, but it did make him pause and consider before going on. Perhaps it would be best to allow Jennings and Margy Stevens a little rest from the machine. The theory ran that the absence of pain for short periods of time made its resumption all the more effective. Devlon smiled and turned off his machine.

"I'll be back," he promised.

J ennings was the first to recover from Devlon's machine treatment. He was used to pain—and there was, after all, less of him to hurt. As coherent thought returned, he gazed across at Margy and wondered how, in his present condition, he could help her. For Black, he could see, there was no help.

A brief struggle against the machine's restraints told him exactly what he could do: nothing. This was not quite true, and he knew that. At the very least he could rest—take advantage of this respite in at least one way by regaining a little strength. His long military training helped him in this. He knew how to take sleep when the time came and how to do without should the need arise. Within seconds of his decision he was sleeping peacefully, or as near to peace as the situation allowed.

When he woke the room was dark. Noises filtered in from beyond the open doorway and next to him in the darkness he could hear Margy's soft breathing. She too had chosen to sleep. It took him a few seconds to decide that something strange was going on. The light being out was not enough, but the door was open too, and there were voices; hushed voices. The voices all held one thing in common, and that was fear.

What was there to fear? It did not occur to him until he tried to move and found himself falling forward into a loose tangle of machinery and then to the floor. The power was gone!

He did not stop to wonder how it had happened. He was free and he moved rapidly to take advantage of the situation. As quietly as possible he disentangled himself from his former restraint. It was an awkward business with only the stump of one arm to work with, but he managed. Next there was Margy. He felt in the darkness toward the sound of her breathing and came upon something soft. There was a sharp intake of breath and Jennings hissed a warning for silence.

"What's happened?" came her cautious inquiry from the darkness.

"The power is down," he whispered in return. "You are free to move about, but do it carefully—and don't make any noise."

He could hear a faint rustling as she disengaged and then felt a touch on his shoulder. "What now?" she asked.

"We hunt for my fingers," he answered bluntly. "They should be over on the control table. Toward the door there."

A faint light was filtering in from outside, perhaps from someone's suit- lamp or an emergency store somewhere. Jennings could see Margy silhouetted against the light as she searched the control panel of the pain machine, groping this way and that. He could also see her stop and hesitate as she found what she was looking for.

"What's wrong?" he asked impatiently.

She turned toward him in the darkness. "I can't give you these," she said, her voice oddly strained. But she brought them to him anyway, in direct contradiction of her whispered words. She even helped to fasten them into place, listening patiently to his instruction as to which finger went into which socket. In the darkness it took several minutes, but he felt like a man again when they were back in place.

"Thank you," he said, and reaching out he kissed her suddenly. He couldn't see but he suspected that she smiled.

"Stay behind me," he ordered softly, moving toward the door. He slid forward quietly, flat on his stomach. With his head pushed a cautious few inches into the aisle he could see lights flickering far down the corridor. Voices carried to him weakly.

". . . and keep up a steady fire," came Devlon's voice.

"But, sir! We can't recharge—not with the *Matilda's* power gone."

"Do as I say, damn you."

Jennings did not catch the grumbled reply.

Margy tugged gently at his leg. "What's happening?" she whispered.

He withdrew his head from the corridor and sat up facing the darkness, his back against the wall. The light from the door was just sufficient to cast a pale arc of light, and he could see Margy seated at his feet, her hands still touching him.

"Some kind of a fight. I can't be sure, but that's what it seems to be."

"What do we do now?" she asked. "Where do we go?"

Jennings did not answer the questions. He couldn't. To move in any direction seemed dangerous, while sitting still seemed ridiculous.

"Follow me," he said, quietly standing up.

He slipped into the corridor, keeping his back pressed against the wall. An occasional flash of light lanced into the darkness as the man far down the aisle followed Devlon's orders. Response from those he fired upon was less frequent and tended to be better aimed. Tiny driplets of molten steel ran down the wall only inches from Devlon's man, who kept himself safe by exposing only his weapon when he fired.

Jennings moved away from the fighting and, glancing back, reassured himself that Margy was following. The first door he came upon was closed and locked, as was the next. They were not power locks, as those on their prison door had been, but older mechanical devices which, although vulnerable to picking, were still quite effective with the power off.

The third door Jennings tested was unlocked. The faint whir of machinery filtered through it into the corridor and Jennings paused cautiously. He motioned with his hand and Margy paused beside him. Muffled voices drifted out to them.

"I sure hope this works."

The reply was muffled.

"A little more to your right. That's it."

The buzzing inside the room increased, rising and falling in pitch. Jennings strained to hear, but the voices were covered now by the increased mechanical noise. Suddenly it was quiet. Thumping. A padded hammer striking the bulkheads perhaps. The thumping stopped and Jennings shifted his position, facing the wall so that his left (and only) arm was closest to the door.

From within the voices resumed their conversation. "Good. Don't knock it out until I get back with Mr. Devlon. He may not want to go through immediately."

Footfalls approached the door, masking whatever reply was made. Jennings tensed. A light flickered through the door as it opened, probing the wall opposite him. As the man stepped into the hall, Jennings moved. He brought his arm down and felt it strike solidly against the back of the man's head. The man crumpled to the ground, his light skittered across the floor and came to rest against the far wall of the corridor. It cast a long thin line of light far into the darkness ahead.

"Douse that light," Jennings whispered. He slipped into the darkened room. He could hear Margy moving in the corridor behind him, but his attention was concentrated on the room. It was filled with bulky-looking equipment which disappeared when the light from behind him died. Only then, in the near pitch darkness, did Jennings notice that there was another door in the room. It was far to the rear, behind machinery, and a glimmer j of light showed that it was opened just a few inches.

He moved across the room quickly, keeping his eyes glued to that tiny sliver of light. Thumping, clumsy movements and an occasional grumble came from behind the door. Jennings considered what to do next, and while he thought, Margy came up behind him and paused there, carefully remaining quiet.

Jennings pushed at the door gently and to his horror it squeaked loudly. There was no turning back now, so he thrust forward hastily and burst into the room half expecting to get cut down in the act. But what he found was even more frightening.

A glow bulb dangled from a hook in the ceiling and illuminated the small room with a light which was harsh compared with what his eyes were used to. He squinted at the glare and dodged to one side as the bulky form took a swing at him. A muffled laugh followed when he was forced to dodge again and stumbled into a pile of equipment. The man in the spacesuit was enjoying himself.

The right hand of the spacesuit was still enclosed in and covered by precision drilling attachments and they whirred into life as the man advanced on Jennings making exaggerated fencing motions with diamond-tipped tools. Jennings dodged again, frantically. He searched the bulky figure for some point of weakness. He couldn't find one. The man was advancing again and Jennings deflected the drill with his hand and it cost him one of his precious digits. But he was in close now and the suited figure groped with its oversized arms, trying futilely for some hold. The best it could manage was a gentle bear hug. The suit's arms simply would not close with the required pressure. If it hadn't been a power-assisted suit, the arms would have been free to do as they wished, but then they wouldn't have had the crushing power to deal with him so easily.

Jennings grunted as the bulky arms attempted to do him in. He worked his own arm up and under the suit's armpit. He worried at the joint there with his remaining two digits. The suited man sensed that something like that was happening and he spun around, trying to fling Jennings away. As the pair swung around in their strange dance, a blazing flash of light came from the doorway and the fight ended as suddenly as it had begun.

The giant toppled, carrying Jennings down with it. He rolled away from the dead man and smiled thanks at Margy, who stood in the doorway limply holding a needle-nose in her hand. He was on his feet, examining the still warm cut and almost-hole in the bulkhead. He did not notice the tortured look on Margy's face.

He gave the loosened plate a solid kick and it clattered to the floor beyond the opening. He stepped through into the darkness. Light poured in after him and he crossed a musty-smelling room to the door opposite. He opened this door and found only darkness in the corridor on which it opened.

"Looks like the power is out all through the ship," he said to Margy as she stepped through the hole to join him. When she did not answer, he looked around. She was at his side and as he turned her hands slipped around his waist and she was suddenly sobbing against his shoulder. He felt awkward and stupid at the same time, with his one arm and the tight knot in the pit of his stomach.

"What's wrong?" he asked foolishly.

Even in the darkness he could feel her looking up at him, her head moving away from his shoulder. "How can you kill so easily?" she asked, and he could tell from the tone that it wasn't really a question. He felt like cursing under his breath, but refrained when he realized that Margy was no longer armed. She had left the needle-nose behind.

He tried to disengage himself, but her grip only tightened. "No," she pleaded, "leave it behind."

"But we need it. If you hadn't used it a moment ago . . ." He let the sentence hang.

He could feel her head against his shoulder again and the warm moisture from her tears soaking through his uniform. When she spoke her voice was strangled, muffled against his body. "If that man hadn't turned ..." She couldn't go on.

"You couldn't help that," he said. Then her meaning hit him. Like an icy knife, it sent shivers down his legs and up his spine. She had been aiming at him and not the man in the spacesuit

The *Matilda* moved through space quietly now. She was following the last set of instructions she would ever follow. They had come to her indirectly, through Anna, but her programming allowed for that. Already *Matilda* was shutting down power, saving it for her last descent, her last landing. In a few hours she would reach her destination and there, where her main drive had first kindled into life, it would flicker and die for the last time.

There was no way to alter what was to happen. Her course now had been dictated long ago; had been planted deep in her mechanical intelligence with the intention that once the fateful words were spoken, by anyone, there would be no turning back—no chance to change heart or mind.

CHAPTER 8. HIDEAWAY

The planet was not dead. There were patches of green here, patches of brown or yellow there. The surface of the oceans teemed with the irrepressible activity of life in its most primitive stages. There were even a few fish —or what passed for them on Belmar. But there was definitely something wrong with the planet. Its cities were empty, slowly giving way to the fern and the ivy. No animals wandered its desolate plains or hid beneath the sand of its great deserts. And the water, when it fell, still occasionally stirred a noxious patch of ground and the fumes would rise up. Blown by the wind they would wreak havoc for a while until, through death and dissolution, they were spent. The fumes were less frequent now and the noxious grounds were fewer and farther apart.

Someday, the Quaker mused, human life would be able to return to Belmar. He would live to see it, and when that day came, he would have to move his base of operations elsewhere. But that was in the future. The planet served him well now; not merely a convenient body about which to orbit, but as a burning fuel with which to stoke the fire of his undying passion; his dedication in life.

Once people had lived down there; built those cities. They had all died though, like rats in a trap, when the Hursk had come upon them. The Quaker knew, for he had been among the Hursk. They had paused in their tampering with him; paused and allowed—compelled him to watch the planet die.

The Hursk had been methodical in their own way. The human animal was a pest to them—a nasty pest whom they'd only just discovered, and Belmar was their huge and nasty nest. Extermination was the indicated policy, and extermination it would be. There was no fighting, no dignity in the way Belmar had died, only a slow and painful agony.

A quiet knock on the Quaker's door interrupted his thoughts. "Excuse me, sir," the man said, "but we've got visitors. Two of them."

The Quaker stirred. His massive bulk turned in the semi-darkness of the observation room and glided toward the door. The man stood aside and let him pass, closing the door quietly behind him.

When the Quaker arrived in the control room a few moments later, his officers were standing about looking serious. "The *Nina* dropped out of station to let us know, sir. Two ships are approaching."

The Quaker nodded. "Let's take a look for ourselves," he said, and his officers hurried to comply with the request. A few seconds later the Quaker's big black warship was sliding into main drive.

The planet Belmar and its two small moons vanished from sight, and against the starry background their two visitors appeared; two ship-blips moving toward them.

"The closer one," one of his officers indicated, "is the *Matilda*."

"Yes," the Quaker sighed. He watched without surprise as the second blip slowed, dropped from the screen for a moment, and then reappeared as a pair. The pair split, one resuming its course after the *Matilda* while its partner reversed direction and sped away from them.

"Shall we dispatch an interceptor?" the weapons officer inquired.

The Quaker shook his head slowly, "No, let them go. I expect the IXT would have discovered us here, in time, anyway."

Silence fell over the assemblage. Everyone was watching the two blips which continued their approach, and thinking about the IXT dispatch ship which the Quaker was allowing to escape. The Quaker turned to his communications officer. "Have the *Nina* take care of the IXT warship following the *Matilda* if it tries to interfere with us. Otherwise, ignore it."

"Yes, sir," the officer answered, turning back to his instruments and preparing to send out his message to the *Nina* the moment they dropped back into normal space.

The Quaker's ship, anticipating its orders, was already aligning itself along a course which would intercept the *Matilda* when it dropped out of drive. The minutes of waiting ticked by and men suited themselves for vacuum, prepared for boarding and taking a ship where opposition could come in any form. The *Matilda* wouldn't be returning here with an IXT escort unless something was very wrong aboard her.

When the *Matilda's* drive did shut down, the Quaker's ship was running a close parallel course and the two of them assumed nearly identical orbits around Belmar.

Anna paced the darkened aisles of the *Matilda* restlessly. She was alone now, and frankly lost, but that didn't really matter. She continued her search for some way down into the sealed spaces below. Again and again she'd gone down and found what she thought to be a way, only to find it blocked in the end.

She kept trying, though, and for a very good reason. Somewhere far below she could feel the spark of a life, a life she'd thought gone forever. How he had survived, she did not know. Eyeada was alive. But now that he lived, why didn't he come up and take charge of the situation? She was determined to find out. But determination was not enough. It did not open the doors locked against her, nor did it show her the way in the dark. So she wandered.

There was fighting above her now. Somehow the deadlock had been broken and Devlon's men were no longer confined to their little section of the ship. They were sweeping through the ship above her, killing or taking alive those members of the crew who would surrender. Soon, when they were done with those above, they would come below and search for any who might have escaped in that direction. Already there were two others who had escaped the fighting above. Anna could hear them, running blindly in the dark, fleeing a fate which was all too obvious.

Down the long corridor small sounds reached her; hushed voices and the steady approach of feet. Anna slipped into a room and pressed herself in among crates and long abandoned machine parts. She waited, aware for the first time that she still held, clutched tightly in her hand, the captain's heavy revolver.

For a second light pierced the darkness, then it switched off. "This way," a voice whispered, and Anna felt herself relax. She knew the voice and now, with her fear gone, she could see that there was no danger.

The footfalls continued their approach and Anna moved from her place of concealment, willing to join forces with anyone against Devlon. In moving, she displaced a small bit of metal and it promptly clattered to the floor. Outside the footfalls stopped.

Suddenly, by so small a thing as a single sound, she was in danger of her life (because *they* didn't know who she was and might kill her before they found out.) She dared not move a step further, for just outside the door a desperate man stood waiting to attack. She stumbled backward, but it was too late. He was already in the room with her, moving along the opposite wall, ready to strike at the first sound, the first movement. She held her breath and she could tell that he was holding his breath too.

He was moving again, closer. She slid her foot to one side and perversely it encountered the same bit of metal that had fallen only moments before. Roll, roll, roll it went across the steel floor; a sound so loud it made her want to scream. Her mouth opened and she groped for words with which to ward off the blow that was falling, but nothing came. Instead a light flashed from the aisle, pinning her with its brilliance.

Jennings stopped his arm in mid-swing. Beads of sweat covered his face, and he wiped them with his arm; an innocuous end for a gesture he had begun with such lethal intent.

Anna remained standing quite still. Her mouth was slightly open and the gun she held with both her hands was still pointed at the ground. She did not protest when Jennings leaned forward and relieved her of the burden.

"Quite a start you gave us," Jennings said, almost amiably. "I can see you still haven't found your voice."

"What is she doing here?" Margy asked from behind the light in the doorway.

"The same thing we are, by the looks of it," Jennings mused, examining the heavy pistol curiously. "What is this thing, may I ask?"

Anna squinted in the harsh light and it obligingly dropped away from her eyes. "Thank you," she murmured.

Devlon glared at the motley group of prisoners. It was not enough for him that his plan of cutting a way out of the "golden suite" had worked.

He and his men had captured the *Matilda's* entire crew, or killed them, but the three people he wanted the most were missing.

"Where are they?" he demanded. The prisoners could only stare at the ground and shuffle their feet; they didn't know. "You—there," Devlon selected a man. "Where are they?"

Several lamps illuminated the poor man. He squinted into the glare, licking his lips and twisting the cap he held in his hand. "I don't know, sir. None of us here seen those two IXTers who got away from you. And as for the girl Anna, Bling was the last to see her—and Bling's dead now."

"Is that all you have to say?"

The little man's eyes darted back and forth, seeking a friendly face among the crowd of his fellow captors. This he failed to find. "Please, sir," he pleaded, "I'll lead you down below. I know the ship pretty well. You — you can get lost down there easy."

"Very well," Devlon said easily. He motioned to two of his League followers. "Have this man lead you down below. Give him the light and see that he stays well in front of you."

"Yes, sir!" one of the two men replied, grinning.

"But—but—" The man was grabbed by the scruff of his neck and propelled from the room before he could finish his protest.

"Now," Devlon said, turning to the other prisoners. "Now we can get down to business." Their screams of sudden terror did not carry far, nor did they last very long.

Jennings held the pistol in front of him and Margy illuminated it while Anna explained how it worked. The mechanism was simple enough and although it contained only three more rounds, it was still the best weapon available to them. Jennings' big problem was that he couldn't use the damn thing. He couldn't even use an ordinary needle-nose now that he had only two digits on his mechanical hand. It meant that he had to trust the weapon with either Margy or the girl and hope that when the time came for a test he had made the right choice.

He looked from one to the other and in the dim light he could see that they were both studying him with as much interest as he was studying them. He smiled finally and handed the gun to Margy.

"Here," he said, "you take this and let Miss Bey take charge of the light."

Margy took the pistol and her hand sagged under the unexpected weight. "It's heavy," she said. "But I think I can manage." Margy smiled a little. "I just hope we don't run into more than one target at a time, or more than three altogether." She paused, and looking at Jennings, she said, "I'm sorry," then turned away, unable to say more.

There was an awkward silence after that. Jennings walked to the door of the room and looked out into the darkened corridor. Margy came up behind him as he stood staring out the door. She slipped her arm around his, leaned her head against his shoulder, and let the gun dangle limply in her left hand. "What are we going to do? Oh, what are we going to do?" She felt like crying again, and almost did.

Anna turned away from the pair in the doorway. She sat on a crate heavily, holding the light in her lap and playing it idly across the floor. She was wondering what would happen when Devlon finally got around to finding them. It was bad enough having to worry about that, without having to contend with Jennings too. His mind revealed to her a strange sense of honor: he would kill her rather than let Devlon do it. And yet, if they somehow escaped, he would just as surely work to see her put away for the rest of her life. What a choice.

Anna sighed. She let her thoughts wander from such dreary contemplation and found that she was looking at something on the floor. It was the same small piece of metal she had knocked off one of the crates and then kicked only a few minutes ago. A tool of some kind, probably, and in her curiosity she stooped to pick it up. It was indeed a tool. Inscribed quite clearly on the side it said: **ASSEMBLY UNIT #23**, **PART #88**, **SUBASSEMBLY #6**. And then, for the layman, it said: **ROTATING CONNECTOR SHAFT.** She smiled and wondered what it would be like to be a workman who knew what all of that meant.

She let herself fall into the temptation. Her light traveled over the dusty crates marked **GREASE INJECTION VALVE,** and over there, **CYLINDER CASING-EXTERIOR.** Just how did those two go together? She smiled again and pictured her poor workman puzzling out the question; scratching his head in dismay. You put the injection valve into the cylinder casing thus—scratch, scratch—then you look around and find the, ah there they are—the **REPLACEMENT BEARINGS,** you inject them through the injection valve and they roll around inside the cylinder casing, turning the rotating connector shaft. What a fantastic machine that would be. Her smile faded sadly and she only wished that her workman and his problem were real; and the solution he sought the most serious matter in the universe. How simple life could be.

Jennings turned from the doorway and caught Anna at her little game. "What are you doing there?" he asked with a note of annoyance in his voice.

She smiled and resumed her work. "I'm prying open the replacement bearing case with a rotating connector shaft," she replied with a straight face.

"Take care that you don't spill the damn—" he began, irritated. After a brief pause he concluded, "Damn!" and almost pushed her to the ground in his hurry to take a look.

"What is it?" Margy asked, a little bit confused by the sudden activity.

Jennings didn't answer. He finished prying the lid off the case. After one quick look inside he was staring down at Anna; squinting at her with a sudden suspicion. Being a telepath didn't mean she was necessarily dumb. "Did you think of this?" he demanded, picturing what he had in mind.

Anna didn't answer but smiled an impish grin.

Half an hour later, after much work on hands and knees, the little case was empty. The corridor a hundred feet in either direction from their little room was now covered with a more or less uniform layer of ball bearings. Spaced an inch or two apart they would make walking through the area somewhat hazardous. A surprising number of half-inch bearings could be packed into a cubic-foot crate.

"There is someone coming," Anna whispered. She doused the light she had been using while helping to spread the bearings.

"Which direction?" Jennings asked.

She pointed to the left and Margy moved to the right side of the door, where she knelt and sighted down the slit between crates of grease-injection valves and cylinder casings. The return fire would have to be pretty good to get at her hiding place.

"Don't fire at the one with the light," Anna added. "But there are two others. Don't let them get away."

"Just two?" Jennings whispered.

"They don't think we are armed," Anna replied.

Jennings crossed over and stood behind Margy. "Use all three shots if you have to."

"I won't need that many," she promised a little unsteadily.

The three men approached quite casually. At least the two men in the rear were casual about it. The man holding the light was jittery. The light jabbed and slashed from one doorway to the next, seeking something the poor man did not want to find.

"Hurry it up," one of the two men in the rear snapped. "We could be at this all day, and tomorrow too." He gave the man holding the light a shove just to emphasize the need for speed.

The shove was fatal. The man with the light lurched forward unsteadily and just as he was regaining his balance he stepped on something round and smooth. His foot flew out from under him and his other foot, desperately trying to compensate for the imbalance, encountered the same problem. He flailed and cried out, his light went sailing through the air; throwing a deadly illumination on the two men behind him. A single shot rang out and the man who had done the shoving jerked backward into the man behind him, throwing both to the ground.

The second man scrambled back to his feet, expecting a shot at any moment. Nothing happened. Had the man with the light not been shoved, and the true cause of his fall overlooked, this second man might have escaped. But he did not know about the ground covering, nor did he take the time to look. He simply dashed forward toward the nearest convenient doorway. He never made it. His first stride put him flat on his face and he was up and down again before he realized what was causing the trouble. Finally, as he was shuffling through the doorway, a second shot rang out, and heavy flopping sounds were the only resistance he would ever make.

"What took you so long!" Jennings groaned. The strain of waiting for Margy's second shot had almost been too much for him.

"This thing hit me in the mouth," Margy complained, her tone grieving. "I think I'm going to bleed."

The man who had been holding the light did not move. He sprawled on the floor in a grotesque tangle, not breathing, trying to sink into the floor as Anna came closer.

"It's all right," Anna called to him, and she could not suppress a smile. "You can get up now."

The man moved. His limbs untangled a little and he lay gasping for breath. "Why didn't you tell me you weren't going to kill me!" he accused, still gasping.

"That is you, isn't it, Bling?" Anna asked, kneeling down and squinting at him. "How did you get into the second officer's uniform? It doesn't fit, you know."

Bling didn't elaborate. "Long story," he said. "And I'll gladly tell you someday, but don't you think we ought to be removing ourselves to safer quarters?"

"And where might they be?" she asked innocently.

"Well—damn it—where did you get all them—" he cursed, kicking at some bearings and then, just as rapidly, forgot about them and returned to the subject at hand. "I have keys—to a freight shaft. With a little luck I can open 'er up and get to a safe place."

"How about us?" Anna asked.

"Us?" For the first time Bling glanced up and saw that Anna was not alone. His mind underwent a quick bit of mental gymnastics, scrapping plans he'd been formulating only a moment before. "The more, the merrier," he mumbled, his smile a little strained.

———————

Jennings took charge of the weapons, stuffing one needle-nose and the heavy pistol under his belt. The other needle-nose he gave to Margy. In return he got a mixed look of thanks and anxiety.

Bling led them toward the shaft for which he had the key, looking glum for someone who had just been saved from an almost certain death. When they arrived he fussed with the lock for several moments before it would open. It was just a small door—a service entrance to the shaft and beyond it there was musty machinery, a metal grille platform to stand on and a steel rung ladder leading up and down.

They all entered and Bling very carefully locked the door behind him. He was on the point of congratulating himself on the superbness of his hiding place when the ship shuddered once and then fell very still.

"That's the drive," Bling groaned, but nobody was listening. They were all straining to hear it start up again.

"It won't be starting again," he moaned. "If that's what you're waiting for. She didn't stop naturally—she blew herself out. He probably planned 'er that way."

"Who?" Jennings asked.

"The captain," Bling said, his whining tone increasing. "He'll not let us live long now he's gone."

"But he's not . . ." Anna stopped herself with an effort. The others were all looking at her: Jennings and Margy without comprehension and Bling with growing suspicion.

"So he ain't dead!" Bling accused. "Then we still have a chance."

He started down the ladder without another word, and they followed. For Jennings the climb was a trial, each rung an unexpected victory. Both Anna and Margy lingered with him and Bling was soon out of sight below them. Only an occasional sound coming up the shaft reassured them that he was still there. The climb seemed endless. It was a shock when they reached the bottom. Bling was already there; his ear pressed against the smooth metal of a hatch and a look of utter frustration on his face.

"It's sealed," he complained. "I thought sure I—we could get through this way. Now we're doomed for sure. It's only a matter of time before they find us—and if they don't we'll starve anyway."

Jennings grunted, flexing the tired muscles in his arm. "I take it we're going to have to climb back out of this hole."

"What's the use!" Bling moaned, kicking the hatch and flinging his battered, twisted cap to the ground.

Jennings tested his two remaining digits and looked at rung after steel rung planted in the wall of the shaft and disappearing into the black mists above. "There is no immediate hurry I guess, but I don't plan to stay down here like a rat and wait for them to come on us."

Anna was not really paying attention to the conversation. She was sure that Eyeada was alive and back there somewhere buried among his ship's machines; almost as if he were hiding—purposely avoiding her. He knew she was out here, and he knew she would know that he was still alive. And yet he persisted in a plan, the very dimmest outline of which made her shiver. If only she could see more clearly. If only. . .

They all noticed the change immediately. Like having the wind knocked out of you—a sudden decompression. Bling covered his ears and exhaled, his eyes mirroring the fear they all felt. Would the decompression stop before it was too late?

It did, and like a bell the ship reverberated with the shock of it.

"The pressure hull," Bling gasped, his voice almost as thin as the air. "It's been breached."

The suspense of what was happening did not last long—at least for Anna. Nor did the battle which began above them. The Quaker's men in full battle armor were more than a match for Devlon's scattered men. Even fanaticism can carry a man only so far. Devlon surrendered with his remaining men the moment he realized that the suited men were not connected with the IXT. He was overjoyed when he found they served the very man he'd been hoping to find—the man who would help him smash the IXT once and for all. Devlon could not know that the Quaker would never help him —that the Quaker disliked aliens and the ideals of the Freedom League even more strongly than the IXT.

I t took nearly an hour for the Quaker's men to find the four of them down at the bottom of the shaft and Anna used the time to good effect, persuading Jennings to surrender without fighting. This was agreed to only when she convinced him that the people coming down the shaft had no connection with Devlon.

In a way their rescue, or hers anyway, came as an anti-climax. Aboard the Quaker's ship Anna was separated from the others and taken to the observation room, where she found the Quaker sitting in the dark and looking out at the *Matilda* and the planet below. His bulk seemed larger than she remembered, but this was the impression she always had on seeing him after a long absence.

"A strange and unusual surprise, this reunion," the Quaker said as he turned to face her. "But things often happen that way; you lose something unexpectedly and in the same fall of the die, you win something equally unexpected."

Anna frowned. The cryptic statement seemed to convey a meaning she could only vaguely grasp. The Quaker regarded her puzzlement with the trace of a smile, his arms folded—as they always were, across the great expanse of his body. His mind remained unreadable; as unreadable as some others were transparent.

"What do you mean," she asked reluctantly, "What have you lost?"

The Quaker's eyes shifted back to the observation port. "That planet out there and the convenience of basing operations here. I have lost those; and that ship you see, the *Matilda,* and her captain—a valuable man. One of a kind."

"Captain Eyeada? But he's still alive—haven't your men found him yet?"

"Alive, you say?" the Quaker responded skeptically. "Perhaps. But not for long; and not in a way you would understand."

Her eyes widened. "You're not just going to leave him out there."

"No," he said, and he realized that she truly did not understand what was going to happen. "In fact," he continued, seizing the opportunity, "I do intend to make one last attempt to change the inevitable."

He departed, leaving her to think, worry. He made the trip over to the *Matilda* rapidly; knowing that Anna would be watching. When he arrived he did in fact visit the captain.

Eyeada lay amid the tangled machinery of what had once been the *Matilda's* medical center. He was alive, but only by the thinnest edge; his conscious mind blissfully unaware. The Quaker knew of the captain's preparations—knew everything that would happen in the next few hours. He could stop it if he wished—go back on his word. But Eyeada had worked for him under an agreement, an agreement which he felt obliged to honor; much as he regretted its termination. He was tempted to arouse the captain; ask him if this one last service would meet with his approval. But he knew that it wouldn't. And he knew that the few moments' consciousness the captain had left were being saved and would be used better elsewhere.

After a suitable time the Quaker departed, glad that he had maneuvered himself into this last farewell. It was to Eyeada's credit that he would go on serving right up to the end.

When the Quaker returned he found Anna standing alone in the observation room, looking out upon Belmar's shaded crescent. He closed the door and remained quietly in the darkness behind her. She spoke without turning.

"What did you find?"

The Quaker did not answer immediately. He weighed many things in his mind and when he spoke it was not without calculation, nor were the effects of what he said unforeseen. But he spoke the truth and he let this be seen. "The captain will not be with us much longer."

"Why?" she asked. "Why is he doing it?"

The Quaker looked from the girl's back to the planet beyond. "Let me tell you a story, Anna, a story that began a long time ago. There was a young man then. He was happy. He had everything; a young and beautiful wife, and for a home the ship of which he was captain and owner. They went everywhere together, cutting their ties from the ground and living a life few are able to conceive.

"Finally the inevitable happened and the young wife grew heavy with child. She could no longer travel and faced with the separation our young man did the best he could. He provided for his wife in every way and for himself he did as much. He changed the name of his ship to hers, and to ease the loneliness replaced its mechanical modulation with the voice so dear to him.

"And so prepared he departed on a trip no different than all the others, save that he made it alone. Amid all his passengers and crew, he felt alone. The trip was routine in every way, and like all others, it was named for the date of its scheduled return; the five-oh-five, or fifth of May.

"For two weeks he was gone, a mere two weeks. And when he returned he found . . ."

The Quaker's voice trailed away into the darkness, and the planet below them seemed to grow in the magnitude of its murky light.

"Only the combined effort of its crew and passengers kept the ship sealed after its landing on Belmar, and it was against his own will that the young man survived that day. The ship returned with its news of death and destruction—news that helped to save the human race—but its owner was no longer capable of command. He disappeared from sight after that and for thirty-five years no one knew or cared that he was still alive.

"When I found him, he was barely alive; dying of starvation and apathy. But there was still a spark left—a spark I could use and needed. He was the first man I recruited and the only one I ever allowed to join me in the kind of life I lead. Our reasons were different, and we did not always agree on methods, but together we did quite a job on the Hursk."

He paused and out in the darkness around the planet he watched the *Matilda* moving, making its long delayed descent to the land of its origin, the soil from which it had sprung.

"Stop it!" Anna cried. "Bring it back. Don't let it go. Can't you even do that?"

"I could," the Quaker answered, "if he wanted me to. But he's made up his mind."

"Why?" she asked again, her voice choking, "Why, after so many years?"

The Quaker glided forward through the darkness and took her limp, cold right hand between his. She turned and looked at him, her eyes swollen and pleading.

"Don't you understand?" he asked, and could see that she didn't. "It's because of you. You reminded him, and stirred the ashes I'd tried so hard to bury. His wife—her talent was like yours, matured—and she was able to share it with him."

CHAPTER 9. REUNION

W hen the *Exeter* returned to the IXT Complex with the *Ambol*
a meeting took place to decide the IXT's policy in the case
once and for all. The concluding speaker was Admiral Keel
of Justice. He was prepared to recommend action which the IXT had
never undertaken before.

"Gentlemen," Keel began, "we are faced with a very difficult problem.
On the one hand we have the Quaker—an unknown quantity for the
most part, and on the other we have Mr. Somack and the *Ambol.*
Separately we might be able to deal with either one of them in our usual
way, but they are linked in such a fashion as to make this treatment
impossible.

"Consider the Quaker. With one ship he has proven he can take
anything we can give out. Through good fortune we have located him
again and find that he has yet another ship, a planetary base, and some
possible connection with Devlon and the Freedom League. All of this is
bad, but we have overcome worse in the past. However, there are
complications. The *Ambol,* for instance, has some properties we would
very much like to study.

Then there are Mr. Somack and Miss Bey, both of whom were
removed from Justice custody over my loud protest. We are not sure how
these two people fit together, but we are sure that the Quaker is interested
in getting his hands on one or both of them. His interest was deep

enough to make him reveal his existence to us, and demonstrate to us that there is little we can safely do to interfere with him.

"We have gambled with one of our assets—the girl, and in return have managed to relocate the Quaker. He is aware of this and doesn't seem to care. We have a ship watching his base and his actions near Belmar and he has not attacked it."

The admiral paused in his talk. His case was a strong one and he knew that after the bungles made by Intelligence and Enforcement his views would be taken seriously.

"The real question," Admiral Keel continued, "is what to do now. The Freedom League is interested in only one thing—our destruction and unlimited contact with aliens. And *this,* more than anything else, is what we must prevent. Before I give my recommendations for action, I want to show you what our computers have come up with."

Keel paused to thumb through some papers. "The probabilities they point to are as follows:

"1. The Quaker is in contact with aliens unknown to us. This is substantiated by his use of weapons about which we know nothing.

"2. The Freedom League, although in contact with the Quaker, has no contact with unknown aliens. This is substantiated by lack of action by the League. If they had access to knowledge and weapons, they would not hesitate to use it.

"3. Somack and his ship *have* been in contact with unknown aliens. This is substantiated by the following set of facts: A. Malfunction, for no known reason, of numerous reliable devices placed aboard the *Ambol.* B. Attitude of Somack toward the IXT. C. Willingness of the Quaker to reveal himself in pursuit of Somack and the *Ambol.*

"4. The Quaker wishes to communicate with Somack or the *Ambol* and does not wish to destroy them. The log aboard the *Ambol* and our own records of our recent battle with the Quaker show he did everything in his power to protect and *not to destroy* the *Ambol* and its passengers."

The admiral smiled as he finished reading. "What I am going to propose is something that has never been done before by the IXT. We cannot allow people like the Quaker to get ahead of us. We can no longer be content with simply protecting and isolating the human race. We must reach out and acquaint ourselves with what is happening out there.

"Specifically, we must discover the nature of the being or beings which have effected such a change in the *Ambol,* and which the Quaker is so interested in contacting.

"It is no longer possible for the IXT to fulfill its duty by simply waiting. We have seen that the dangers which stumble upon us are not the only ones that exist. They must be sought out—when they come to our attention —and dealt with. We cannot hide from the fact that the world out there progresses, and we must do the same to survive."

The room was quiet when Admiral Keel finished. What he proposed was dangerous, unheard of. In searching out this alien threat, the IXT would be doing what it was supposed to prevent—and yet—something had to he done. It was this need that brought agreement to the group. Action must be taken.

C aptain Abraham Kane, Commanding Officer of the IXT *Exeter* and now officer in charge of a situation no one else wanted, glanced around the room. Captain James Merrick, Justice, was seated to Kane's left. Across the table sat William Somack, until recently a pilot for the Heinmann and Schultz Transport Company.

"Well, Mr. Somack," Kane said, pausing to pluck one particular report from the many arrayed in front of him, "I understand you terminated your employment with the H&STC the moment you garnered sufficient credit to make your purchase of the *Ambol*. Is that correct?"

"Yes."

Kane thumbed through the report he had selected. Occasionally an eyebrow would lift, otherwise he made no comment until he had finished reading.

"You are a qualified pilot," Kane stated. "In fact you are more than that. It says here that H&STC offered you an executive position when you informed them that you were resigning. A twenty-year contract with a guaranteed renewal option. This is also correct?"

Somack smiled, remembering the scene Kane spoke of. "Yes, it's true." The H&STC liked to retain good men and what they had offered in private was a good deal more than a guaranteed renewal option.

Kane dropped the report on the table with an audible thud. He leaned far back in his chair and his eyes narrowed. "You turned it down for what, Mr. Somack? Just what did you intend to find on your trips with the *Ambol?*"

"Something valuable."

"Valuable enough to warrant the sacrifices you've made just to begin your search?" Kane let his skepticism show through.

"Certainly," Somack answered. He leaned forward to emphasize his point. "Valuable enough to make me willing to accept even your help."

"You make that sound like an insult."

Somack nodded.

"Very well, then," Kane resumed, "I think we understand each other pretty well. I will let Captain Merrick explain the situation to you."

Merrick paused before speaking. He took a long hard look at Somack. "You have something we want, Mr. Somack. We are not sure exactly what it is, but we suspect it involves knowledge of a kind the IXT is interested in. We often expend many lives in obtaining information about alien races. You can help us prevent such an unfortunate loss in this case. We haven't the time nor the manpower to search countless stars for the kind of information we want. That is why we let them come to us, and the meetings are usually painful for everyone involved. If you know the location of an alien race, that information is of vital importance to us. We want it."

Somack let the words flow over him. His mouth remained pressed in a tight line. "You know what *I* want," he commented dryly. "All you have to do is give it to me."

"I'm afraid that's impossible."

"Who made it impossible?" Somack asked simply.

Merrick glanced at Kane and the *Exeter's* commander shrugged indifferently. "Very well," Merrick continued. "If you are not willing to cooperate we will have to find another way."

"I never said I wouldn't co-operate," Somack corrected. "I simply said I wouldn't do it for nothing. All I can do is promise you that if *you* can recover the girl, I will do my best."

"Impossible. We know where the Quaker is, but there is no way we can fight him."

"I am not asking you to fight him," Somack sighed. "All I want you to do is let me know where he is. You must realize he is waiting for something."

"You mean he is waiting for you?" Merrick suggested.

"Possibly."

Merrick drew a thin envelope from his pocket. "We are willing to trade you the information in this envelope—Miss Bey's location, for the location of your alien race."

Somack sat very still. "I have never claimed to know the location of anything."

Kane raised his hand before Merrick could say anything sharp. "Please, let's not quibble. We will help you if you will help us. It's as simple as that."

"On my terms," Somack insisted.

"On your terms," Kane agreed.

Somack extended his hand across the table for the envelope. Merrick hesitated to release it. Only Kane's nodded assurance—order—compelled him to do it.

"One man," Somack said. "I will allow one man to accompany me aboard the *Ambol.* You can follow us with anything you want, but only one man can come aboard the *Ambol.* And he must be unarmed."

Kane rubbed his chin. "If we co-operate with this plan of yours, you will co-operate with us later on?"

"If she is alive and well, yes."

Kane considered a moment the possibilities and risks involved. He had a chance to unbotch a job which for the longest time had looked hopeless. If this meant taking a few more chances than usual, so much the better. He was a fighting man and not averse to taking chances. Besides, he had a feeling that Somack could be trusted.

"Then we will begin at once," Kane decided abruptly. Turning to Merrick, he added, "And you will be the man to accompany him. I will follow with the *Exeter.*"

There was no argument.

The *Ambol* followed Somack's instructions without comment and seemed almost upset at not having been consulted on the arrangements. It showed its displeasure by remaining stubbornly silent. Even when Merrick was asleep and out of the way it maintained its boycott on communications. Only after four long days, when they were within hours of the Quaker's base, did it make its displeasure known visually.

WHAT YOU ARE DOING IS DANGEROUS, it flashed in the early hours of the morning, while Merrick slept.

"How so?" Somack retorted, in no mood for an argument.

TOO MANY UNKNOWN VARIABLES. COMPUTATIONS DO

NOT SUGGEST PROBABLE SUCCESS. THE MISSION YOU UNDERTAKE IS UNNECESSARY. ALLOW INITIATIVE AND WILL PROCEED DIRECTLY TO MAIN OBJECTIVE. FOLLOWING SHIP CANNOT INTERFERE.

"Go back to sleep," Somack answered shortly. "Your suggestions are not wanted, nor were they solicited."

The ship surprised him by remaining quiescent. It seemed resigned to a course which it considered to be wrong. The few remaining hours passed quickly and Merrick, who had been asleep, emerged from his light sleep refreshed and ready to face whatever action they were about to encounter.

The star grew rapidly and the *Ambol* slowed. There were no other ships in the area—at least no other ships with their main drives on. The *Ambol* cut its drive and the planet of Belmar snapped into view. A few minutes later the *Exeter* followed suit and made its appearance next to them. By that time the *Ambol* had located the three other ships already in orbit around the planet.

"Which one is it?" Somack asked anxiously.

THE SHIP *MATILDA* IS NOT PRESENT, OF THE THREE SHIPS WHICH ARE PRESENT: ONE IS OF IXT DESIGN; ONE IS OF UNKNOWN DESIGN—QUAKER SHIP PREVIOUSLY ENCOUNTERED; ONE IS OF UNKNOWN DESIGN—QUAKER-TYPE SHIP NEVER PREVIOUSLY ENCOUNTERED.

Somack felt a sinking in his chest. Anna was aboard the *Matilda*.

AM RECEIVING REQUESTS FOR COMMUNICATION FROM IXT *EXETER* AND FROM QUAKER SHIP PREVIOUSLY ENCOUNTERED.

"Let's talk to the *Exeter*," Merrick suggested.

"No. We'll see what the other ship has to say."

The *Ambol* immediately devoted a portion of its screen to the incoming transmission, visual and audio. A face appeared, heavily jowled, with eyes so sunken in flesh that their color could not be discerned.

"Ah!" the face said, though there was no visible motion of the lips. "Billy Somack! I had not hoped for so fortunate an outcome."

"Who are you?" Somack replied dryly, ignoring the proffered familiarity.

The face seemed to be squinting at him. "There is someone else with you, isn't there? Ah. I see now. An IXT uniform. I commend your caution, but there is no need."

"What is this?" Merrick demanded. His suspicions were aroused by the familiar way in which the Quaker addressed Somack.

Somack looked from the screen to Merrick and back again. "There was another ship here not long ago, the *Matilda*. Where has it gone?"

The Quaker began to say something, but the *Ambol* cut him off. Knowing the answer, it simply supplied it.

THE IXT *EXETER* HAS BEEN ATTEMPTING TO CONVEY THAT INFORMATION TO YOU. THE *MATILDA* HAS DESCENDED TO THE PLANET'S SURFACE AND IS PRESENTLY RESIDING THERE. AN UNKNOWN NUMBER OF PERSONNEL WERE REMOVED FROM SAID SHIP, BEFORE IT DESCENDED, AND TRANSFERRED TO THE SHIP WITH WHICH YOU ARE COMMUNICATING.

The Quaker seemed anxious for a reply so Somack said, "I understand that you have taken certain personnel from the *Matilda*. Perhaps that is how you obtained my name."

The Quaker paused to consider his answer. He could tell that things were not going in exactly the way he had planned. But he had the advantage of a well-laid groundwork and nothing to lose. This latter asset, of course, was his most valuable.

"Yes," he said quietly, "she is here. She wants to see you very much. Perhaps you will join us for the evening meal—or whichever meal you happen to be needing at this moment."

"No!" Merrick ordered.

"I will be glad to join you," Somack replied without bothering to acknowledge Merrick's interruption. The *Ambol* responded to the implied order and began drifting in toward a rendezvous with the Quaker's black ship. The *Exeter* followed, but not too closely.

S omack paused in the *Ambol's* control room hatch. Merrick wanted to go with him, had argued vehemently against his leaving the ship at all, but to no avail. He was going aboard the Quaker's ship alone and Merrick was staying behind. The inner hatch slid closed and for a moment Somack stood by himself. The dim light and the cramped space inside the chamber reminded him of the time he had spent lying on the floor of the tiny room, bleeding and wondering if his life were about to end. It was strange to think that those events lay only a few waking days behind him.

He shook his head as the outer door opened and he stepped through. Two men were waiting for him and they saluted formally.

"This way," the dark-haired man said. "The Quaker is waiting for you."

Not another word was spoken on the long walk through the dark ship. The route was not direct. Many turns and twists convinced Somack that the Quaker was taking no chances. He was not going to see any vital part of the ship during his long walk. It was just as well. He had no interest in the black ship, its secrets, or its personnel. All he wanted to do was see Anna and get her back aboard the *Ambol* if possible.

His two guides paused finally. The door they stopped in front of looked no different from the many they had passed already. Just another door, but it was obviously their destination. The dark-haired man rapped on the door lightly and a small green light appeared in the ceiling above them.

"You can go in," the dark-haired man said, his lips twisted slightly in silent amusement.

The door opened and Somack stepped through. The two guides remained outside and the door closed behind him. The room was dimly lit, a table and setting prominently located at the center. Somack glanced to his right and his gaze went no further. Anna stood not five yards away. Her back was against the wall and she presented him with a beautiful profile. Her gloved hands rested beneath the small of her back and she was looking down, her head bent in contemplation.

Somack felt his tongue thicken. He tried to say something, but nothing happened. He realized now that his memories of her were only pale reflections of the real thing. Her youth struck him more forcefully now than it ever had. He felt a twinge of regret—of doubt almost, that his memory had misled him and things as he remembered them were not things as they were. He did not recollect her being this . . . and he groped for a word to fit what she was. And what she was wearing, he had never seen anything like it worn to better advantage. It was almost as if, and he couldn't stop the thought, as if he were looking at someone he had never met before.

From the shadows on Somack's left something glided forward. After pausing to watch in silence for a few moments, it said; "Come, come, my children. Let's not keep the food waiting."

Somack heard the voice and recognized it, but he did not move to follow its suggestion. Anna, however, glanced up at the sound and for the first time she looked at him. Somack quailed silently and he felt his heart sink. He remembered those soft dark eyes and the compassion they had given him once. Now they were hard and they looked right through him. And the mouth was set and firm. It smiled at him beautifully, but it was not pretty.

He turned away and could only wonder at the difference a few days could make. He saw the Quaker then, and though he should have been repulsed by the sight, he wasn't. He only smiled a little bit sadly and nodded.

It was the Quaker's turn to be surprised. It was not often someone could see him for the first time and show no reaction. Again he felt himself to be dealing with someone he could not be sure of. There was nothing more dangerous to the Quaker's mind than a man whose reactions you could not calculate. He covered his momentary discomfiture with the smile of a welcoming host and gestured toward the table.

"The meal awaits us," he said, and added to Somack, "I hope our humble fare will please you."

"I'm sure," Somack muttered. He assisted Anna to her seat and tried to brace himself for what he was sure would be the worst meal of his life.

Although the table was set for three, food was served only to Somack and Anna. The plates and saucers before the Quaker remained empty.

"Go ahead and eat," the Quaker chuckled when he noticed Somack's gaze on the empty setting. "I take my nourishment in other ways—and besides, as you can see, I needn't worry about starvation for some time to come."

Somack looked from the Quaker to Anna, who was dabbling with her food and keeping her eyes averted. "I came aboard your ship for only one reason," he said, turning back to the Quaker, "and that was not to eat. It seems I was mistaken in what I had hoped to find."

The Quaker frowned. "An evil-tempered remark for so pleasant an evening. What more could you want? I've done my best to provide you with pleasurable company and a good meal. Surely you will not refuse them after I've gone to so much trouble."

"Perhaps if you left I could bring myself to eat."

The point was made so bluntly that the Quaker could not help laughing. He rumbled and quaked. His whole body was set into an uneasy rippling motion and it was some time before the motion subsided enough for him to speak. "Certainly, certainly," he conceded jovially. "If you wish to be alone with Miss Bey, I shall be obliged to leave. How much simpler it would have been if you had made your wish plain from the start."

The Quaker withdrew as quietly as he had appeared. When the door sealed Somack turned to Anna. "What is wrong?" he asked simply. "What has happened?"

She looked up at him and he saw again that her eyes were hard, but there was something more. Her face showed signs of strain and now, with the Quaker gone, a trace of fear. "Nothing is wrong," she said, glancing away quickly. "Nothing at all."

Somack tasted his food unenthusiastically. He was trying, unsuccessfully, to find a reason for what was happening. Anna looked on him with an unexplainable fear and yet she was determined on some course he could not fathom. He forced his eyes to inspect the room, the table and the food, but they always came back to her. He could see every shadow cast by the smooth features of her face and her hair fell in the same dark cascade he remembered so well.

"You are very beautiful, Anna," he said, unable to help himself.

Her head came up with a snap and the fear he saw there was more pronounced. "Don't say that!" she pleaded, and her eyes dropped again. "Please don't say that. You have no right."

"Who is the Quaker?" he asked. "Or perhaps I should say, what is he? And what has he been doing to you?"

He knew even before he finished speaking that he'd said the wrong thing. She looked at him for a long moment before answering. If her determination had been on the point of breaking a moment ago, there was no trace of the weakness now. "Who," she said very slowly. "Who. Not what." It was too much; this fighting an opponent he could not see on a battlefield he could not find. He could flail at shadows forever and still never find what there was standing between them. She would not tell him and he could not pluck the answer from thin air.

He stood abruptly. There was no point in staying. But he revised this thought quickly. His legs would not hold him. He lowered himself back into his chair, looking from the food to Anna and back again. She accepted his accusing look without flinching.

"It's too late to stop the inevitable," she said calmly, almost sleepily.

For a moment his vision blurred, but it cleared again and he looked at Anna more closely. Her lashes hung over her eyes heavily and her lips were slightly parted. She seemed on the point of saying something, but there was no sound. Even her expression, held so constantly through the evening, was gone now. He was seeing her now as he had never seen her before—a child's face innocent of the trouble which lay beneath. And he could see those troubles—even as his eyes were closing he could see them. The sensation was strangely familiar, so much like a rainy night long ago. It all came to him clearly in those last few moments—what they were doing to him —what they would find out. Anna's eyes were closing too and she was slipping forward onto the table—sliding sideways—dropping toward the ground.

He wanted to stop her—help her—but he could only hear a distant voice saying, "Take them into the next room and make them comfortable. They have a long hard time ahead of them."

The night was a long one. The Quaker was the only one in attendance and he watched the two sleepers with weary eyes. He felt no pride in what he had done. The drug, though illegal, was easily made and produced a period of sleep filled with unusually vivid dreams. But for a few, a very few, these dreams were not the random products of imagination. They were glimpses of another's mind; chunks of memory lifted out of context and dropped haphazardly among one's own. Often the chunks were irrelevant, meaningless trivia. But because prominent memories were more easily snatched, they were often obtained—and important memories from Somack's mind were just what the Quaker wanted.

The Quaker knew that there might be no result this first time. The information Anna gathered might not be what he wanted. If this was the case, then the whole thing would have to be repeated—and repeated again and again until he got the desired result. He hoped that there would be no need of a repeated application. Too many treatments with the drug and the subjects would begin to lose their sense of identification—begin to confuse stolen memories with their real ones. He had no wish to destroy either Somack or Anna. And most of all, he grudged the time these extra treatments might take. He had every reason to hope for success this first time—for everybody's sake.

Time passed slowly and there was no movement in the little room, save an occasional toss or mumbled word from one of the sleeping pair. The Quaker watched it all. Every motion or mumbled word was recorded in his perfect memory for later use. A trivial sound now might be the key to a memory later, when he was questioning Anna.

He did not sleep. It was one of the many prices the Quaker had been forced to pay for his unwanted immortality. He never slept, just as he never ate in the ordinary sense. Though he might feel weary for years on end, the weariness could not be ended by sleep. It was something he seldom thought about—a tribute to the discipline he clamped on his mind, twenty-four hours a day.

The vigil ended abruptly. Anna opened her eyes and stared at the darkened ceiling. The Quaker waited several seconds for her first word, her first reaction to what she had experienced, but nothing happened. She continued to stare into the emptiness above her and occasionally she would blink slowly.

He glided to her side and touched her hand gently. "Are you all right?" he asked.

Her fingers reacted to his touch with a crushing grip. She turned her head on the pillow and looked at him. Her eyes seemed to be sunken and she blinked again before they registered recognition.

"I'm tired." That was all she said, but there was something in the way she said it, in the way her eyes closed and the grip on his hand relaxed, that made him react swiftly. Within moments she was receiving medical care unmatched in its competence and skill. With the Quaker watching everything, none dared give less than the best.

"I don't understand," the head of the medical team said. "There is nothing wrong with her. Just a little fatigue, perhaps."

The Quaker looked at the man for a long moment without speaking. Some of the confidence in that medical face ebbed visibly. It was gone entirely by the time the Quaker spoke. "Just see that she lives," he said quietly, and turned to look at Anna. Her face seemed relaxed now, although still a little pale. "It is important that she live. You understand that."

The medical man himself looked a little pale now. "Yes, I understand."

"Good." The Quaker withdrew, sure that the best attention would be given the case. He returned to the darkened room and was happy to find that Somack was still asleep. He seemed to be reacting to the drug normally. There would be no cause for worry in his case.

S omack awoke in the darkness blinking at the ceiling. His mind was filled with bits and pieces; glimpses of a life he had no right to share. There was a flash of grief lost in the mist of a childhood filled with mild sadness —happy illusions and dreams helping to fill the lonely days when the Quaker was away; illusions of dark and handsome faces, always shattering on too close approach.

Many things are private and are meant to be. Little things. They are important and yet they shrivel in the garish light of exposure. Somack believed in privacy. It was a part of his personal philosophy and it saddened him to have seen so much Anna—so much that only she, of her own will, should have given away.

Always Somack had held himself back. He'd never desired to see so deeply into another person. And not Anna. Not someone he'd wanted to give of herself freely. He did not want to steal things which she might have given.

But it was too late. Just as it was too late for her. She had seen things she could never understand. It made him shiver to think of what she had done. She had seen parts of his dream—she had pricked it in tiny places and it had run forth like the yoke of an egg; to congeal and harden on exposure. What she had seen frightened him. They were bright spots— bits of warning; terrifying even in their full context. To see only them would be like seeing a film on Earth history where only wars were shown, wars shorn of their origins and outcomes—carnage, senseless in its aimless intensity and continuity. He had seen a film like that once, and had not enjoyed it. The sensation would have been the same for her, only worse. Much worse. She would not only have seen and heard—she would have *lived* the most frightening portions of his dream. He longed to correct the situation, to share it all with her, but he could sense that Anna was no longer close enough to hear.

He sought to move and found himself weak. He turned and discovered he was not alone. The Quaker's bulk showed even in the darkness. It took a moment, but Somack adapted quickly to the Quaker's lack of presence. Somack had always been able to sense when other people were near. But the Quaker was different. The Quaker's body was there, before his eyes, but he could sense no mind within it. It must be there— somewhere, but he could not sense it. He accepted this just as he had accepted the Quaker's unusual physical appearance.

"You have enjoyed your rest?" the Quaker inquired.

Somack did not answer. He struggled into a sitting position and rubbed his face. His mouth suddenly felt dry and sticky. He wanted a drink and this thought lodged itself in his mind, ironically combating with his desire to sink a fist into the Quaker's face.

"Where is she?" Somack asked at last.

The lights in the room brightened gradually and the Quaker studied his face for a few moments before answering. "I can see that you intend to take her with you when and if you leave."

"Yes," Somack said, and he waited.

"Perhaps she does not wish to accompany you. Have you considered that possibility?"

Somack set his jaw. "When she tells me that herself—and we are both light-years away from you, that is when I will begin to consider that possibility."

"Confidence is a wonderful thing," the Quaker said, and he rotated toward the door. "You shall have your chance to speak with her, perhaps."

The Quaker paused at the open door, rotating to face Somack again. "I'm sure you understand. You're an astute man, astute enough to realize that things would be so much easier on her, on yourself, if you would simply cooperate and tell me what he told you."

"He who?"

The Quaker sighed. "You see. Stubbornness. You know what I'm after, just as you know that I am the only one who really knows what happened on that rainy night when you were five years old. If you co-operate and give me the information he passed on to you—or lead me to where I can discover it for myself—then we'll not have to go through another session like the one we just finished."

Somack felt himself burning and he restrained himself only because he knew that violence would get him nowhere. "I will speak with Anna first."

"Certainly," the Quaker said. "It will be arranged."

Anna sat propped up in bed. Physically she was perfectly normal, but her face still showed signs of strain—the only residue of a protracted struggle she had fought with herself. The outcome had been a drawn truce of exhaustion and she had been carried back from the brink by the combined momentum of youth and a healthy body. There were shadows beneath her eyes because she now tended to avoid sleep as much as possible and closed them only when a weary and dreamless sleep was assured.

She was aware that she was to have a visitor and she was also aware of who that visitor would be. She heard him enter but did not look to the side where he would be standing. She had insisted on that condition. She would not have to look at him unless she chose to.

"How are you feeling?" Somack asked.

"Very well, considering," she answered, and frowned. It was easier to talk with him than she had dared hope. Too easy.

"You'll be up and around soon?"

"Yes."

"You're a brave girl," he said gently.

Anna stiffened and for a moment her lips seemed to quiver. "You came to ask me a question. Please ask it now, then go."

Somack stepped toward her and the unexpected motion made Anna do something she had resolved not to do. She turned her head and found him looking down at her, smiling.

"You've answered my question," he said. "You won't come."

He turned and left the room quietly.

She stared after him and then at the cold grey door that closed behind him. She trembled and for just a split second forgot the horrors she'd seen and been dreaming about. She called out. But it was too late. He was gone and was not likely to be back.

"Well?" the Quaker asked, although he could tell by the expression on Somack's face that everything had gone as he had known it would.

"I'll take you where you can learn for yourself some of what Anna has learned."

The Quaker did not smile at what Somack said, but he did feel one step closer to his goal and for him it was much the same. "I'm glad," he said, "I don't think she could have taken another session. What did she see?" the Quaker asked. "She couldn't tell me much—only that there was a creature —a creature which had a terrible power."

Somack looked at the Quaker and shook his head. "You don't even know what you're looking for. The IXT wants to find it because you seem interested, and you want to find it because the IXT was interested forty years ago. And because of power. Both you and the IXT expect to gain some of that from me. From what I know. Why don't you just fight each other and leave me out of it?"

The Quaker turned and pointed toward the screen where the IXT *Exeter* lay watching them. "You see that ship? It's no match for me. They know it, you know it, and I know it. But any second I could give an order and that ship would disappear. You want to know why I don't destroy them? I could tell you that it is simply a matter of expedience; that I don't destroy them because I don't want to waste the time fighting off the swarms of ships they would send in its place. Right now I have all the advantages. I can outrun them if I don't want to fight. But every time I beat them at something they will learn. Science is mainly a matter of learning what is possible. Every time I do something they thought was impossible, they will begin to look and eventually be able to do it too.

"But expedience is not the reason I am letting the IXT alone. Everything I have done in these last few weeks has strengthened them or will eventually strengthen them. They are doing something good for the human race and the only quarrel I have with them is that they do not go far enough.

"The IXT merely separates humanity from potential alien enemies. I *destroy* those enemies."

"You expect me to lead you to yet another kill, don't you? You expect to learn as much as you can from it—add to your power—and then destroy it."

"Exactly," the Quaker admitted.

Somack stepped toward the door. 'You will find it difficult in this case."

"I think not."

Somack did not argue. 'You will allow me to return to the *Ambol* now?" he asked, stepping through the door.

The Quaker followed him into the corridor before answering. "Certainly. You will be allowed to go your own way once you have shown me where this creature of yours is. I can't speak for the IXT, of course. They may have other ideas."

"What if I assured you that it represents no threat to anyone? That it has only shown itself because it wants to help."

The Quaker did not show his amusement. "The precedent would be unique. A kindly creature—yet merely knowing about it affects Anna so adversely? I cannot imagine such a thing."

Somack shrugged. There was no point in argument. He could only regret that things had not worked out as he had planned. For the first time in his life he'd allowed his personal ambitions to overrule what he knew was the right course. He had gone out of his way, placed himself in the Quaker's power—all in the hope of seeing Anna again and the result had been disaster. Everything he had ever worked for was now in jeopardy. But he would do it all again. He was not fool enough to wish he'd done it differently, but he could still feel the regret. It was a regret and sadness he could look forward to feeling for a long time to come.

T he *Ambol's* hatch opened as he approached, and Merrick, showing signs of strain and uncertainty, stood anxiously waiting for him to enter.

"This is the damnedest ship I've ever been on," Merrick commented the moment the hatch sealed behind Somack. "It won't do a thing. The controls haven't functioned since you left and now it's suddenly alive again."

Somack sank into the control chair. He did not feel up to explaining anything at the moment.

"It has some type of personal sensing device?" Merrick half guessed. "It is certainly better than anything we have been able to come up with."

Somack noticed that Merrick sounded just a little bit odd in a way he didn't like. "I think you had better leave the bridge while I prepare to set the ship in motion." Outside, the hull of the Quaker's ship was already opening to let the *Ambol* out.

"What about our agreement?" Merrick asked, his voice hardening.

"Damn your agreement. Just leave." Somack's head ached and he felt heavy all over. He leaned forward wearily and spoke to the ship. "There have been attempts to tamper?"

CORRECT, the ship answered, **INTERNAL ATTEMPTS WERE**

MINOR AND EASILY CORRECTED. EXTERNAL ATTEMPTS WERE SOPHISTICATED. THEY HAVE NOT YET BEEN CORRECTED.

"Can they be?" he asked, brushing the hair back from his eyes.

THE PROCESS OF CORRECTION BEGAN THE MOMENT YOU WERE SAFELY INSIDE. TO COMMENCE EARLIER WAS DEEMED AN UNACCEPTABLE RISK.

Somack smiled. It was good to see that someone, or something at least could throw a monkey wrench into the Quaker's all-knowing plans. He sat quite still for a moment and contemplated the impossible. He visualized the little *Ambol* crashing through the surrounding bulkheads and snatching what he so helplessly wanted and needed. The daydream was nice, but that was all it was.

He tapped the console with his fingers, impatient at his own hesitation. He looked to his right, out into the waiting darkness of space. He gripped the controls and fired the secondaries gently, nudging the ship toward the opening. Nothing happened. The *Ambol* would not move.

It was too much. The last straw. He pounded the face of the console with his fist, once. He would not have the will to leave again, not on manual.

"Do it yourself then, damn it!" he shouted.

The ship did nothing.

THIS SHIP CANNOT PROCEED UNTIL THE FULL COMPLEMENT IS ABOARD. TO DO SO WOULD BE CONTRARY TO PRIME DIRECTIVES.

"What is that supposed to mean?"

THE PRIME CONCERN OF THIS SHIP IS TO BRING CERTAIN PERSONS, HUMAN BEINGS, TO A CERTAIN POINT IN SPACE SAFELY: WITHOUT REVEALING UNNECESSARILY THE UNIQUE AND UNUSUAL ASPECTS OF THIS SHIP. UNTIL RECENTLY ONLY ONE PERSON OF THIS TYPE EXISTED. YOU. DUE TO ACTIONS BEYOND THIS SHIP'S CONTROL, ANOTHER SUCH PERSON HAS BEEN CREATED.

MISCONCEPTIONS ON CERTAIN MATTERS CANNOT BE TOLERATED. IT IS EXTREMELY IMPORTANT TO CORRECT THIS SITUATION. MISSING COMPLEMENT MUST BE BROUGHT ABOARD OR DESTROYED.

PART III

PURSUIT OF THE DREAM

CHAPTER 10. A VERY DELICATE PROBLEM

The Quaker's mind changed gears in a hurry. When a plan is foiled, scrap it. Don't waste time trying to salvage something. Fortunately the Quaker had a lot of material to work with. When the *Ambol* refused to move—and when all the control devices his men had imbedded in the ship failed to function, there was nothing he could do but give in; conditionally. When Somack demanded Anna and made it clear that the ship would not move without her, he agreed—conditionally. The condition was Devlon. Somack had to take Devlon if he wanted to get Anna, and since Somack knew nothing about Devlon, an agreement was reached. The Quaker rubbed his hands together. Everything would work out after all.

Self-satisfaction is a strange thing and it does strange things to some people. Devlon congratulated himself. For nigh on a week after he'd come aboard the Quaker's ship things had not gone well. He was treated well enough; he had no complaints in that department. But even his most persuasive arguments had not moved the Quaker in the proper direction. In fact, the Freedom League and all he, *Devlon*, stood for, seemed to leave the enormous man unaffected.

Finally the Quaker had come around. Devlon realized now that he had been mistaken in his under-confidence. He could look back on his worry as a wasted effort. Persuasion was his business and the Quaker was just like any other man when it came to being persuaded.

Giant and grotesque though he was, the Quaker would make a formidable ally. Devlon could not help feeling exhilaration at winning the man over. At last he had everything he needed. The Quaker would supply the power and he would supply the following—the Freedom League—the great mass of people. Only one more thing was needed to tip the scales against the IXT. And that was an example of their injustice; an example that the simple people—the ones who counted—could understand.

How well everything had fallen into place. A creature—single and unique—came to mankind hearing gifts of unknown magnitude and lo, the IXT intervenes. Once again the people are denied access to a treasure of knowledge beyond compare. But the IXT is not satisfied with this. In its blind arrogance of power, it cannot tolerate such a threat to its position. The creature must be destroyed! The IXT seeks it out, using all of the sly craft at its command. Hated telepaths—mind leeches, are employed. One in particular, beautifully seductive, is used to ferret out the creature's location from the only one who knows; a veteran pilot who has fallen hopelessly into a betraying love. Witlessly the pilot leads the Jezebel to the creature; and the IXT, following, destroys them all.

It was a perfect story of tragedy and loss on an individual and universal scale. At this very moment the Quaker was beginning to compile the film record that would eventually be shown to the public. All that remained was locating the creature and destroying it in a suitably spectacular manner. It was a small price to pay for the freedom of the entire human race.

A knock at the door interrupted Devlon's thoughts. He knew that it was time now to begin the final act. Everything was ready and he stepped into the corridor, joining the Quaker.

"Are you ready?" the Quaker inquired.

"Shouldn't I be?" Devlon parried lightly. 'Whatever you did for my neck certainly worked. You wouldn't know from looking at it that it had been strained and cramped only a few days ago."

The Quaker nodded modestly. "Just one of the many things my years of dealing in alien arts and trade have given me."

Devlon smiled. 'What is that you have clutched so tightly in your hand?"

"Oh, this," the Quaker murmured. He turned the small object slowly in his hand. "This is for you. It is the little gem of alien technology I was telling you about."

Devlon squinted. The black cube the Quaker was holding didn't look like an alien camera—or anything else for that matter. "It looks like a paperweight to me," he grumbled. "Where are the controls? How do I turn it on and off?"

"Nothing so crude as that," the Quaker explained. "You don't need to turn it on and off. It is always working. It will record in detail everything that happens within nearly a hundred yards of it—in any direction. Walls and other obstructions don't interfere with its operation. Only its range is limited. Just remember to keep it with you whenever you leave the *Ambol*."

"How can it do so much?" Devlon asked, rubbing his cheek. He wasn't quite sure just what he was getting into. He finally asked the question that had been bothering him for some time. "The girl—you said she was a telepath . . . Then how can we pull it off? She'll take one look at me and know what is going to happen."

The Quaker shook his head slowly. "Now that you've raised the question, I might as well explain. This recording device has side effects, because of the way it works. It disturbs telepaths, similar to the jamming of a radio or the overloading of a receiver with a signal too powerful and too meaningless to understand. Anna will not be able to read your mind so long as you stay close to the cube."

Devlon fingered the black cube gingerly. "Ingenious," he muttered, reminding himself that the Quaker was now an ally. He dropped the thing into his pocket. "What if they object to me bringing it aboard?"

"I doubt they will," the Quaker reassured him. "Neither of the men aboard know you personally, and I don't think they will consider you a danger. More of a puzzle and a nuisance than anything else. That is one advantage of being an important and well-known person. People are more likely to think about you—and less about what you can do. Especially when you're an orator and leader, not a man of action."

Devlon almost blushed. High praise was something he was used to, but coming from the Quaker it was something more. "Thank you," he said, "but what I am doing is little enough. You are doing far more. This cube—it is so small."

"Just another of the forbidden fruits," the Quaker said modestly. "Having it is illegal because the hands making it were not human—but we could do as well if the IXT would only let us."

"Well, what you are doing won't be illegal much longer," Devlon promised. "Soon everyone will be able to trade with our brothers in intelligence—no matter what their shape. We will all be able to share in the knowledge gained. There will be controls, of course, but the knowledge will eventually seep down to the least of our people. It will be a new golden age!"

"Controls?" the Quaker asked, raising an eyebrow.

"Certainly," Devlon acknowledged. "You can't get rid of something as large and powerful as the IXT without leaving a vacuum of some kind. I, and the government we establish together, will take its place. We will provide the guidance and control—a unity of direction for the human race—something the IXT has never pretended to do. Instead of negative isolation, we will provide growth and direction. The proper use and distribution of the knowledge we control will set humanity on a path never before dreamed of."

"Yes," the Quaker said seriously, "I think you're right. But that is in the future. At the moment we have other things to worry about."

The two men reached the corridor branching toward the *Ambol* and paused.

"Well," the Quaker said, "here we part. Anna will follow you aboard in a little while."

Devlon suppressed an impulse to protest. He had never been forced to trust anyone so completely before and he didn't like it. But the Quaker had everything to lose and nothing to gain by helping the IXT. There was no one in the universe with less reason to double cross him than the Quaker. With that thought he was reassured and started toward the *Ambol* with every reason to expect success.

S omack recognized the man immediately. So did Merrick. The two of them exchanged glances; they finally had something to agree on. No words were necessary. Anyone with an ounce of common sense and a schoolboy's knowledge of history knew Alexander Devlon for what he was: a fool. But knowing this about him did not make the man any less dangerous.

Devlon could speak, and he always spoke with conviction because he always believed what he said. Anyone could see his sincerity and for those without common sense or a schoolboy's knowledge of history, sincerity was enough. Those people followed Devlon because they were bored, or because what he said sounded right—a noble cause. They were his greatest strength and he loved them for giving him that. When he spoke to them they could feel his love and returned it with their devotion.

"What do you suppose he wants?" Merrick asked, and Somack shrugged.

Together they watched the man stride along the ramp toward the *Ambol*. Devlon's very walk spoke of confidence and a knowledge that proper arrogance did not offend those who really mattered.

Somack activated the outside intercom and waited.

"Open up in there. I'm coming aboard." Devlon pounded at the hatch impatiently.

"What do you want?" Somack growled, and it came out sounding even harsher on the other side.

Devlon stepped back and eyed the offending intercom plate. "Everything's been arranged," he said, scowling. "Or are you going back on your agreement?"

"*You* are the man the Quaker chose to accompany us?" There was disbelief in Somack's voice. He had a sudden premonition that Devlon was no joke after all. He was real and he wanted in. What was more, Somack had to let him in. It was something he did with reluctance. He punched the hatch control and turned to welcome his guest.

"No," Anna said. "I don't have to do a thing. Not this."

"Yes," the Quaker insisted gently. "You know you have to. He won't leave without you."

"I don't believe it."

"It's true, and you know it," the Quaker stated flatly.

Anna turned away and clenched her teeth. Tired and weary, tired and weary. The words ran through her mind and all she wanted to do was rest. But rest would not come.

"Why?" she asked, and it came out sounding like the plea that it was. "Why me?"

"Come now, Anna," the Quaker chided gently. "You know we can't find and destroy this danger without his co-operation, and he won't co-operate unless you go aboard the *Ambol*."

Her resistance was gone; she'd used it all up. Her shoulders slumped and she sat down on the edge of the bed, "When do I have to go?"

The Quaker did not try to offer comfort, he simply told the truth. "You'll have to leave right now. Don't worry about clothes or anything—there are still plenty aboard the *Ambol* from your first stay. Just try to remember that we all have a duty to ourselves and to each other. You know now—through what you have seen in Somack's mind—the kind of thing I've been trying to do these many years. You know what I and my friends have been fighting. You have an opportunity to do in a few short days what has often taken me many years. I'd never ask it of you if it weren't important, and you know yourself just how important it is. This alien of Somack's must be destroyed."

Anna did not answer, but his words brought to her mind the wasted planet drifting just beyond the bulkhead and the men like Eyeada who fought to prevent others like it. She knew she'd do what the Quaker wanted, for the thing she fought each night in her dreams was far worse than what the Quaker could conceive. She might not survive it, but so long as it was there, she would fight it.

She stood up and looked at the Quaker. Her mind was closed to him and his to her, but they understood each other. The Quaker understood her so well that he felt a tiny regret at her leaving and it was tiny only because his store of regret had long ago ebbed low.

D evlon examined his quarters aboard the *Ambol* with contempt. They were small; hardly fit to move about in. He thumped his cot and was rewarded with a plume of gray ship's dust. He sneezed and stepped away, out into the tiny corridor.

The hatch to the control room was closed. Somack had made it clear that he was not welcome aboard the ship and that the control room was strictly off limits. It was the same with the hatch leading down into the engine spaces.

Thus confined, Devlon concentrated on what he had left. There were six little rooms along the corridor. The two nearest the control room hatch were occupied by Somack and Merrick. He himself had chosen the room farthest down the aisle on Somack's side. Across from his was the room he was interested in.

It showed signs of recent occupation. The small closet and drawers were stuffed with clothes and other junk. He removed all the men's stuff and was surprised to find that what the Quaker had said was true. The clothes did fit him. He carted it all back into his room and dumped it on his bunk. He went back for one last look. He glanced around at the small room that would soon be Anna's. Smiling, he fingered the small black cube in his pocket.

The Quaker had said that it would record everything. He took the cube out and slid it into the far corner of the room, under the bunk. It was a good spot and one where no one was likely to find it.

Satisfied, Devlon returned to his room and relaxed on his cot. He rubbed his neck and silently thanked the Quaker again for freeing him of that hateful brace. In a few days time even the residual pain would be gone and in a sort of ironic way, so would all those who were connected with giving him the injury. It was only a small thing, but it always helped to clear a cluttered table before you settled down for important business.

The small cube which lay on the *Ambol's* deck, beneath Anna's bunk, was examined. The ship was aware that Devlon had placed it there. But the *Ambol* could not determine what the cube's function was. It seemed to do nothing. It operated on a level beyond the ship's comprehension. The *Ambol* noted where it lay, classified it as harmless, and turned its attention elsewhere.

Anna walked toward the *Ambol*. She did not want to go and she took each step with a mixture of dread and duty. What was known and what was not known; they both frightened her. And yet, she held her head high and her back straight. There is nothing so long as the last walk and she felt something of this now. A premonition perhaps, or some instinct of her talent told her that there was no joy ahead of her, no fulfillment of dreams or hesitant wishes. She felt like turning back and running.

Then it was too late. She entered the *Ambol's* hatch and something descended on her with an almost physical violence. A cloud of darkness and confusion pressed down on her mind. She stumbled and almost fell;

clutching for support. She reeled. Unseen blows shook her and blackness rushed in and then receded.

Only the *Ambol's* hatch closing saved her from a public fall. She was inside the airlock, her hands outstretched. But there was nothing there; only cold steel, cool air, and the blessed privacy in which to die.

But she did not die. The agony and blindness which the cube imposed on her were worse—oh, far worse.

The inner hatch opened and Somack's heart almost stopped. Crumpled in the corner—he would never forget that sight. Nor the helplessness and the beauty she was and how it frightened him to see her so.

He did not remember much. She was alive and in his arms; and weight was nothing to the burning forehead pressed against his cheek. He carried her and the way must have been clear because he did not remember slowing, only laying her gently on the small bunk and brushing away her hair.

For a long time he did nothing but watch her and occasionally touch her fevered brow. Slowly the flush subsided and she no longer burned. She began to rest comfortably.

Merrick finally took it upon himself to interrupt the silent watch. "The *Ambol* is all set to go," he said. "Hadn't we better leave while we still have the chance?"

Somack looked up and for the first time he let the anger he was feeling show. "We will leave when I say we will, and not before."

Merrick very sensibly remained silent and stood aside when Somack stood up and stomped from the room. Back in the control room, Somack slammed the transmitter and a startled face appeared on the screen.

"I want to speak with the Quaker."

When the startled face began to argue Somack leaned forward and said very quietly, "Now."

The Quaker's face appeared on the screen. "What is wrong now? I am surprised—"

"Surprised! You have been expecting this call from the moment Anna came aboard the *Ambol*. Otherwise you wouldn't have been available the moment I called. What have you done?"

The Quakers eyes narrowed. "How is she?"

"How should I know! You're the one who did it."

The Quaker shook his head. "I haven't done a thing to impair the girl's health. Are you sure there is anything wrong?"

Somack swallowed hard. Merrick laid a hand on his shoulder before he could speak.

"Don't press the point," Merrick cautioned. "She's here and she's safe, sleeping restfully even. He has done his part in this bargain. Now let's get the *Ambol* out of his ship before he changes his mind."

Somack looked from the screen to the man at his side. Somack would keep his part of the bargain with these two all right, and he hoped that both Merrick and the Quaker enjoyed what they got.

"O.K.," Somack said bluntly. "We will leave immediately."

The Quaker smiled. "A wise—"

Somack cut the connection.

The Quaker blinked once at the blank screen. He sat in the safety of his vast ship, but he could still feel that Somack was a dangerous man. It was something he would have to keep in mind. He pondered the question as he glided toward his next engagement. He had one last plot to set in motion before he could rest easy. With a problem as important as the one Somack represented, he wanted to leave no stone unturned.

Jennings and Margy Stevens were waiting for him. He could see that their feelings of anxiety were relieved somewhat by their present treatment and by being together. They had been separated the moment he had taken them from the *Matilda* and brought them aboard his ship. Now they were together again for the first time since.

"I am glad to see that you are comfortable," the Quaker said when he entered the room. The statement was followed by a moment of awkward silence. Neither of them had seen him before and the sight shocked them as it shocked most people.

"I am . . . we are grateful for the help you gave us when we needed it," Margy said, recovering from the sight of him first.

The Quaker chuckled softly and set his whole body to shaking. "Nothing," he muttered with a gesture of self-abasement, "it was nothing at all. My helping you was more of an accident than anything else."

"Who are you?" Jennings asked, cutting through the sweetening atmosphere. He wasn't about to place much trust in this "accidental savior," especially after having been kept in virtual solitary confinement since leaving the *Matilda.*

"They call me the Quaker." More chuckling helped to illustrate the point. "I've been very busy lately and haven't had the time to check up on all the people I took from the *Matilda.*"

"You can recognize an IXT uniform, can't you?" Commander Jennings insisted.

The Quaker smiled. "You mean the rags you were wearing when I picked you up? They did resemble IXT uniforms, but I like to be sure before I make up my mind about people. Not everyone wearing an IXT uniform turns out to be a part of that great organization."

"I see," Jennings said, "and it has taken you all this time to decide that we are the real thing after all."

The Quaker shook his head sadly. "Commander Jennings, your skepticism does your training justice, but we have very little time for that sort of thing now. You must decide, and decide quickly, whether or not you can trust me."

"Just like that? An enemy of the IXT for three hundred years and you want me to trust you."

"Exactly," the Quaker admitted.

"Let's hear what he has to say," Margy said, striving to break the verbal deadlock.

The Quaker snapped his fingers gently and two of his men entered the room. One of them carried a sheath of photographs and the other a small cylinder. The man with the photographs handed them to Jennings. Half of them showed a small ship, and taken from different angles they clearly identified the *Ambol.* The rest were of two people seated at a dining table. Jennings recognized the girl as Anna Bey, and the man looked familiar.

He handed the pictures to Margy for inspection and then turned to the Quaker. 'Well?" he asked.

"You recognized the young lady, I assume," the Quaker said.

"Yes. And the ship." Jennings paused. "When were those pictures taken?"

"A few days ago."

"Impossible!" Jennings protested. "The *Ambol* was in IXT custody less than a week ago. You couldn't have taken it from us—not without its destruction."

"I didn't take it—your people let it go." The Quaker selected one of the pictures and pointed. "And Mr. Somack, here. They released both the ship and its owner."

"Why? Why were they released?" Jennings examined the face in the picture, shaking his head.

"He is a dangerous man," the Quaker continued. "If I'd known how dangerous he was, I would never have let him come aboard my ship in the first place. But if he can talk himself away from the IXT, how can I be expected to do any better?"

"He was aboard this ship?" Jennings asked in surprise.

"Of course," the Quaker said. "Until just a few minutes ago."

"And you let him get away!"

The Quaker smiled ruefully. "No. As I was trying to say, he and his ship are more than they appear to be. Together they forced me into surrendering Miss Bey and presently they are departing for places unknown."

Jennings' face became grim. "I can't believe this is true! If it is, then you must follow them at any cost—they cannot be allowed to escape. Not again!

"It is really none of my business," the Quaker said, shrugging. "I have my crew and other things to think of. However . . ." He paused and motioned to one of the crew members who had entered with the pictures. The man hurriedly attached the cylinder he was carrying to a socket in the wall and stepped back. The lights dimmed and the cylinder projected light upon the opposite wall.

"This is a partial view from my ship's screens," the Quaker resumed. He did not mention that the view carefully excluded two IXT warships and another one of his own. What it did show was a view of the *Ambol* leaving the Quaker's ship's launch hay and slowly drifting away from them.

"Let them go."

Both the Quaker and Jennings turned to stare at Margy. She returned Jennings' blazing glare without flinching.

"They haven't done anything," Margy continued. "Let them go."

Jennings looked at Margy for a second longer and then turned to the Quaker.

"You can destroy our ships easily enough," he said. "Why don't you do the same with the *Ambol?*"

The Quaker shook his head. "You don't seem to understand. That ship —the *Ambol*—and Mr. Somack have been in contact with alien powers that make my ship and what it can do impotent beside it." It was a lie, but the whole conversation was a fabric of the same. He was maneuvering the two IXT people into a position from which they could act only as he wished them to.

"I can't believe it!" Jennings said. He was shaking with his inability to do anything. "I saw how you destroyed one of our best ships!"

"Can't you understand?" the Quaker said softly. "I wasn't trying to destroy your ship—it was the *Ambol* I was after. Somehow it deflected the destruction I was throwing at it onto one of your ships."

Jennings was shaken. "How can I believe you?"

The Quaker shook his head. "I can understand your concern, but this whole thing is just a little bit out of my line. I only attacked the *Ambol* in the first place because of what I heard about it from the Dash Hounds."

"Dash Hounds?" Jennings queried. "You mean the Avligesh Dye, don't you?" They were the only alien race with which humanity traded on a normal basis. Having been defeated in a war before the Hursk Encounter, they were considered weak and safe. They had even helped to fight the Hursk.

The Quaker nodded.

"But what could they know that we don't?" Jennings wanted to know.

The Quaker shrugged indifferently. 'You would be surprised at the number of things the IXT doesn't know."

Jennings felt frustration rising in him. It didn't matter if what the Quaker said was true. The *Ambol* was getting away—and that was the only thing that really counted. He had to persuade the Quaker to follow it—to help the IXT.

"You can't let them get away," Jennings pleaded. "Regardless of what your part in this is, they are too dangerous—if the IXT can't stop them, given time there will be nothing you can do either. You've got to do something now. You've got to follow them—and wait for an opportunity. They've got to make a mistake some time, and you *have* to be near by when they do!"

The Quaker considered what Jennings had to say for a moment. And while he did the *Ambol* drifted further off. Finally, reaching a safe distance, it disappeared into main drive.

"Quickly!" Jennings urged. "You can't afford to wait any longer. You'll lose them!"

"Very well," the Quaker agreed with a show of reluctance and he ordered his ship to follow the *Ambol*.

A board the *Ambol* everything was quiet as the ship went into drive. In Anna's room a black cube was laying in the darkened corner beneath her bed. It functioned, and in its functioning it disrupted the space around it. A short time before, the cube had almost been interrupted in its functioning. Anna had boarded the ship. In doing so her mind had interfered with the smooth operation of the cube; but only for a moment. Now it was working perfectly again.

W hat is it for a blind man to lose his hearing? Or an ordinary man to lose his sight? Did they feel as she felt now?

Anna stared into the darkness above and about her. Was it true what they said? Would her eyesight improve now—to compensate, in part, for what she had lost?

She buried her head and cried as she had never done before—with all her heart and soul. She shook to the very foundation of her life.

S omack turned from the console, letting the *Ambol* run as it saw fit. The main drive hummed in the background and he was glad to be free of the Quaker and his machinations. Now there was just Anna to worry about, a far different and more important task.

"You think she is all right then?" he asked Merrick.

The IXT officer shook his head. "I'm no doctor. But there is nothing wrong with her that I can see. Unless you count the little bump she got in falling. It's probably just the strain of her hurried departure."

A voice came from behind them and Somack remembered he had left the corridor hatch open. Devlon was slouched in the opening and speaking casually. "A touching show of concern for the girl," he drawled at them, "especially on the part of the IXT."

"No one asked your opinion, Devlon," Merrick said stiffly. "I think you'd be better off staying out of the way as much as possible for the time being."

Devlon smiled strangely. "Why, I would never knowingly get in your way, sir, but for the concern I feel for my fellow passenger. By the noise she is making, I'd say that she had recovered her wits—or a part of them anyway."

Somack moved. "You have a long way of saying something simple."

Devlon stepped aside to let Somack pass, then turned and followed. "There is no great hurry," he muttered. "I fear she may not wish to see anyone in her present condition. As a matter of fact she was quite upset when I tried to comfort her."

"You did what?" Somack turned sharply. "I thought I told you to confine yourself to your room."

Devlon came up short. He looked at Somack and was about to say something when Merrick came up behind him. He changed his mind and smiled instead. "I'm sorry if I've done anything wrong. I was just trying to help."

Somack snorted. "I'll ask for your help, Devlon, when I need it. And I don't think that is going to be very often."

Devlon shrugged and slipped away, back into his room.

Somack shook his head and turned to knock quietly on Anna's door.

"May I come in?" he asked.

There was no response, but a sudden silence told him that she had heard him knock. He waited a few moments before knocking again and entering the room. The room was dark when he entered and he turned on the light, shutting the door behind him. Anna was sitting on the bunk to his right. She was sitting up and that fact alone eased his mind a little.

She did not look at him. Instead, she concentrated harder on what she was doing; combing the tangles out of her long dark hair. She pulled at it so violently that he winced in sympathy with the pain she must be feeling. It looked like she'd been crying, but he couldn't be sure. She was careful to keep a curtain of hair between his eyes and hers.

"Are you feeling all right?" he asked at last.

She did not answer immediately and he was about to speak again when she said, "No."

Somack choked on the bitterness of that one word, and though it was meant to be hard on him, the hardest part was that her voice had almost broken in saying it. For the longest time he could say nothing and when he spoke at last, it was only to ask, "What have I done to deserve that?"

For a moment there was no reply, only the convulsive shaking of her shoulders, ending with a strangled sound. "Oh, what haven't you done!" she cried. "You have taken my freedom, my heart and my soul. What more do you want?"

Any further speech was muffled by the tangle of her hands and hair, or lost in the sob that racked her.

"No!" was all that Somack could say and he bent to comfort her, but she jumped so violently from his touch that it frightened him.

"Get out! Get out!" she screamed, and she showed him her eyes. They were bright, terrible; verging almost on the insane.

He was rooted to the spot, but he could not look away. Slowly, very slowly, her breathing returned to normal and her eyes dropped.

"I'm sorry," he said quietly and left.

She was very much alone when he was gone.

The *Ambol* dove through space at a deliberate pace, toward a destination known only to itself. Following close behind were the Quaker's ship and the IXT ship *Exeter*. The computers on both of these ships made occasional attempts to project the *Ambol's* ultimate destination, but course changes on the *Ambol's* part made the attempts little more than machine exercise.

Aboard the *Ambol* Somack maintained a lonely night watch. The only sounds came when he shifted in his chair and the only light came from the full array of screens around him. They cast the strange light of stars seen as only ships in drive can see them. Core-bright and sharp-edged.

For two hours now he'd been alone with the naked stars. It was nearly half a day since his abortive talk with Anna. He still couldn't reconcile himself to the present state of affairs. If only things weren't happening at a pace beyond his control, on a scale he had never imagined. Barely three weeks ago he'd set out on a trip that should have been as uneventful as it was profitable. Then, from nowhere, people had coalesced around him, like beads of water on a cold glass. It was something to make him wonder —to make him think and worry more than a little.

Where had they all come from? All his life he'd been pretty much alone; alone and consoled a bit by the thought that before he died he'd be able to do something for all the people he'd never gotten to know. Now he was entangled with people—with one person in particular—in a way he'd never hoped or wanted to be since his family had been shattered so many years ago. All of these people wanted the same thing. It was the same thing he had hoarded to himself all this time. He'd never looked on it as hoarding before, but that's what it was. He'd hoarded his money, and worse—his life; all to make a gesture that was now impossible.

Once he would have revealed his great gift to humankind in a master stroke of altruism. But now there was Alexander Devlon—a man who could do the same thing so much better than he could. And the IXT—who would see them both dead to stop it all. Or the Quaker.

It was enough to make a man wish for simpler times and simpler things; to watch the stars for a few moments and let the whole mess take care of itself. And for just a few moments he could think about Anna and pretend the rest was just part of a bad dream. But the few moments would always pass and he would still be facing problems that didn't go away all by themselves.

He turned to check the screens behind him and there was something in the way; something silhouetted nicely against the image of the star field.

Even half-seen, like this, she was beautiful, and he turned the lights in the room up slowly so as not to shock his or her eyes.

Anna was standing quietly before the passageway hatch; a hatch which had opened and closed for her as quietly as it had ever done for him.

"I've come to talk with you," she said, and though the words were for him, he did not hear them. He was too struck by her presence and the way the violet in her dress matched the strange light in her eyes.

Somack was on his feet suddenly, uncertain of what to say. "You look so much better now," he mumbled. "Have you rested well?"

"Rested?" She gave a little laugh. "I haven't rested since—a very long time."

"What can I do? Is there anything I can do?"

"Oh. How can you make it so hard? Can't you see I've come to beg?" Suddenly she was on her knees. "Please, please! Give me back my sight, my life. Take back your dream, terrible dream. I can't bear it longer."

"Don't do that!" he groaned. "Don't do that!"

But she had already done it, groveling at his feet before he could more than speak. He knelt and jerked her back to her knees.

"What are you doing!" he grated. "Why are you doing this to me?" He was shaking her violently, hardly aware of what he was doing.

"I knew you wouldn't!" she cried, and great tears streaked her face.

"Don't," he moaned, and wrapped her in his arms. She was a child to be protected and for a long time there was nothing to say. She cried and shook against him and he held her, helpless in his inability to comfort her.

She was quiet finally. Her eyes were wide; looking at him through tangles of hair and searching his face. She was so close their eyes almost touched and he realized he was holding her so tightly that her breathing moved against him strongly. He relaxed the pressure, but she continued to watch him, uncertainty touching her face. He brushed the hair back from her eyes, and then, embarrassed, he rose and brought her up with him.

"You can go now?" he asked gently. "You must get some sleep, or those rings there will grow darker." He ran his thumbs beneath her eyes, moistened them with the tears she had shed.

She almost smiled. Almost. She turned and let him walk her to the door of her room. There, as he held the door for her, she said, "If you can sleep with all of your dreams, then I must sleep with mine."

CHAPTER 11. THE JOURNEY BEGINS

Anna lay curled in the soft green grass. The sun warmed her fur and it was an effort to keep an eye open. Comfort filled the meadow and she peeped and winked. Her cubs paid no heed to her ever-watchful eye. They romped, attacking each other, rocks, and bushes with equal abandon. The day was bright and the air was clean— not a time to waste in rest, and the cubs knew this without thinking.

But Anna had spent the night in worry. She did not understand her worry, it was just something carried in her breast and with each passing day it grew heavier and weighed her down. Her mate felt it too and he prowled the wood; watching but never finding what it was. It seemed to lurk above in the day and below in the night.

A lazy bird winged its way across the sky and her eye followed. She hardly saw the bird and her eye returned to her cubs when it was gone. They chased a fluttering bug, the foremost ever thwarted by a tail stumbled upon and vandalized by those behind. How could life be more than this? She sighed and her tail twitched, flicking away a bumbling buzzer.

The fluttering bug came to rest suddenly and it did not move, but the cubs no longer chased it. They stood frozen in the green field and their stiff little legs trembled. The fur on Anna's back rose and she sprang to her feet, snarling. But there was nothing to fight, only the sense of wrong and spreading silence. Her paws slashed the air, her eye caught the sun and held there.

The sun. It bulged and heaved most unnaturally. She cried in protest and the lonely sound went unanswered, for the sun would not stop. Great jets of orange and yellow flame distorted its former shape and it grew, blooming out and growing—spreading its grotesque petals across the sky. There was nothing to do but watch and this she did, the sight burned forever upon her dying eyes. She did not turn away, for there was nowhere else to look. The pain was easing because the sun no longer burned bright. First an angry dull red and now black, it spread across the sky. Stars shone in the daytime sky, but only a few—a dreadful few. The spreading black blotted them out one by one, touching the horizon with its stubby fingers.

The sky turned white and blew away.

The hot wind touched the ground and the trees were gone, the grass was gone, and her cubs were gone. But she remained. Her fur, it burned, and her eyes, they left her. But she did not bow before the wind.

Anna screamed and so good were her reflexes that no sound came, only a choking cough. Her hand covered her mouth and after a moment her breathing slowed. Her sleep was over and as she sat up in bed she was half thankful that she had awakened before she had lived through more of Somack's dream.

To be awakened in agony and defiance was something she was getting used to. If only she could get used to the cause of her wakefulness, the dreams themselves. But they were not dreams. She lived them as surely as she had lived anything in her life.

It was a symptom of her trouble that with the passing of each night she must feel an arm—seek out a mirror and reaffirm to herself her human form and living warmth. Each morning the echoing thoughts died more slowly. They left her touched with sorrow for the creatures whose lives she shared and who she would never see.

It was not easy and she grew weary.

She rested now, after her sleep, and let the tension drain away. Its going left room for the sounds of the ship around her and the small beat of her own heart. Her mind filled with softer things.

D evlon stirred a cup of coffee. It was bitter; everything that came from the food slot was bad. He poured the coffee into the disposal and threw the cup in after. It was the last cup he would try while aboard the *Ambol.*

Sleep had not refreshed him and neither had bad coffee or bad food. He was feeling angry and restless, a mood his closer aides had come to respect with quick departures and faraway places. But there were no aides now, only four bleak walls, a bleak roof, and a bleak deck. He paced, paced, and glanced at his watch. Slipping the door open, he glanced into the corridor. Everything was quiet. He stepped out, moved down the aisle, and tested the control room hatch. It was well secured. He listened briefly at the door of Somack's and then Merrick's room—not a sound.

He returned to his own door where he stood and contemplated the room across the hall. It was obvious that the telepath could not read his mind now, nor could she have at any time during the trip so far. The Quaker's plan did not call for her survival. If she could see that, she certainly would not remain quiet. Nor would she if she could see into his mind right now.

He let his mind dwell on her for a while, testing to see if there would be any reaction. There was nothing. The room across the hall remained quiet. Devlon smiled. He owed her a thing or two, that was certain. She'd played him for a dupe, manipulated him—and almost got him killed. He could never forgive humiliation.

Devlon fell to examining the simple lock mechanism on his own door. It was sturdy and effective, but a person might forget to use it—especially someone upset by the recent loss of a sense they were used to having. He rubbed his chin in thought, then slipped his shoes off. This was no light undertaking. He realized that as he shut his own door and moved to hers. He tested the latch and his half-formed resolution to do nothing dissolved when the latch moved. The door was not locked. Indeed, it opened and closed without a sound and the shaft of light from the corridor was gone almost as soon as it appeared.

Devlon braced his back against the inside of the door, breathing hard. What in the world was he doing, he wondered. Risking everything—and for what?

The room was dim, but not totally dark. His eyes adjusted to the light and he suddenly knew what he was there for. He remembered now that Anna was a beautiful girl. Seeing her reminded him forcefully.

She was covered lightly and it did more to attract than hide. Her shape was suggested nicely by the blanket and her quiet breathing.

Devlon moved forward quickly, then faltered. Her eyes were open. They had been open since he entered the room, following him, and yet she hadn't made a sound.

"Who is it?" she asked hesitantly.

Devlon laughed quietly and the sound set her to moving faster than anything else could have. She leaped from the cot, dodging, almost slipping by. He caught her shoulder and she spun against the wall. Jumping after her, his right hand caught her by the throat and hair. He pressed the advantage and pinned her to the wall.

"Not again, you don't," he whispered. "This time you will not get away."

She did not answer, but her eyes stayed on him; threatening pools of darkness. He looked into her eyes and smiled. She was not afraid of him. He would see how long that lasted.

He parted her hair so he could watch her face more closely. She was wearing something white and flannel; soft. He tightened the grip on her throat and lifted. She was on her toes and then nothing. Her eyes stayed on him; larger, perhaps, but still no fear.

Her breathing became ragged, strained by his grip. He pressed his forearm down against her, forcing air from her lungs. They fought against him, slowly losing. Her eyes clouded, but did not waver. Devlon's smile broadened. He could feel her heart pounding against his arm and the same pulse against his wrist and finger tips. She would die if he held her much longer.

The lights brightened abruptly and Devlon twitched. He looked around, but they were still alone. No one had entered the room.

He let Anna's feet slip back to the ground. She could breathe again, but he kept his grip on her throat. She would not scream. Her eyes cleared and though they blinked twice, they still watched him.

He grinned. "Black little eyes; black little heart. We will see how much longer they stare at me."

There was a noise. Devlon's grin froze. He looked around quickly. It was just water dripping in the basin.

Drip, drip-drip; the rate increased, becoming a steady stream.

What was happening? It was ridiculous, but he watched anyway, fascinated. The water gushed, darkened. He shook his head. The water was thickening, turning red, splashing against the sides of the basin—trying to get out.

Devlon swallowed hard and stepped back. Anna's eyes followed him.

Impossible, he tried to say. Where did so much blood come from? Why did it want to get him? He stumbled, then ran toward the door. He opened and closed it behind him, then tripped. Someone was standing over him, kicking him. He crawled, was thrust back into his room. The door slammed and bolted behind him.

Anna still stood with her back against the wall. She breathed in great gasps and her heart pounded in her ears. She was alive and had not expected it. Even as she sank to the ground she wondered and did not know what had saved her.

Deep within the *Ambol* consciousness stirred. Once again it had managed to help one of its charges. It had brightened the ship's lights in Anna's room. It had turned on the water.

But Devlon had seen blood—and the *Ambol* could never sense the real reason he had run.

Anna felt so comfortable, so warm. A gentle touch brushed her temple, stroking back wisps of hair rhythmically. She sighed and stirred. Pain seemed so far away—a dream, like this. Her eyes remained closed and she willed this dream to stay.

The minutes passed slowly and Anna dropped into a heavy and untroubled sleep; the first in a very long time. The warmth moved closer beside her and planted a kiss before departing.

Anna had unknowingly saved Devlon's life. Somack realized this as he carefully closed her door. The time he had spent caring for her had diverted him from killing Devlon. He was calmer now, content to remove the threat in another way.

Somack moved to the hatch leading down into the depths of the ship, and began to descend. He had not foreseen what had happened. He knew Devlon was a dangerous man, but he had always considered it a political danger—nothing as personally sick as it turned out to be. Fortunately he had instructed the ship to keep an eye on the man and report anything unusual. Only his own grogginess in responding to the ship's warning had allowed things to go so far. If he'd been a few seconds earlier . . .

Somack searched through his cargo until he found what he wanted. Up until now there had been no weapons shown aboard the *Ambol*, but the time for games was past. He held in his hand a cutting torch similar to the one which had almost ended his own life. It was a miner's tool, really, but lethal none the less.

He returned to Devlon's room and opened the door to make sure Devlon was still there. Devlon saw the torch in Somack's right hand and the length of steel in his left. He screamed.

"Shut up," Somack said. He pointed the torch.

Devlon whimpered.

"That's better," Somack said, lowering the torch again.

"You can't kill me," Devlon said, trying to muster his dignity. "The Quaker will destroy you all if you do that."

Somack ignored the comment. "Listen," he said coldly. "Listen very carefully. You are going to be confined to this room for the rest of the voyage, however long that takes. Your door is going to be welded shut, and it won't be opened until we get where we are going. If, for some reason, I have to unweld it before then, well, that means you won't be alive when the voyage ends. Don't think I won't take my chances with the Quaker, because I will. So, for your own good, be very quiet for the rest of the trip. I don't want to hear any noise coming from this room. Can you understand that?"

Devlon nodded twice. He had not expected such lenient treatment, but he did not let his relief show.

Somack stepped back out into the corridor and closed the door. Two spot welds were more than enough to hold the door against Devlon. When he finished, Somack returned to his own room, locked the door, and tried to resume his sleep.

The crewman walked with great care. He was careful to stay out of the Quaker's line of sight. There was nothing more dangerous than disturbing the Quaker during one of his "moods," as the crew so aptly named them. The Quaker never slept in the ordinary sense, but occasionally he would slip into a mood. For hours at a time he would stare into space, or at a spot on the wall—catatonic to all appearances. But he was not catatonic. The Quaker remained aware of what was going on around him, but he chose to ignore it. The crewman knew this and he was careful to do only what he had been instructed to do.

He laid the exhibits out in front of the Quaker and arranged them in the proper order. When he was done, he departed quickly.

The Quaker hardly noticed the momentary presence. He was concentrating, only semi-conscious of the surrounding room and the hum of his ship in the background. For long moments at a time he attained something resembling a computer's ability in correlating and calculating. His speed was not electronic, nor were his calculations precise; but no computer could have come close to what he was doing. The variables his mind worked with were people and the equations he used were of his own making.

For a moment he suspended the jumble in a corner of his mind and paused to look at the exhibit laid out before him. He had ordered it for just this moment, knowing that it would help his mind solidify the soft and changing pattern in his mind.

The exhibit consisted of six objects. The largest was Eyeada's heavy black pistol. To the left of this lay four expended cartridge cases. To the right was a single cartridge, its charge and projectile intact.

The Quaker's abstraction swirled and coalesced around the imagery he had selected. The pistol bulged and stretched, assuming in its distortion the role he himself played in the continuing action. He was the motivator, the man who set things into motion. The four expended shells; they changed and became the forces he had already set in motion—forces all set upon different courses and colliding this very moment within the confined spaces of the *Ambol*. Every passing second brought this volatile mixture closer to the point of explosion. The four people aboard the *Ambol* were all moving in different directions toward the same goal. Their opposing momentums would grind and chum, and at the proper moment they would detonate. But the Quaker took no chances. He reserved his final shot. He primed it with a double charge and would ensure its success by making the projectile explosive, not solid like the others.

Six chambers and only five shells to fill them. Eyeada had been a careful man and the Quaker was not unaware of the danger to all his plans. It lay in that one empty chamber. The unknown. The one force he could neither control nor predict, and it was getting closer with every passing minute. When the *Ambol* arrived where it was going he would have to face that problem and overcome it, just as he had overcome problems of a similar nature before. The unknown was a threat. Anything powerful and unhuman was a threat that could not be tolerated. He would destroy it.

And after this one, there would be another. The Quaker realized that his work would never end. With each passing year he would grow older and the weight of trying would increase, but he would continue. He was not meant to die. The Hursk, in their arrogance, had thought to use him —to make him into their tool—and he had destroyed them. No trace remained of the Hursk, but space was filled with their cousins; relatives in the danger they posed for humanity. If one race was to survive and accompany him through time, it would be his own.

———

Jennings tossed in the agony of his uncertainty. The Quaker had offered him everything—the impossible. There was no crime more heinous, and yet he contemplated committing it. He tried to tell himself that he was doing it because it was the right thing to do. It would enable him to do his job so much better. But he knew he was lying to himself.

The operation would be painless. The Quaker had promised him that. But the decision to go ahead, to throw away a lifetime of belief, made him wish for the distraction of a physical and more easily bearable suffering.

The punishment for what he was doing would be capital. His best friend would shoot him on the spot for the act he was contemplating. There was nothing more abhorrent to the IXT mind than the thought of gene manipulation. The human race had nearly died fighting off the Hursk and the human variants they had so effectively produced. There was nothing more frightening—nothing more likely to raise the hackles of the basic man, than having to fight men who were not entirely human. It was no accident that the werewolf and vampire were so widely and uniformly effective as symbols of terror. Perhaps the Hursk had realized this fact dimly, and had produced their terrors because of it. They would have been better advised to leave off while they were ahead. With conventional weapons they might have won.

Jennings thought of this. He thought of all he was risking, and he still did what he did. Even as he removed his shirt and looked at the stump of his right arm and the metal extension on his left, his mind continued to war with itself. Only a merciful shot from the Quakers medical attendant put an end to the strife.

"Very interesting, Miss Stevens, but time presses us on." The Quaker spoke slowly. He sounded almost apologetic at having to change the subject.

"It does?" Margy responded, puzzled by the sudden turn in the conversation.

"Yes, I'm afraid I must speak of certain things that have come to my attention."

The Quaker waved a hand toward the door and the crewman standing there nodded silently. The door was opened and a scruffy-looking person stumbled in. He was clutching something in his gnarled hands and wringing it nervously.

Margy frowned. The man looked vaguely familiar, then she remembered. "Why, that is Bling, Captain Eyeada's—"

"Quite right," the Quaker cut in. "He's been saying disturbing things about you, Miss Stevens. That your connection with Alexander Devlon and the Freedom League was not an altogether clear one. I am surprised that an IXT officer would allow personal problems to cloud professional judgment."

Margy's eyes came up and she met the Quaker's accusing gaze. "What have my personal problems got to do with you?" Her eyes sharpened as she asked the question. She was tired of playing cat and mouse with this man, especially since she was being forced to play the part of the mouse.

"I don't mean to be abstruse," the Quaker apologized. "All I meant to say was that this man holds your life in his hands. One word from him and the IXT isn't going to like you any more."

Bling shifted uneasily at the reference to his future testimony. If he came out of this thing with a whole skin he would be highly satisfied. Co-operating with the Quaker presently seemed to offer him the best chance of that.

Margy didn't say anything. What could she say?

"Let's not look so glum," the Quaker said cheerfully. "All is not lost. After all, I'm not a completely heartless man. I just wanted you to understand your position."

"I understand it very well," Margy said quietly.

"I am glad you do. I think you will understand even more later on, but right now you're going to trust my judgment. If you don't, there is not much I can do to save the two of you."

"What do you mean—the two of us? Commander Jennings had nothing to do with the Freedom League!"

"Commander Jennings!" the Quaker mocked gently. "I am sure he would appreciate your defense, but he doesn't really need it. He has chosen his own course and it is just as likely to lead him to disaster as yours is. The IXT is a harbor to which neither of you can return."

"What are you talking about?" Margy asked. She tried not to show the fear that was growing in her.

The Quaker shrugged, not answering. "I'm sure you will appreciate the situation when you see him. He's already decided to do what he can. Talk to him and see if you can find it in your heart to help him."

The Quaker's closing words were clearly a dismissal and she returned to her quarters, numbed. The Quaker was trying to tell her that she was going to help in stamping out yet another race, whether she wanted to or not. She understood him. She knew what he was—something the Hursk had made. A person once, but now he was a changed thing. He would go on killing—taking his revenge for something an extinct race had done to him.

Margy could understand the Quaker and his unshakable resolution, but how little *he* understood *hers!* She would face the IXT and all its injustice, rather than help them put another chunk of mortar between people and the rest of the galaxy. Didn't they understand that it was time to grow up? Maybe the Freedom League was the wrong way to do it, but it was something. No one else was even trying.

Alexander Devlon was a disease. She had never thought differently, but the vehicle he was riding to power—the League itself, and what it stood for—they were the things she fought for. When Devlon was dead and gone, the League would remain to pick up the pieces. It would carry on where Devlon and the IXT left off. The thought was a fond one. She worked for it. She lived for it.

———————

Margy did not remain in her room long. The Quaker's veiled threats gnawed at her. She had to discover if there was any truth in them. She slipped down the hall and entered Jennings' room without knocking. What she saw made her tremble.

Jennings was sitting off to one side, his whole posture radiating apathy. He was holding something in his hands, but she did not see what it was. All she could do was look at the hands themselves. They were a pale white —sickly, yeasty-looking—but they were still hands; hands where no hands should be.

"What have you done?" She spoke with an unreasoning horror, hardly thinking of what her words might do to him.

Jennings moved his newly formed right arm weakly. "How do you like it?" he asked, his voice heavily slurred. He flexed the pale fingers on both his hands. "Beauties, aren't they?" His head sank back and he raised a glass to his lips. "Cheers."

Margy felt suddenly sick. What she had done against the IXT was nothing compared to this. Nothing short of death would satisfy the IXT in this case.

"How did he do it?" she asked. "How did he convince *you* to do it?"

Jennings' head bobbed and the glass dropped from his fingers. "You don't like them." His voice was resigned and he looked at the pair of hands resting in front of him. "They are ugly. White."

Margy crossed the room, knelt, and placed his left hand between both of hers. "No," she whispered softly, "they are not ugly." The hand she held was cold and she was lying, but her words helped him anyway.

He brightened and looked at her for the first time. His eyes were dilated with drugs and alcohol.

"The Quaker said they would be like this at first," he said hopefully. "It takes some time for my body to replace the symbiot's DNA with my own."

"Yes, I know," she said sadly.

"You do?" His drunken surprise was pitiful to see.

"The technique is well known," she answered, dully. "The Freedom

League has been using it for some of their more important people." She didn't say that the Hursk had used it first—on people like the Quaker.

"Freedom League!" he roared, pushing her away clumsily. She tumbled backward as he rose to his feet. "Damn them. I'd have my own, weren't for them."

Margy climbed to her feet. She did not argue; that would only make things worse. She watched him sway for a moment as he stood there and it made her throat thicken. He was so confused; his motives hopelessly mixed together—helping him obscure from himself the real reason for what he had done. She knew what it was and thinking of what it had done to him made her eyes sting. Someday he would figure it out too. Then she would have real cause for sorrow.

She watched him totter back and sink into his chair, exhausted. "Tired," he said, and his head lolled to one side. He closed his eyes and in a moment she was alone with her worries.

Bling scurried down the corridor. He had freedom of the ship. What a laugh. He had about as much freedom as a rat in a maze. So long as the Quaker was satisfied with him; as long as he did exactly what the Quaker wanted—that was how long he would be "free."

He was beginning to wonder just what advantage there was in his present condition. He could wander the aisles and corridors of the Quaker's ship as much as he wanted, but there was nothing to see and nowhere to go. All the important sections were closed off. And Bling was careful now to stay away from places marked with forbidding warning signs; especially the ones done in red paint.

He was approaching the area he knew best. It was the area where he lived and where he saw the Quaker occasionally. He knew the door by heart and he stopped to admire it. That very morning he'd been in there, doing his very best for the Quaker's cause; lying to one and all alike. Lying was something he was pretty good at. Sneaking around—he wasn't as good at that, but he liked it a lot more. That was what he was doing now.

He listened at the door into the Quaker's audience room. It was sound-proofed of course, and Bling couldn't hear anything, but it made him feel good just to be listening without anyone knowing.

Swoosh. The door opened.

Bling stumbled back. "Ah—Ah—I was—"

Explanations weren't necessary. The officer who exited had other things on his mind. When he saw Bling stuttering and trying to look innocuous, he merely frowned and went about his business.

The officer had been carrying something and although it was wrapped loosely in cloth, Bling recognized its outlines immediately. He'd seen it a hundred thousand times before and the sight of it brought back fond memories of his previous employer: Eyeada's pistol.

Bling really didn't give his action much thought. He followed the officer; half out of curiosity and half in the hope of getting his hands on something he could use in an emergency.

He didn't exactly start out thinking that he was going to steal the pistol, but somehow the idea grew on him. Why not? No one was likely to miss the gun and he was even less likely to use it. It was just something he would like to have. Captain Eyeada would have hated the thought.

Bling couldn't help smiling and licking his lips.

The officer continued down the corridor, and then turned to the left. Bling lagged behind, walking slowly with a purposeless shuffle. He had almost reached the turn when the officer re-emerged from the side corridor and walked past him. Bling turned and watched as the man moved briskly back toward the command section. The officer was returning without the little bundle and Bling was quick to see his opportunity.

He entered the same side corridor the officer had just left, then he hesitated. There was a notice painted on the floor entrance of the corridor and the wall on each side. It was written in faded blue lettering; **DO NOT ENTER.** Bling squinted, then shrugged. After all, the lettering was in blue, not the red he was required to obey. He moved quickly down the corridor, unaware of his mistake. The lettering was not blue; it was etched into the body of the ship and there were no guards at the entrance of the corridor because none were needed.

The lighting elements in the roof above became more and more widely spaced as Bling moved further. By the time he reached the end of the corridor his eyes were fully dilated to make use of the reduced illumination. The corridor ended in what looked like a vault door and Bling paused to wonder. Should he go on, or turn back now? The door would decide and Bling reached out, tugging reluctantly on the handle. It moved, massively and without resistance. Bling stepped back and let it swing open. His hands were suddenly covered with sweat and he wiped them uselessly on his clothing.

The room that opened to him was dark. Only the light from the corridor, falling in a murky shaft through the open door, brightened the gloom. Bling shivered involuntarily. Something caught his attention and he took a step forward. There was dust on the floor. He stared at it. The interior of the room was clearly marked by the layer of dust which began where the vault door normally ended. This fact and the stale odor of the place told Bling that for some reason there was no air circulation within the vault.

Footprints in the dust exposed the metal of the deck and showed Bling exactly where the officer had gone when he had entered the room. Bling followed them only because he could see they ended a few feet away and then returned again. A dusty shelf lined the right-hand wall of the vault and it was piled high with obscurely outlined objects; one of which had to be the pistol. Each object seemed to be wrapped in cloth and placed carefully so as not to touch any other.

A smear in the dust on the shelf showed Bling what he was hunting for. The recent disturbance could only have been caused by placing the pistol on the shelf and he lifted the cloth bundle nearest the smear. The heavy pistol shifted position and tumbled out of his hands, crashing back to the shelf, and other smaller objects rained down with it, spilling onto the floor and rolling away into the darkness.

Bling froze. He stood motionless and let the darkness absorb the sound until finally it was quiet again. Beads of sweat formed on his forehead and he strained his ears for the sound of his certain capture, but he couldn't hear a thing.

Suddenly all his ambition was gone. All he wanted to do was put everything back the way it had been and get out. He fumbled with the gun and then began to feel around on the ground for the objects he had spilled. He found one almost immediately and touching it he realized that it was an empty cartridge case. That meant there were four, maybe five more he had to find before he could go. He dropped the empty into his breast pocket and searched frantically for another. He found two more easily and then no more. Perhaps they had rolled all the way across the vault.

Bling stood up and searched the dim area with his eyes. It was a deeper recess and the light from the open door was hardly adequate. A bulky oblong box seemed to occupy most of the area on that side of the room. He might have looked at the box more closely, but he noticed a curving trail in the dust. It was the path one of his errant cartridge cases had taken. He got down on his hands and knees, feeling under the great box to the full reach of his arm, his cheek pressed up against the box. It was cool and smooth against his skin and one part of his mind was telling him that the box was made of glass, while the rest of it concentrated on retrieving the bullet. He finally had it, and gripping it in his hand, he realized that it was indeed a bullet—not an empty cartridge case like the others.

The discovery startled him and he tried to extract his arm quickly, only to snag his shirt on the underside of the box. He cursed silently and strained to see what had snagged him. It was some sort of supporting structure. Bling's eyes bulged. He was looking into the box! His eyes were so adjusted to the dark now that he could see his arm and the supporting underside of the box—but he was seeing them through the box.

The hair on the back of his neck prickled and his eyes searched higher. There was something else in the box. It was suspended right before his eyes and dimly resembled a volley ball—even to the suggestion of a yellow color.

Bling swallowed hard. He began to squirm and tug frantically. There were two eyes in the yellow volley ball, and they were looking at him. His shirt gave way, ripping impossibly loud in the panting silence and Bling was on his feet, stumbling backward—away from the box! He collided with a wall—a switch—and suddenly the lights came on. Bling slid along the wall and the lights went off again, but too late to remove the horror of what he had seen. He tried to scream, but his throat was constricted and no air would move. He ran. He ran out the door and along the dim corridor, screaming silently at the top of his lungs.

Behind him the volley ball head moved—and a few feet away the body, separated from the head by a tangle of cords and fluid pumps, began to squirm. The head moved and the body squirmed, but separated as they were, the motions were as useless as they were harmless. The Hursk—the last of its kind still alive—finally sank back into the apathy from which Bling had awakened it. Its thoughts were dim and feeble; coherent only in their consistent wish for revenge. A revenge it would always wish for, and never get.

Bling finally stopped running. He was totally out of breath and he couldn't scream now if he wanted to, which he didn't. His wits were back and he realized that he was standing within a hundred yards of his room and he was holding in his right hand a pistol and in his left a bullet. How impossibly lucky he had been to have run so far without passing a single crewman, but his luck was running out. Two crewmen were walking toward him right now and he turned around quickly to conceal what he was holding. Only another hundred yards and he would have been safely hidden in his room, but now he was trapped. He couldn't, wouldn't go back and replace the objects he had inadvertently taken. Nothing would make him re-enter that vault. He would just have to think of something else.

Fortune smiled on him. A door to his left opened and Margy Stevens stepped out. She looked at him and her face immediately registered contempt, then surprise. Bling moved quickly. Three strides placed him next to her, directly in front of the room she was leaving.

"What—"

"Here!" Bling whispered urgently. He thrust the pistol into her hands and pushed her back into the room, tossing the bullet in after her. Then he closed the door, turned, and strolled toward the two approaching crewmen.

They looked at him, at the sweat running down his neck and covering his shirt.

"Just out for a little exercise," Bling grated out from behind a frozen smile. He began to jog weakly past them toward his room.

The two men looked at each other, then shrugged. It takes all kinds.

For a second Margy simply stared at the pistol thrust into her hands, then she stared at the door slammed in her face and hurriedly sat down.

The pistol and its single bullet took her back to the short period of time she'd spent aboard the *Matilda*. It seemed so long ago and yet it was only a few short days. How much had changed in that time.

She looked across the room at Jennings slumbering heavily in his chair.

Yes, how very much had changed in such a short time. It was strange, in a way, the situations people got themselves into without really trying. She watched the man across the room, and the way his head rose and fell with his breathing. Did he realize what she had gone through in the three years since that awful accident? Not likely.

Everything she had done since covered her feelings and made it easier for him.

She could still remember seeing him every day in that long-ago hospital; watching him recover steadily toward a life without his wonderful arms, and her heart had sunk lower with each day as she came to realize in the depths of her pragmatic mind exactly what would happen when he recovered and exactly what she would have to do to prevent it from happening. She had stayed with him every day in his delirium and he had somehow known it and gained strength from it. He had smiled at her so often with foggy eyes that she cried even now at the memory. She had cried and finally the doctor told him about his arms.

She never saw him after that. She had transferred to planet duty, saying things about him and knowing he would hate her for leaving him. But he would survive. He would hate her—and not himself. It had come full circle, and this time she could not run away to save him—or herself.

"What's that?" Jennings asked.

Margy turned, nearly startled into dropping the bundle she was holding.

"Nothing," she said, taking a deep breath. "Just a few things I have managed to collect—personal things; combs and such. The Quaker has been kind enough to help make up for my initial destitution—now that he trusts us so well." She tried not to make the sentence sound ironic. If she failed, Jennings didn't notice the failure. He rubbed his face and eyes uncertainly.

"I don't remember you bringing anything with you when you came . . ." he mumbled.

"You were in no condition to notice much of anything an hour ago," she said, tossing the gun in its makeshift disguise onto the padded chair behind her. "You still aren't very coherent." She looked pointedly at his right arm and then back at him. Her face was completely expressionless.

Jennings felt himself growing hot and his jaw began to twitch. "I'm surprised you don't approve," he growled. "I never knew you enjoyed seeing me without them so much. You should have told me—but then you couldn't, could you? Not and mean it."

"I never said I didn't approve," Margy said in a small voice. She felt weak, and very tired.

"You looked it—and I think that must be just about as honest as you can be."

"Don't blame me," she said, "please don't blame me if you're beginning to have second thoughts."

"Second thoughts!" Jennings raised both his arms and clenched his fists in front of her face. "You see these. I had to have them both—to undo all the trouble you and your friends have started."

"I, my friends?"

"Yes, you, and your Freedom friends. If you hadn't started this whole thing by staging that escape . . ." Jennings stopped. He realized that he was shouting and there was no need. "It's done," he said quietly, looking at his new arms and hands. "There is nothing either of us can do about changing that. But if you can find it in your heart to help me—you could make it so much easier."

"I can't," Margy said, closing her eyes. "I can't help the IXT any more. It has taken everything I ever wanted in life and thrown them away. Can't you see how useless it is to fight against the change that is coming? People are tired of being protected. They want to go places again, do things."

Jennings' face hardened as she spoke and he stopped listening. "I can't understand it. How can only three years have changed a person so much? Once, for a little while, I thought I hated you. Now I can see that it was only pity. You couldn't take it three years ago so you ran away from me. Now you've gone all the way. You have always been beautiful, and now I can see that is all there ever was to it."

He turned slowly and left the room.

Margy sat down when he was gone. She didn't cry, because her eyes were empty. She'd used her tears already.

CHAPTER 12. INTERLUDE

Somack lay awake. Sleep just would not come. Finally he gave up trying and decided to find out something once and for all. He dressed and returned to the control room. He sat there for a while, looking at the console. When he had purchased the *Ambol* Somack had realized that the ship was old. His experience with it so far had convinced him that it was a good deal more than just old.

He had been drawn to the ship right from the start and now he realized it had all been planned that way. The *Ambol* had been a part of the dream, a part he had not been able to recall consciously. The *Ambol* knew what it was doing and where it was going—while he did not. It was doing things no ordinary ship should be doing, and until now he hadn't questioned it.

Well, the time for thinking like that was gone. There was too much at stake now. There were too many forces opposed to what he was doing. He could no longer operate on the dream alone—not in a ship which he did not understand and on a trip to who knows where. Somack stood up abruptly and left the control room. An idea had come to him. It was an absurd idea, but one that explained a number of things. The *Ambol* had claimed to be a **"STANDARD LONG HAUL PACKET, #856-CX49."** It was a claim Somack had never taken seriously, and one he had finally uncovered a way of testing.

There were a number of hatches leading down into the *Ambol's* engine spaces and Somack opened and relocked each one in turn as he descended. When he reached the lowest level Somack paused for breath.

Ninety per cent of the lowest level's space was occupied by a single object; the ship's power supply. A small metal disk, made prominent by its polished surface, labeled the huge, squat cylinder. Emblazoned on the disk were the letters and numbers, **R.B. AMBOL; CX49.** Somack smiled. It was all very consistent. The *Ambol* was slow and with this power supply it should be. A **CX49** was just about as low as you could go and still move something like the *Ambol* through space at an economical speed. There would be very little power left over for other things. A weapons system was unthinkable with so little power, and yet the *Ambol* had one.

Somack examined the disk label. It was perfectly smooth and set into the surrounding metal without a visible flaw. All in all, it was a perfect forgery.

Somack made a quick circuit around the base of the power supply. There was nothing at all suspicious. It looked like and was exactly the size of the engine it claimed to be.

Returning to the disk label, Somack studied it again. He ran his hand over it and his fingers probed the inset lettering. He examined the initial B. There was something wrong with the letter; a slight rounding at the top and the bottom of its back; almost as if the letter had originally been a G or C. A quick look at the B in *AMBOL* showed the same rounding. The hair on the back of Somack's neck tingled. The left-hand leg of the M had a bulge at the bottom as if it had been stamped on over a period. The O had a similar bulge at the bottom. *R. B. AMBOL* was an overprint and what lay beneath was either an R. C. A. C. or an R. G. A. G.

G. A. G.

The initials seemed to flash at him and Somack swallowed.

GENETICALLY ACTIVATED GUIDANCE

They were words out of the nightmare past. They were a part of history and something Somack could do without. As a pilot and a history buff he knew what the initials and the words behind them meant. The thoughts they brought to mind dried his throat.

The Hursk War, fifteen years of the most brutal fighting mankind had ever endured, and the *Ambol* was a relic of that war. It was one of the ultimate refinements; a killing machine without equal. The Hursk had been so good at creating *things* that resembled humans and so good at planting them in places of importance that the war effort had been a nightmare of sabotage and death from behind. No one was safe and no one was sure. Only people you knew from childhood could be trusted and they only after careful questioning. Physical appearance was not enough.

G.A.G. had been the answer. Their development had been secret and when everything appeared lost—when the Hursk were winning in the field and creating chaos by proxy on the planets still able to resist—the G.A.G. had been deployed. There were literally hundreds of the small vessels and the attacks they carried out were something that the people who lived through them would never forget. The G.A.G.'s attacked Earth and every other human planet, and they slaughtered hundreds and thousands—millions of people. But most of the people they killed weren't really people.

Nevertheless, even though their use had turned the war around, the people wouldn't abide them. No pilot who used them during those dark days would ever admit the fact. To do so would be fatal.

Somack looked around him. The ships had been designed too well. They had been designed to kill. A job they had done to the extreme. In order to protect themselves and their pilots, the ships had been forced to kill many people, people who thought they were defending themselves from a Hursk attack. The whole operation was one of the darker aspects of the war. Something most people didn't want to think about when the war was over and something that eventually became a sort of horror story —one of the many to spring from the Hursk's great rampage.

Somack shook his head. He remembered one particularly important fact about the ships. They were programmed with an almost paranoid regard for the safety of their pilots. They would do anything to protect the safety of their operators. Somack wiped his forehead. His hand came away covered with cold sweat. Just who, he wondered, did the *Ambol* plan to protect? Someone had gone to an awful lot of trouble to cover the *Ambol's* real nature and that someone was most probably dead—having died on a rainy night many years ago.

What did the ship do in such a case? Somack tried to remember if there was anything in a G.A.G.'s programming which enabled it to select a new "owner." Funny how memories failed you when you needed them most. There was nothing in the vast welter of information he could recall that gave him a clue. The ship itself wasn't any help. The *Ambol* was probably quite capable of lying. All of the more sophisticated computers were capable of it. This was especially true of one with the sensory equipment to distinguish between a human and something that looked an awful lot like a human.

Glancing around, Somack considered the walls and decks around him. Every one of them probably contained hundreds of tiny sensory devices. Perhaps the entire surface of the ship was one giant and perfectly integrated system. It seemed likely and yet impossible. How could an organization like the IXT miss something like that? How could the *Ambol* keep its identity so well hidden? There was more to the question than met the eye and Somack suddenly had an insight into the answer.

At one time the *Ambol* had been equipped with an intercom system. According to the ship's papers the system had been removed by the previous owner for reasons of economy, leaving only the silent console as a means of communicating with the computer. Somack had never given any thought to the modification before, but now he had suspicions.

Taking his time, Somack returned to the cargo deck, the deck right below the control room and the passenger compartments. Here he found what he was looking for; the terminal and translating box for the non-existent intercom system. The box was set into the wall and the plate covering it showed signs of wear, scratches and dents where careless workmen had left their marks. Somack removed the plate carefully and found just what he had expected to find; nothing. The expensive equipment which had once filled the near cubic foot of space was now gone just as the ship's papers said it was.

Somack extracted a small pencil light from his pocket and began a careful examination of the back and side paneling. At first glance there was nothing unusual in the metal plating, aside from the scraped sockets of course, but Somack was sure he would find what he was looking for, so he kept at it. Finally he found what he was seeking. A hair-thin line, almost invisible except when directly under the light, traced a tiny square in the upper right- hand corner at the back of the box.

Somack tapped at the square of metal and nothing happened. He tapped harder. The tiny square dropped out of place. Somack shined his light into the hole; it was a startling effect. He shined the light in, and nothing came out. The hole was filled with a little patch of darkness. Somack strained for a better look and finally he got a glimpse of something. The space was not entirely filled with darkness. There seemed to be a small sphere in there, about an inch in diameter, and its edges nearly touched the tiny compartment walls. There was an illusion of motion. The sphere seemed to be spinning, twirling in one direction and then another. No, that wasn't right. The thing seemed to be spinning in many directions at once and the directions and speed were changing and dividing before his very eyes.

Almost instinctively Somack reached forward and touched the sphere. The sensation was incredible. His finger tingled and felt cold, like it was pressing against a lump of ice, and then he gulped. It was like a crust of air giving way. His finger sank into the tiny sphere and he yanked his hand back with such force that he nearly cracked his elbow.

He could only stare at his finger and wonder how it had come out again. It seemed none the worse for wear, and looking back into the space, Somack could see that nothing had changed there either.

Somack's hands shook as he replaced first the tiny plate and then the larger one. It was secure again, flush with the cargo deck's wall, before he began to breathe freely.

Strange. He had expected to see something like it and yet the actual confrontation was more than he cared to repeat. The tiny thing he had just seen was something from his dream—something that had been put there. He began to understand now why the *Ambol* was such a uniquely endowed ship. The little object he had seen was nothing man-made. Its function was something special. It worked as a governor on the *Ambol's* computer. It gave the ship something closely akin to a conscience. The ship acted according to a set of rules. Somack understood this. *He knew it.*

There was something there that reassured him. The alienness of the tiny, speeding, spinning sphere of nothing—touching it had given him the peace of mind he had been searching for. He could finally return to his room and sleep.

The tiny chip of consciousness and intelligence considered what it had done. The need to reveal itself to Somack had been imperative. But now the need was fulfilled. No one else must find it.

Something began to happen. The molecules of the small metal plate covering its resting place began to fuse with the metal of the surrounding surface. The process was slow and it took all the energy of the tiny entity, but in time the thin line which Somack had noticed in his search was no longer there. Secure, the chip relaxed and emulated what everyone else aboard the *Ambol* was doing. It did not sleep, of course, but what it did was a good imitation.

For two long days the *Ambol* dipped and swerved through space, changing speed and direction whenever it chose to. The narrow corridor of human-explored space was receding gradually into the distance. The *Ambol* was entering an area of space closed to the human race since the earliest days of the Hursk War, an area none had entered legally since.

At the end of these two days nothing had changed aboard the ship.

Devlon was still locked securely in his room and Anna was only now deciding to end her own self-imposed exile. Her decision was slow in coming and complex even in her own mind. She was about to leave her room for the first time since her unfortunate encounter with Devlon and she was determined to make the best of it.

It did her good to see Devlon's door welded tightly shut, but just thinking about him would cloud her mind and she hurried on lest the mood she had so carefully built be destroyed. She was almost happy. For two days she had been carefully convincing herself that she could live with her loss; live with it at least until she could undo it. But she knew herself well enough to realize how fragile her peace of mind was. It simply would not take too many thoughts about Devlon.

Somack was alone in the control room when she entered, and he turned, startled at her light step. It was a long time before he spoke.

"You look very well," he said simply.

"Thank you," she said. There was no way she could help feeling a warm sensation and a prickling in her neck, not when he looked at her so long and spoke so softly.

"It's going to be a pleasure talking to you without a door between us," he continued.

Anna smiled, but the words he spoke brought her back to earth. She was reminded that many of the things she wanted to learn might not bring pleasure.

"Can I ask a favor?" she said timidly, knowing already that he would help her in this as he had helped her without knowing it in more troubled times. "Once before—I came to talk, but I never got around to . . ."

Somack stood up abruptly. "Come with me," he said, walking from the control room. Anna followed, uncertain, and watched as he opened the hatch leading down into the ship.

"Come here," he said, taking her hand and leading her to the open hatch. "I want you to climb down the ladder there and wait for me at the bottom." She hesitated. "Go on," he urged, smiling a little. She watched his eyes and they seemed to be filled with humor, laughing at her and happy watching her react to the awkward situation.

She climbed down more out of self-defense than anything else. It preserved her self-respect and the mood she wanted so much.

He waited until she reached the foot of the ladder and then started down himself, pausing to secure the hatch as he came. "Sit over there," he said when he reached her level. He pointed at an equipment crate and set an example by sitting down on one himself. She did as he said and watched him as he idly toyed with one of the elastic bands securing his crate to the deck. "Now," he said, "we can talk. This is one place where we won't be interrupted by anyone."

She looked around at the cargo hold and was reminded of the first occasion she had spoken to him here. The lighting was mediocre this time, instead of non-existent. That and the time lying between them were the greatest differences in the setting.

"You remember the first time you came down here?" Somack asked, and startled her by picking the thoughts from her tongue. "You were wearing white then, too—and what you did was dangerous. You tried— and failed to get something from me that night. Instead of remaining quiet and trying again, you came and told me. You apologized, even though you thought what you were trying to do was right. You still can't make up your mind about me, can you?"

"No." It was an admission that came hard for Anna. She was torn between *knowing* that he was not evil and *knowing* that what he carried in his mind was. How could she like him, and hate what lay buried within him? It was an impossible situation and one that tore at her more steadily and painfully than any thought of Devlon ever could. "I'm sorry. I just don't know what to think."

Somack shook his head. "You have nothing to be sorry about. I can understand a little of what you must be going through and that's why I want to do my best. I want to make it as easy on you as possible."

"What do you mean?"

"The *Ambol* is going somewhere. Do you know what we are going to see when we get there?"

Anna couldn't answer. She fought down the images of horror that swam up in her mind and she tried not to remember the brief snatches of dream she had taken from his mind. She closed her eyes and waited for it to pass.

"The Quaker still wants you to help him. He was the one who got you to come aboard the *Ambol* in the first place, wasn't he?" Somack pressed.

"Yes! And I would do it again! He needs my help—and what he is fighting is evil. That—whatever you are leading us to—must be destroyed! Can't you see, can't you understand how terrible it is? How can you live with those terrible things in your mind—those horrible memories?"

"They are terrible, and horrible," Somack admitted, "but you only saw a part. No, don't shake your head. I know what you saw, and I know you only saw a part—the worst part."

"I don't want any more! If there is any more, I don't want to see it."

Somack sighed. It was going to be harder than he had expected. How could he explain what she was going to face without making her fear greater instead of less. The silence stretched into an awkward minute and Somack finally gave up. He slipped down from the crate he was sitting on and walked over to Anna. "This isn't getting us anywhere, is it?"

She looked up and shook her head.

Somack took the hands from her lap and pulled her into a standing position. "Then let's go back up and get something to eat."

"I am hungry," Anna said. She was really very happy that things had not turned out badly after all.

Somack served the food slowly. There was nothing special about the meal, except that it was the first one the three of them had eaten together aboard the *Ambol.* Merrick did not ask why he had been invited. He was also careful not to ask what had happened. It was obvious, though, that something was going on. The girl was in high color and her eyes were clear of panic for the first time since she had come aboard.

Anna looked back at him boldly. Merrick cleared his throat, discomforted by the frank scrutiny. "It's nice to see you looking so well," he said, to fill the air with something beside the smell of food.

"Thank you," Anna answered, but her eyes did not leave his face as he had hoped they would.

"A shame that Devlon can't be here with us," Merrick countered. He was probing, unsure of what was going on aboard the *Ambol.*

Somack sat down heavily and spoke quietly. "He won't starve."

"How long do you plan to keep him locked up?" Merrick asked, now that the subject had been safely broached.

"Until the trip is over," Somack answered bluntly.

"I see," Merrick said, and he turned to find the girl still watching him. "Is there something wrong?" he asked with a touch of irritation.

She smiled ever so slightly. "Wrong?" Her smile faded into puzzlement. "No. I was just wondering what hard labor was like."

It was Merrick's turn to look puzzled. "Hard labor?"

"You forget," she accused quietly, "that I am a criminal, escaped for the moment, but still a criminal. How long is a life of hard labor, for people like me?"

Merrick felt embarrassed, for himself and for the IXT. How could he sit here and tell this girl that the knowledge in her mind was dangerous and because of it she was likely to suffer a great deal. Knowledge of the Encounter Program—and of aliens outside of its protective screen—both of these things were scarce and the IXT wanted to keep it that way.

"*You* would probably live quite a while," Merrick said lightly, "hard labor or not."

The intended compliment fell flat. Anna did not smile as he had hoped. Instead, she took the comment seriously and conceded the point. "Yes, I suppose I would."

Merrick squirmed a little and Somack saved him by entering the conversation. "If the IXT can afford to let me go after this whole thing is over, then they can afford to let other people go too."

"Quite right," Merrick agreed, glad for a way out. What Somack said was true, but the logical conclusion drawn from it might not be the one Somack had drawn.

It was quiet for a while. The food was the same as always, but eating it together like this seemed to make it better. Even the cramped little room, one of the two not occupied as sleeping quarters, seemed warmer and more comfortable. It was strange how such a little thing could change the atmosphere so much, replacing strain with normality.

Finally Merrick asked the question that had been gnawing at him. "What is it going to be like, this place we are going? What kind of alien intelligence is waiting for us there? You might as well let me know. There is nothing I can do to change our destination."

"I really don't know what it is going to be like," Somack said. "I can't answer either of those questions."

For the first time Merrick caught the girl's eyes watching Somack. She was interested, and judging by her reaction, just as disappointed when Somack failed to answer. Her eyes dropped again and her lips curled in disbelief.

Somack frowned. He was about to speak again when the *Ambol's* drive shifted, dropping an octave. They were all used to the sound. It meant the ship was slowing to make another course change.

"I had better go to the control room," Somack said, rising heavily. "There is always the chance that this will be the end of the road."

Merrick rose also. "Why don't you have an audio system installed in this old dump. Then the ship could call you when it needs you."

Somack didn't answer. There was nothing he could say, so he kept his mouth shut and left the room. Merrick followed him and Somack began to worry that there would come a day when questions would not go away and answers could not be avoided. Deception was a two-edged blade and there were some people he did not wish to cut. He entered the control room and forgot his worry. The console was alive with activity.

CONTACT WITH DESTINATION HAS BEEN ESTABLISHED. PLANETFALL WILL BE MADE IN SIXTEEN MINUTES. PLEASE MAKE NECESSARY PREPARATIONS FOR PERSONAL SAFETY IN UNASSISTED LANDING. NO ENVIRONMENT CHECK IS NECESSARY. DESCENT WILL BE IMMEDIATE UPON DRIVE SHUTOFF. LOSS OF GRAVITATIONAL ORIENTATION WILL OCCUR IN NINE MINUTES. HEAVY DECELERATION WILL BE EXPERIENCED DURING DESCENT.

"This isn't reasonable procedure," Somack mumbled under his breath.

"What's going on?" Merrick asked.

"We are going to be sitting on the surface of a planet in sixteen minutes. If you want to make the ride in comfort, you'd better help me unlimber these webs."

The acceleration webs sprang up from the deck in a matter of seconds and the two men had them ready for occupation almost as quickly. Somack moved quickly to get Anna. She was still sitting at the small table waiting for the two men to return.

"Throw that stuff into the disposal chute," Somack said, setting an example with his own half-consumed meal.

Anna stared at him, not comprehending, then complied reluctantly. The meal had been a tiny oasis of the ordinary in a world swimming around her. Now, even that was gone.

"Hurry," Somack urged, and pulled her from the room.

Within moments she and the two men were securely strapped in place. Only then did Merrick have time to think of the fourth person aboard.

"What about Devlon?" he asked in an urgent whisper.

Somack was intent on the controls. "Who?" he said in a mildly puzzled tone.

The *Ambol's* main drive shut down and the ship began to rock. It steadied abruptly as the computer completed its calculations. The ship shed its excess momentum in a series of brutal decelerations. The planet grew and then disappeared as the *Ambol* plunged into its atmosphere. It was all over in a matter of minutes.

CHAPTER 13. SPEAKER

The *Ambol* had certain natural advantages over the two ships following it. It was designed to land on planets without the help of modem facilities and to leave again on its own power. This was something neither the Quaker's ship nor the IXT's *Exeter* could do. With their great space-to-weight ratios they could never withstand the stress of a descent without help. Of course, both ships were equipped with small craft, and these could do what the *Ambol* was doing—and do it better—but it would take time to man them and set them loose.

When the *Ambol* settled to the ground it was all alone. Somack unstrapped and contemplated the view from the screens. It was hard to say exactly what he had expected, but what he saw certainly wasn't it. A green meadow stretched in all directions, forming a shallow bowl around them. The not too distant ridges were dense with trees and these thinned away rapidly at the meadow's edge.

Nothing stirred within sight and Somack wondered if anything could look anything more like a park—that wasn't a park.

The console lit.

PRESENTLY RECEIVING REQUESTS FOR COMMUNICATIONS FROM *EXETER* AND QUAKER SHIP OF UNKNOWN DESIGNATION, THEY BOTH DEMAND IMMEDIATE RESPONSE.

"Allow communications with the Quaker's ship," Somack said.

The Quaker's face appeared. "Ah," he said, "I'm glad to see that we have finally arrived—somewhere. I hope you aren't trying to deceive me. My instruments have already informed me that this planet is devoid of anything faintly resembling a civilization. I find it hard to believe that a race—or a single being—of any importance could exist without at least some sign of its origin. Since I can find no trace of a ship, or any other mechanical activity, must we assume that this creature of yours was abandoned by someone? Left on this planet to fend for itself?" The Quaker sounded disappointed.

Somack shrugged. "Assume what you wish. This is the place I promised to bring you. Stay out of the way and it will . . ." Somack paused, at a loss. He had no idea what was going to happen.

"It will what?" the Quaker asked without humor, or much curiosity. "I expect to keep out of the way, just as I expect you to take Devlon with you whenever you leave the *Ambol.* Is that clear?"

"Very clear," Somack said, cutting the connection.

The IXT came next. "Let me speak with Merrick," Kane, the *Exeter's* commander, said.

Somack stepped aside, letting Merrick assume the command chair.

"Yes, sir?" Merrick said, flicking the transmit switch on the *Ambol's* visual pickup.

Kane squinted at the unexpected visual display he was receiving, then smiled. "Looks pretty nice down there. I see you managed to get the girl away from the Quaker."

"Yes, everything's fine," Merrick said quickly. "We got something else from the Quaker: Alexander Devlon."

Kane's jaw dropped, then his face lit with pleasure. "Where is he? I don't see him."

Merrick explained the situation as quickly as he could, adding that Devlon would be accompanying them whenever they left the ship.

"I see," Kane said, nodding. "And when do you plan to go out? The planet looks pretty tame and empty from up here. Too tame if you ask me."

"When we go out is up to Mr. Somack," Merrick said judiciously. "But I expect it won't be too long."

"Keep me informed," Kane said in parting.

Devlon staggered to his feet. Blood was running from his nose, putting indelible splotches of color on his shirt. He wiped at it, then sniffed and began rubbing the bruises on his arm and leg. His whole right side had suffered in the descent; only quick thinking had saved him from a fractured skull.

He sat down heavily on the edge of his bunk and looked at his hands. They were stained red and he chuckled at the sight. This time the blood was his, but the next time it wouldn't be. Everything they did to him—every insult and injury—just added to the pleasure he would get in the end.

He'd given plenty of thought to how that was going to be. The Quaker's clinical methods of killing would not be satisfactory. Films could be doctored and the records of what he did changed. There was no reason to forego the pleasure he would get from doing the job personally. It would take time his way; a little extra time. Certainly, the Quaker could not object to that. Activity at the door broke Devlon's concentration. Visions fled from his mind and the glassy look left his eyes. He changed shirts quickly and cleaned the drying blood from his face and hands. There was no reason to show them how much they had hurt him.

Somack stood in the doorway. He was holding the same cutting torch Devlon had seen him with last. Devlon did not miss the way the torch's aim lingered in his direction.

"We've made planetfall," Somack said briskly. "You're coming with us."

"I couldn't help noticing the descent," Devlon said. His voice was dry and he did not disguise the implied threat in his tone. There was nothing they could do to him—no way they could avoid what was going to happen to them.

He followed Somack down the short hall and into the control room. Anna and Merrick were waiting there, and by their dress, Devlon could see that no extraordinary precautions were being taken. Looking around at the countryside shown in the screens told him why. Nothing seemed more pleasant than what he saw; green against blue. Even the sky was softened and the heat of a perfect sun broken by a scattering of cloud.

"We are going out through the control room hatch," Somack explained. "The distance from the freight hatch would be less, but I prefer not to open that compartment."

Merrick nodded in understanding, while Anna ignored Somack. She was keeping all of her attention on Devlon and he was returning his, adding a slight twist of the lips.

"You first," Somack said, motioning Devlon toward the hatch with the torch in his hand.

Devlon smirked in mock embarrassment. "There's something I have to do first. That rough ride down seems to have shaken something loose inside—I wouldn't want to make a public display of myself down there in the open."

Somack frowned. "Be quick about it, then."

Devlon backed a step, then turned and hurried back down the aisle toward his room. When he reached the door, however, he turned to the left and entered Anna's room. With a quick dive and a brief groping search under her bed, he came up with the small black cube. He was back in the hall within seconds and he paused to catch his breath before returning to the control room.

"That was fast," Somack commented. "Now get going."

The hatches to the outside opened and a breath of fresh air swept into the ship along with a shaft of reflected sunlight. The ship's screens were off now, and the only view of the outside came through the open hatch. It was beautiful, like a tunnel of light leading somewhere nice.

Devlon slouched forward and blocked the view for a moment as he fumbled for a toe hold and began his descent. Somack was the last one out and the hatches closed behind him. It was quite a distance to the ground and the small handholds in the *Ambol's* side required all of his attention, so Somack was forced to place the torch in a makeshift holster he'd rigged for it. He jumped the last few feet to the ground and landed facing out.

"You first," he said to Devlon. "Keep a good twenty feet ahead of us."

Devlon smiled, but he turned and started toward the distant ridge none the less.

"That was a good idea," Merrick commented. "I wouldn't want him behind me either."

"You're next," Somack said quietly.

"What?" Merrick's eyes bulged a little as he watched the open muzzle of the torch swivel and come to rest on him.

"Don't argue."

Merrick didn't argue. He suddenly realized that a quiet voice and a steady gaze was as far as he wanted to go with Somack. He turned and followed Devlon.

Anna watched the two men go. She was half expecting him to turn the torch on her next. She knew he wouldn't, but she knew it with her heart and not her mind.

"Am I next?" she asked.

Somack turned to stare at her. "You still don't trust me?" he said, voicing bitter disappointment.

For a long second they looked at each other, then Anna turned and started after the two walking men.

"Answer me!" Somack demanded, pulling her around to face him again.

"Why should I?" she said, shaking loose and taking a backward step. Her lips made a sharp line in the silence. "Why should I answer you? Why should I trust you? You brought me here—I didn't ask to come. You make me travel with them." She pointed toward the walking men. "Either one of them would be glad to see me dead. Tell me now—why should I trust you?"

If she had shouted, yelled at him, it would have been far better. But this cold speech and calm questioning were more than he could take. "You can do any damn thing you want." He turned and walked away.

She followed, blinking and wishing she were somewhere else.

Jennings took a careful look at his left hand. There were traces of color in the hand and it didn't feel numb anymore. If he touched something with it he could feel texture and temperature as well as every shade of pressure. Even the occasional twitching was gone. It was just like his own hand. It was his own hand, or would be when his cells finished replacing those of the symbiot.

His right hand and arm were another matter. It would take a much longer time before they began to act and feel truly natural—another week perhaps. The white, pasty color would linger for half that time. Still, it was little enough to pay for the use of two arms again.

His mouth compressed at the thought and he reminded himself of the real price he would eventually pay. It made him wish all the harder to get the thing over with. The Quaker was being very secretive about the activities down on the planet. Jennings shook his head. Only his forceful insistence had gained him the chance he was going to have this morning. The Quaker had promised to let him see something he was likely to remember. It was a new technique in observation—according to the Quaker. He would know for himself in a few minutes.

The Quaker entered the room. "Thank you for your patience," the Quaker said jovially. "Everything is ready now."

Jennings stood up.

"No need to go anywhere," the Quaker said quickly. "We are in the observation room right now."

Jennings looked around at the blank walls. "Really?" he said. He was too used to surprises to sound skeptical.

The Quaker slid forward, toward the wall behind Jennings. "Notice how this wall bulges out slightly. There's a spherical chamber on the other side."

The opaqueing disappeared and confirmed the Quaker's word. A black abyss filled the area beyond the wall. It was a spherical chamber about two hundred yards across. A bright spot of light was located at the center of the sphere. The spot was increasing in brilliance and Jennings realized that the chamber was not empty after all. It was filled with millions of tiny filaments radiating out from the center. These were meshed with others cutting tangents across the hollow sphere. As the light increased Jennings could see that the chamber was nearly filled with shining fiber, like the lair of a giant spider gone mad with web productivity.

"What is it?" Jennings asked.

"Just watch," the Quaker said, enjoying himself.

Something was happening near the center of the sphere. Jennings squinted. It almost looked like a man walking in mid-air. Then Jennings recognized the man with a start: it was Alexander Devlon. Jennings was about to speak when a patch of ground appeared beneath Devlon's feet. It was covered with grass. Slowly the picture began to fill in. The ground extended and before long another figure appeared. He was walking behind Devlon and neither man seemed to be gaining much ground. In fact, Devlon never seemed to leave the center of the sphere. When the sphere was finally filled, a kind of sky background appeared on its upper half. Its lower half was obscured by grass and the dirt beneath it. The figures in the sphere were partially transparent—you could see one through another, just like you could see a few feet into the ground.

"This is incredible," was all Jennings could think to say. "How do you do it?"

"Nothing really spectacular," the Quaker said modestly. "I'm sure you've noticed that our friend, Alexander Devlon, never moves from the center of the scene. That's because he's carrying the device that makes this projection possible. Notice the way he seems to rotate around his right-hand pocket, just a bit. I managed to plant the device on him, before I was forced to turn him over to Somack."

"What about sound?" Jennings asked. He was beginning to appreciate the possibilities this device offered.

"Of course," the Quaker said, "we can get sound—but the processing is a little more difficult. There is a slight delay. But that really doesn't matter. Everything is being carefully recorded and we can always go over everything again, with sound."

Jennings was about to say something in response when his eye caught a flicker of motion on the edge of the sphere. His mouth dropped open.

"What the hell?"

The Quaker turned to see the cause of Jennings' contorted face. The sight he found was enough to make even the Quaker flinch.

<hr />

D evlon's pace slowed. The grass was thinning and the trees were growing more numerous as the ground rose. Here and there rocks poked through the soil, exposing the ridge's tough spine.

Devlon turned and looked back on the others following him up the slope.

It occurred to him suddenly that the weapon Somack held was essentially useless. It was deadly enough within a few yards, but beyond that the cutting torch was just so much hot air. A well-thrown rock would be more effective. He turned the thought in his mind and hurried toward the crest of the hill. There, in the shade of a large tree, he knelt to pick up a handy stone. As he was straightening, something caught in the corner of his eye and he shifted to see.

"I am Speaker."

Devlon's mouth worked at a scream, but nothing happened. He toppled, his eyes rolling, and he hit the ground without feeling it.

Merrick was next. He saw Devlon fall and came on the run, but stopped abruptly.

"My God!"

Speaker did not move. It was now aware that its appearance was frightening—motion on its part would only make things worse.

"Do not fear," it croaked, "my form is mere convenience. I will change."

Merrick watched the huge and lumpy toad melt and struggle into a manlike form. "No. No!" Merrick choked. "The other one was better." He tried not to gag.

Speaker melted helplessly. It resumed the toad form. "I fear I have frightened you," it said, "but to speak, I must have form."

"That's right," Somack said calmly. He approached from the rear with a firm grip on Anna's arm, but she was making no attempt to hold back.

Merrick stepped to one side. His legs were still weak from watching Speaker change into something almost human. He shifted his eyes away from the form on the ground and kept the conversation going, hoping the words would distract his mind.

"So, *this* is what we've come so far to see?" he said, swallowing hard.

Somack did not answer. Speaker was not what *he* had come here to see. He could sense that it was a part—a small physical manifestation of the greater thing he had come to find. Speaker was like a porthole—a way of looking into the great storehouse of knowledge and experience which lay somewhere near. Somack could feel that greater presence and its power made him tremble.

He watched Anna, watching her reaction to Speaker's squatting form, trying to see if she could feel anything of what he was feeling. But she gave no sign. Her face was set and her lips made a thin line as she faced Speaker. She did not turn away.

Speaker gurgled. "Excuse me," it apologized. "My shape has caused distress. Your arrival was sudden and I was hurried to get here in time. I am sorry."

Somack smiled. "I understand," he said, "but there was no need to hurry. We have plenty of time."

"No," Speaker disagreed. It shifted its pseudo eyes to Anna. "I am here only because I have to be. Speech is necessary where it should not be. I am here to help you eliminate that necessity."

"What does it mean?" Anna asked. Her voice trembled and when she looked at Somack for an answer there was something like hope in her eyes. Could this mean that she was going to recover the sense she had so recently lost?

"Do not expect such a thing," Speaker said to Anna. "You have brought much trouble upon this meeting. You have caused delay and worse—you have come bringing others—uninvited, like yourself."

Anna shrank back a step and something went out of her. She sagged and Somack found himself supporting most of her weight.

Speaker watched impassively. It must be harsh with this one—because this one was the closest to realizing a terrible power and to do so without a full understanding of the power's implications was more dangerous than any other happening. Speaker's job was to see that understanding came before power—and, if possible, to impel restraint.

"You have no reason to sorrow," it said harshly. "What you have lost is better gone. You will *know* this!"

There was a silence in the clearing for a few moments and Somack found himself in an awkward position. His arms were supporting Anna and yet she was trying to push away. He could feel the weakness of her effort and it made him ache.

"You can't run away," he whispered. "I've lived with it so long—I can't claim to see it the same way you do. I was young; if I'd known then . . ." His words failed him. He wanted to say that he had given away what she was fighting to hold—what she had grown and nurtured throughout her life. But he couldn't. She was losing a most precious part of herself—and he could not tell her why.

She was still, resting against him, and though he looked beyond—at the others around him—he could not see them clearly. He could only see one thing, and that was with his heart.

S peaker moved, breaking the spell that had settled over the group. "I have said what I came to say." Its pseudo eyes remained focused on Anna. It was clear the creature was speaking to her and no one else.

"Not so fast!" Merrick ordered as Speaker began to move away. Merrick had something very small in his hand and it was pointed at Anna. "I don't know what all this talk is about, but no one—or thing, is going anywhere until I say so."

Merrick gestured with the object he held. Somack dropped his torch and stepped away from it, taking Anna with him.

Merrick retrieved the torch with his left hand and trained it on Speaker. "So far as I am concerned," Merrick growled, "you are just a blob of jelly that talks a lot—and that's not enough to justify all the trouble we've been through to find you."

Speaker was unruffled. "I am sorry," it said. It did not seem to care.

A loud boom sounded overhead and Merrick grinned. "Just remain calm," he said, "and no one will suffer. In a few minutes we will all be leaving this place and we can discuss things in a more leisurely manner elsewhere."

The IXT craft swooped low, vibrating the leaves with its passing. It was a launch from the *Exeter*. Banking, it curved to the left and began circling toward the *Ambol*.

Anna watched for a moment, then her eyes darted back to Merrick and the object he was holding in his hand. She was alive to the danger now, to how wrong everything was going, and she found herself watching Somack—hoping that he would do something. But Somack merely stood and watched as the IXT ship circled lower.

"It seems that you believe our agreement is at an end," Somack said, looking at Merrick for confirmation.

The IXT officer nodded. "The agreement ended the moment your friend here showed its face—if you'll excuse the expression. You've done your part and we did ours a long time ago."

"Then Anna and I can go," Somack said flatly.

"No."

"You misunderstand," Somack corrected. "I did not ask if we could go; I *told* you that we were going." To emphasize the point Somack turned and pulled Anna with him.

"Another step and you're dead." Merrick was deadly serious. "This thing I am holding may look like a toy, but one touch of the poison it fires and. . ."

Somack ignored the warning and continued to walk. Merrick aimed the pencil-shaped weapon at Somack's back, taking careful aim.

"Don't!" Anna cried. "Don't!" She pulled at Somack's grip and dug her feet in, pulling him around. "What are you doing?" she pleaded. "He means it."

"I know that," Somack smiled, "but there's nothing to worry about."

"No!" She pulled free and placed herself between Somack and Merrick. Her eyes were wild and she looked frantically for some way to stop what was going to happen. "You!" she cried, pointing at Speaker. "You're so terrible—so powerful. Do something!"

Speaker's pseudo eyes retracted. It quivered. Never had it experienced command so close—so close to the memories. Nothing else would have made it act against its practice of ages and do something it had never expected to see done again.

It melted; reforming into a near perfect sphere—an enormous eye. "I can do *nothing*," it said. "*I can do nothing, for you!*"

Focusing its wholeness upon one small rock, Speaker contracted convulsively. The convulsion ended and Speaker suddenly regained control of itself again. Two quick spasms returned it to its more familiar toad shape.

Merrick watched Speaker's actions with a skeptical frown on his face. All of this frantic shape changing had wasted time and nothing more. He returned his attention to the girl and Somack. He was about to repeat his warning when he saw the rock.

The rock Speaker had focused on was drifting up from the ground. Ever so slowly it rose, a few inches, then a foot. Merrick watched and his mouth dropped open. The rock continued to rise, gaining speed.

There was a dead silence as the rock bumped and bounced its way through the branches about them. When Merrick finally spoke, it was very quietly. "Get moving," he said to Somack and Anna. "I don't care where you go, just so long as it's out of shouting range of this Speaker thing. If it tries to follow you, I'll kill you all." Both of the weapons he held were now trained on Speaker.

'What happened?" Anna asked. Merrick had let them go. She couldn't understand. She looked back at the ridge. She wanted to see, but Somack wouldn't slow down. He pulled her along. "Why are we going this way?" she asked, voicing her confusion.

The question was a good one, but Somack ignored it. He continued to walk down the slope in a line directly away from the *Ambol*. The trees were thinning rapidly and soon they were walking in an open meadow again; this time a completely empty one.

Somack slowed. "We are not going back to the *Ambol*," he said finally. "I'm afraid we are not through with what we came here for, yet."

"You mean the IXT would stop us—don't you. Once they take your Speaker thing away, they will change their minds and want us again."

Somack stopped. "Yes. But it doesn't matter what they want; not here."

She looked at him, more puzzled now than ever. "I don't understand," she complained. "Shouldn't we be doing something—hiding? How can a floating rock be so important?"

Somack took a deep breath. "What we witnessed with the rock was different, terribly different. That was a violation of the laws of gravitation, a negation of those laws rather than a use."

"But Speaker said it couldn't do anything for us."

"No," Somack corrected as gently as he could. "Speaker said it could do *nothing* for *you*—and that is just what it did. Speaker eliminated the effects of gravity on that rock, so it floated away. He created a little bit of space where the laws of gravitation did not work! Merrick realized that—he realized the danger of that—and that's why he was so shocked and frightened."

"Danger? What danger? How can a floating rock be dangerous?"

Somack tried not to think of what he was about to do. "There is no danger in a floating rock, but the same thing can be done on a larger scale. If you took gravity away from a planet—it would fall apart. If you took it away from a star—the star would explode. And if you did it to a whole universe . . ."

Anna swallowed hard. Something clicked in her mind. Her sudden understanding came as a physical shock. Her mind rocked with the horrible memories of her dream—of the dream she had taken from Somack. A blackness shook her. She looked at Somack, she looked at trees, grass. She tried to hold on. But she slipped. She fell out of the world.

CHAPTER 14. THE DIM PAST

The dream was upon her. She swirled in a maelstrom of darkness and conflicting images. Something rose up out of the chaos. Enormity. Age. A vast darkness which spread out in every direction and rippled back again. Anna whimpered.

YOU ARE HURT.

The words echoed around her and within her. She could feel a groping, an awkward attempt at comfort from the darkness around her. Then she knew why. It was the awkwardness, the gentleness of a machine so close to life that it ached on the edge—and yet knew it could never cross.

SORROW, *it said,* **SORRY, THE BURDEN I CARRY, YOU MUST LIVE IT WITH ME. YOU MUST SHARE.**

The words left an emptiness behind them, but there was an expectancy too. Something was going to happen. Something *was* happening. Anna felt herself swell and grow enormously huge. She was taking on the existence of the giant mechanical being all around her—going back to the beginning of its memories. Everything was quiet. Everything was dark. She was very young. She was being built.

Tap. Tap. The first sound. It came from all around. Everywhere tiny living creatures swarmed around her. They were tiny. Human-sized. So small. They were nearly finished, but they hurried—faster than they had ever hurried before.

Light. She could see and all around her the tiny builders rushed. Hurry. Hurry. She wondered. Even inside her, they were forever moving, never stopping, never slowing. But she could scarcely understand why. It was enough to hear, to see. Could there be anything more important? It was her job. To see. To hear. To remember. *Everything.*

Sorrow. She could suddenly feel it. All around her. It came from them —the little builders. She tried not to feel it, but there was no way she could shut it out. They had built her to feel. They wanted her to hurt. They wanted her to remember everything that happened. Their sorrow burned in her. She tried to comfort them, but they could not respond. They could not see or feel the way she could. That was part of the reason for their sorrow.

Slowly she learned. Builders were different. They weren't like her, the great machine they built. They could not see—not like she could. All the other races looked down on them because of this. They were builders and could not see into each other's minds. But they could build. They could see the danger and they would do what they could. Others had used their deep powers. Run them wild. If only the builders had known of the danger sooner—if only they had known earlier.

They finished just in time. The darkness spread toward them. They did not try to save themselves. They couldn't. Only a few stayed with her —just enough to start again, if there was another chance, somewhere, sometime.

There was another planet—another people. They knew the builders and disdained them—for they had the power to do things the builders could not do. They were horrified by what the builders had created. She frightened them; terrified them. The builders have turned on us, they thought, they have come to destroy us. She tried to warn them. She tried to tell them of the blackness. But they closed their minds. She fled onward; continued to search, and behind her the darkness spread, engulfing all she had known and leaving her memories as their only trace to existence.

She came upon another race—and discovered the way that darkness spread. It was a weapon, a tool. To break a law, to nullify one—for just an instant—it created so much energy and did so little damage. What harm was there?

A Black Dwarf, for instance. A useless star, and wasted matter. Eliminate the nuclear force. Instantly the dense matter broke down and became hydrogen. Restore the force and a new star was born to replace the burned-out husk of what had once been there. A wonderful thing. A wonderful thing. But the same thing—what it did to a planet and living things was not as nice.

Eliminate electromagnetic force and change lead to gold, soil to platinum, and people to dust.

All of this, and more, she saw. Here—and there—tiny places; the fabric tore. The order was destroyed. Black pools spread and matter, energy, everything fell, slipped in and never returned. She tried to stop them, tried to warn them, but no one would listen. Finally the builders realized their mistake. She—their creation—was too big and too frightening. They hurried to correct their mistake and she helped them. Together they made Speaker. Speaker was small. Speaker could go first. Speaker could become one of them—one of anything, and it could convince them from within. Speaker could convince them and do what she was failing to do.

It worked, a little. Some would come with her. Some were convinced, but never enough.

They tried. Many times she and her living companions would turn and fight the spreading edge. But there were never enough—always too few to stop it and they would flee again.

The end came slowly. There was nowhere left to go and nothing left to fight for. The waves of darkness lapped at her and each time there were fewer of her companions left behind. Finally there was only Speaker—and Speaker was really just a part of her. Speaker was not really alive, just as she was . . . memories. A machine of memories—surviving the death of the universe into which it had been born.

I AM SORRY.

The apology flooded over Anna and she felt something of herself again.

She was no longer a part of the great presence that surrounded her.

YOU ARE STRONG, *it told her,* **I HAVE GIVEN YOU MORE OF MY MEMORIES THAN ANY OTHER. YOU WILL CARRY THEM AND PASS THEM ON—AS YOU CAN. YOU WILL HELP.**

It was over. Anna could feel the grass again, the warmth of the sun, and the shadow of someone leaning close to her.

Merrick stood, with his eyes narrowed, watching Speaker. He was expecting trouble. Ever since that rock had floated away he had been expecting trouble. Only a few moments ago that same rock had come tumbling down through the trees, nearly striking him on the head, but nothing would change the fact that the rock had once been weightless.

The men from the *Exeter's* shuttle were finally approaching. Merrick could hear the fall of their running feet coming up behind him. Any moment now he'd be relieved of some of the responsibility weighing him down. He heard a twig snap and then the sound of someone trying to slow down in a big hurry.

"Ugly!" someone choked.

"What is it?"

Someone began to empty a good meal onto the grass.

"Cut that," Merrick grated. "Get up here and give me a hand with this thing."

"Yes, sir," was the reluctant reply. A young officer approached and stood hesitantly on Merrick's left. The young man's face was covered with beads of sweat and he held a Mark-6 Thermal in a hand that trembled ever so slightly.

"Watch where you point that!" Merrick snarled. "We don't want fried frog. We want the thing alive."

"But, it's ugly, sir. God, it's ugly!"

"I've seen worse," Merrick lied casually. "Now, get those men up here where they belong."

"But—but, what do we do with it, sir?"

"Move it!" Merrick snapped. He was running extremely short on temper. "Damn—what now?"

Speaker's pseudo eyes shifted from one of the men to the other and then to the group milling around in the distance. It blinked, leaned to one side, and slushed to the ground—dissolving into a glob of jelly as it went.

The young officer stiffened his arm, extending his weapon uncertainly.

"Don't shoot, you fool!" Merrick's face was becoming flushed. "Get those men up here and pick the thing up. We'll carry it out, if it chooses not to co-operate."

"Sir?"

"You heard me."

The men approached slowly and formed a reluctant circle around Speaker who now resembled a translucent jello pizza about five feet in diameter.

"Pick it up, damn you."

The men exchanged glances. They leaned—more or less in unison—and gripped Speaker's edge. Their faces, as they began to lift the limp body, varied from stoic acceptance, through disgust, to near sickness. Speaker sagged in the middle. Its center dragged along the ground as the men began to move toward the shuttle.

"Lift it higher," Merrick ordered.

The men obeyed, but it did very little good. Speaker sagged again and it was still touching the ground, even when the men had their hands well above their own heads. Pseudo eyes began to form along the surface facing out; a pair for each man. One man yelped as the eyes stretched out toward him, another cursed and let go of his section of Speaker. Within seconds everyone followed suit and there was an extended plop as Speaker dropped to the ground.

The young lieutenant looked at Merrick helplessly. Merrick sighed and looked around. They had managed to drag the limp body about a hundred yards and it now lay in an area largely free of trees.

"Get the shuttle to move up here. We'll load it directly into the cargo hatch."

Clear relief showed on the lieutenant's face as he gave the necessary orders. The job of loading turned out to be relatively easy—relatively. When the shuttle was finally gone Merrick wiped the sweat and some of the dirt from his face. Two of the shuttle's crew had remained behind with him. One of them would stay beside the *Ambol* and stop anyone from entering. The other would help him round up the *Ambol's* missing complement. The *Exeter's* second shuttle would be down eventually to pick them all up.

Until that time he would have to make do with what he had.

The walk back up the ridge took only a few minutes; minutes that may have made the difference. Devlon was gone.

The discovery did nothing to improve Merrick's mood. He cursed himself for not having tossed that nuisance into the first shuttle along with Speaker. He simply hadn't thought of it. Speaker had kept everyone so busy.

Well, it just meant that he had twice as much work to do. He began immediately, searching the ground for some trace of Devlon's movement and the direction he might have taken. Of the three people he had to round up, Devlon was probably the most dangerous and Merrick decided that it probably wouldn't hurt to secure him first.

Devlon panted for breath and flung himself against the trunk of a tree for support. He was winded. He had never run so hard in all his life. He rubbed his eyes, trying to erase the nightmare of what he had seen. Speaker had been a hideous creature, worse than anything he could have imagined.

He plucked the small cube from his pocket and thought how useless it had been. For the IXT to kill the thing—how could that be made to look wrong? He would do it himself given half a chance and something powerful enough to do it with.

Devlon stumbled away from the tree and resumed his flight. He was walking now, and thinking a little. He had to escape the IXT. Nothing else mattered at the moment. He glanced at the surrounding foliage. As long as he remained on the gently sloping ridges he was safe from visual observation, but once the IXT began to look for him in earnest there was no way he could avoid detection and capture. If only the Quaker would do something. The Quaker had the power, why didn't he use it?

Something buzzed in Devlon's hand and he instinctively flung it away. Then he realized that it was the black cube. He approached the spot where it had landed cautiously. The cube was laying in a pile of leaves, inert. Devlon knelt to pick it up and it buzzed again. He snatched his hand away and waited. Nothing. Then it buzzed again, this time in an undulating pattern of sound; almost like talking or trying to talk. Devlon picked the cube up and frantically pressed it to his ear.

"That's better!" the cube buzzed, sounding like the Quaker. "I thought you were going to sleep through everything. If I hadn't started sending with this thing, you would probably have remained unconscious. Merrick would be using you for an IXT information source right this moment."

Devlon ignored the Quaker's comments. "Why didn't you tell me this thing was a communicator too!" he shouted at it.

It buzzed at him ineffectually until he finally calmed enough to put it back to his ear.

"We all have our little secrets," the Quaker said bluntly. "I just want you to know that I'm doing my best for you. I have to go now, but one of my men will stay with you and tell you when anyone gets within the cube's range. Follow his instructions and they will never find you—not as long as you stay under cover. Good luck."

Devlon shouted. He cursed, but he knew that the Quaker was no longer listening.

He was right.

The Quaker had more important things to do. Already he was moving toward the control room of his ship. The platform upon which he rode moved faster than any man could run and the trip took less than a minute.

"Their shuttle is coming up, sir," one of the officers on the screen informed him. "They should be within pickup range of the *Exeter* in approximately three minutes."

The Quaker nodded. His eyes were concentrated on the small spot on one of his screens which represented the *Exeter*. For almost an hour now the two ships had been watching each other. Both were in stationary orbits above the spot where the *Ambol* had landed, and both ships had already sent shuttles down toward the surface; the IXT first, and then the Quaker.

"They are beginning to maneuver, sir," someone called out.

The dot on the screen moved imperceptibly and the Quaker smiled. His respect for the *Exeter's* commander rose a notch. The man was obviously no fool; he expected something to happen.

Silence settled over the large room. Everyone waited and watched as the two dots on the screen moved closer together. The *Exeter* was trying desperately to reach its shuttle and get Speaker aboard and safely away.

"Begin the attack program," ordered the Quaker.

The screens jumped; the Quaker's ship was now accelerating toward the *Exeter* in an excess of ten gees. The dot on the screen grew into a small disk, and then into the faint image of a giant warship. The *Exeter* began to maneuver frantically, moving away from a possible collision and simultaneously unleashing everything in its arsenal. The Quaker's ship took the blows without noticing. Its course was altering to match that of the *Exeter* —an impossible feat requiring accelerations never seen before in a ship the size of the Quaker's.

A small beam of energy left the Quaker's ship and struck the *Exeter* just to the left of its spherical center, boring a hole through its entire length. The *Exeter* wobbled and then did exactly what the Quaker had been hoping it would do. It jumped into high drive and disappeared from the screen. The Quaker's ship reacted to the change immediately. It braked, changing course radically and hurling its bloated bulk at the *Exeter's* tiny shuttle. The men aboard the shuttle never knew what happened. Every weapon aboard the Quaker's ship blasted at the unfortunate vehicle. A brief incandescence marked its end. There was nothing left; only molecules of hot metal and flesh moving in random directions. The Quaker heaved a sigh of relief. He had destroyed Speaker more easily than he had expected. All of his intricate planning and backup scheming would go to waste this time, but that didn't matter. The main threat was gone. That was all that really mattered.

"Sir!"

The Quaker's eyes returned to the screens. There was something there. It looked like a manhole cover; a blackened disk turning slowly in space.

The Quaker's expression darkened. "Pick it up!" he ordered.

The ship responded immediately, swooping down on the inert object and scooping it out of the vacuum.

"Sir!" someone shouted. "The *Exeter* has dropped back down. They're about fifty thousand miles up slope from us."

"Did they see us make the pickup?" the Quaker asked sharply.

"No, sir. They were just a few seconds late."

"Good." The Quaker relaxed a little. He had no intention of letting anyone know that the alien—or whatever—was still alive. If the *Exeter* had seen him make the recovery, he would have had to destroy it as utterly as he had destroyed the shuttle. And that was something he would rather not do.

"Turn toward the sun," the Quaker ordered. "Let's see how well and long this thing can stand the heat. We will jettison it when we get up a good speed, and drop it right into the star."

The officer manning internal communications ripped off his headset. "We can't do that, sir!"

"What!" The word nearly deafened everyone on the bridge. The Quaker was not used to being contradicted, not by one of his own men.

"It . . . it's gone, sir," the officer stuttered. "The men at the cargo scoop . . . they say it melted into the deck. There's nothing left."

The Quaker's face turned to granite. "Turn toward the sun," he repeated.

Every man in the control room exchanged glances of horror. They knew exactly what the Quaker was prepared to do, but there was nothing they could do to stop it. The ship took the matter out of their control. It followed the order. Not knowing exactly how fast it should go, the ship contented itself with a leisurely one-gee acceleration toward the star centered on its screen.

"Maximum acceleration!" the Quaker snapped irritably.

"That won't be necessary."

The Quaker snapped his head around and found himself looking at a pasty-faced imitation of a man.

"Excuse me," Speaker said. "I have assumed this form with insufficient practice. I thought it would cause you the least discomfort. I can see that I was mistaken."

"No! You needn't change your shape," the Quaker said quickly. "I was just startled for a moment."

"There is no need to fling yourselves into the star," Speaker said. "The effect on me would be negligible, but you would suffer irreparable damage."

"No effect?" the Quaker asked sharply. "You could—probably are lying."

"I am Speaker. I do not lie."

"Stop the ship," the Quaker ordered. The ship stopped.

"So, falling into stars doesn't hurt you?" the Quaker asked mildly.

Speaker remained silent. It had already answered that question.

"If you are so all-powerful, why did you let the IXT take you?"

"I was powerless to prevent it. You cannot hurt me—I cannot hurt you. I am Speaker."

"'I am Speaker,'" the Quaker mimicked. "That explains everything."

"Yes."

The Quaker snapped his mouth shut. Suddenly he believed it. He believed that the creature's name did explain everything. This thing was merely a mouthpiece; a spokesman—or spokesthing, for the real power around here. The Quaker looked back at the planet below. Something was wrong. Speaker did not act right—and Somack hadn't cared in the least when Merrick had captured Speaker. The Quaker felt himself grow hot. He had been mistaken. Somewhere down on that planet was the real thing Somack had come looking for. The Quaker closed his eyes and began to think. There was something down there that could make this indestructible Speaker talk for it. Suddenly, the Quaker had a great deal to think about.

Far below, in the planet's upper atmosphere, a small craft rocked as it plunged through the hottest part of its descent. Jennings piloted the small craft. He was still in a state of semi-shock. The Quaker had ordered him from the observation room the minute Speaker had made its first appearance. In fact, the Quaker had literally thrown him out and into the tiny two-man shuttle he was now riding toward the planet's surface.

"You have to go!" the Quaker had ordered, offering no explanation.

Well, he was going—and didn't like it one bit. Neither did his passenger. Margy was distinctly hostile. She had been thrown in with him, given barely time enough to dress and snatch up the small bundle she now carried with her everywhere.

The ground was coming up fast and Jennings concentrated on the controls. He was aiming at a spot near the *Ambol* but not too near. The small craft jerked to the left and skimmed along the edge of a clearing. Jennings was taking no chances. He slowed and let the craft drop into a bay of trees. It was swallowed from sight before touching the ground.

Jennings took a deep breath. Now what? Somehow he had to save a situation that seemed hopeless. He felt like a pawn—once important—but abandoned now as the action swept to a far corner of the board. Well, the Quaker had known what he was doing. Jennings flexed the hands he was only just becoming used to. The Quaker had given them to him. But the condition had been to compromise his loyalty—to make it impossible for him to continue his allegiance to the IXT.

The Quaker was wrong about that, though. He would continue to do his best to keep what was happening under control. He could no longer expect his fellow officers in the IXT to accept him, but he could do something on his own. He could still make use of the Quaker's left-handed gift as he had originally planned. He could stop Somack and Anna from continuing their flagrant abuses and unauthorized contact with aliens. Speaker, here, and who knows how many other aliens the pair were contacting. Something had to be done. He would have to act alone.

"What now?" Margy asked. She had watched him thinking and what she saw in his eyes worried her.

"Quiet!" Jennings snapped. He was regretting her presence more with every passing moment. "Don't ask questions, don't say anything, or do anything unless I tell you to. Understand? Just follow me and keep your mouth shut."

She didn't answer, but her expression told him that he was going to have trouble on his hands. He checked the needle-nose pistol at his side and then opened the small ship's hatch. "Come on," he said, and climbed out.

He moved into the trees quickly and she moved right behind him. He paused only for a second, calculating the direction he had to take, and then started off on the run; being careful to avoid any noise. Two miles of running and fifteen minutes brought him within sight of where he wanted to be. He dropped to the ground and produced a pair of field glasses. He took a good look at the place where the meeting with Speaker had taken place. He frowned. He was sure it was the right place, but no one was there.

"What's wrong?" Margy asked, violating his no-speech order without a second thought.

"There's no one there. We're too late."

"Too late for what?" She had absolutely no idea what was going on and she was beginning to suspect that Jennings wasn't much better off.

He ignored the question and shifted his attention to the clearing where the *Ambol* stood silently waiting.

"What?" Jennings was staring hard at something he could not believe. There was a man wearing the uniform of an IXT Enforcement officer making slow and careful rounds around the *Ambol*. The man wasn't Merrick. Where had he come from? Merrick was the only IXT officer aboard the *Ambol* and the Quaker's screens had never shown any IXT ships.

"This is too much," Jennings mumbled in confusion. Then a thought came to him suddenly. He remembered that Speaker had changed shape when the people from the *Ambol* had first approached it. Could that man down there be . . . He took up his glasses again and studied the figure guarding the *Ambol* again. He just couldn't afford to take any chances. There was too much at stake.

"Come on," he ordered quietly and pulled back into the trees. Margy followed him and they topped the ridge quickly and moved down the slope to search the ground for some sign. He moved back and forth along the edge of the tree line until he found what he was looking for.

"Tracks?" Margy asked. She was standing over him as he bent down to examine the ground. She wanted to know what was going on.

Jennings was in no mood to enlighten her. From the impressions in the grass he could tell that two people had left the forest at this point and headed out across the meadow. If his guessing was right they would be the two people he was most interested in—the two people whom the alien might let walk away from the meeting alive. Merrick's fate, and Devlon's fate; well, he didn't care to dwell on what had probably happened to them. An alien that could change shape would have little use for excess witnesses. Jennings felt his anger building. How could human beings help such a thing!

He followed the tracks for a few feet and made sure they did indeed lead across the wide meadow and toward the distant ridge. Jennings paused to eye the horizon. By circling to the left, and back toward the parked shuttle, he could reach the distant trees without leaving cover. It would be shorter to cross the meadow, but not too smart. He moved quickly, keeping just within the fringe of trees that bordered the clearing. Margy panted to keep up with him. She had nothing to lose, and nowhere else to go—so she stayed with him.

Twenty minutes of hard running brought them to the point Jennings had picked to examine. He found the tracks again and followed them carefully across the second ridge and down to the edge of its forested slope. The tracks led out again, into another clearing, and he followed them with his glasses. His visual search was terminated partway up the opposite slope. Jennings smiled. He could make out two people under a distant tree and they were exactly the pair he had expected to find. Somack probably thought he was safe, and the girl too. Jennings shook his head.

Margy was trying to see without the aid of field glasses. She squinted her eyes and then looked at Jennings, uncertain of what to say. "What do we do now?" she asked, trying to convey in her voice some of the puzzlement she was feeling in her mind.

"We wait," Jennings answered, and his expression was hard. "We wait and we see what happens."

The slow passing of time was an agony for Somack. All he could do was wait and watch, while Anna tossed and moaned beside him. He knew what she was seeing, but the knowledge did not comfort him. She had never asked for what he had thrust upon her. She had dreaded it, and now he worried. It was taking too long—so much longer than he had expected. What could he do? He knew what she was going through—he knew and was not sure. Would it be the same for her? His dream, it was so old, so long ago. Secondhand, and incomplete; did he remember the dream and not the pain that came with it?

Anna's lids fluttered. Her eyes opened and she seemed to look at him. But her eyes were focused on the distance—looking right through him. Her whole body shivered and trembled with cold.

"Anna," Somack moaned. He held her face in his hands, trying desperately to warm it and bring her color back.

She seemed to hear and her eyes searched for him, bewildered and lost. They did not see him. She raised a hand, trembling, and touched him blindly. It was the lightest of touches and her lip trembled. She pulled at him, a tiny tug, and then with all the violence she had within her. He came down atop her and she shivered and trembled against him.

"Help me. Help."

The words were lost, for Somack's heart drove all else from his ears. His mind blurred. She was so strong he hardly breathed. He realized that she could not. He stirred, but she only pulled him closer.

"No . . ." The word seemed all she could manage. Her strength faded with the sound and the tension left her body. She was quiet, and though he might have feared, he didn't. She was warm again; she breathed and the eyes beneath her lids were still.

So quickly. It seemed a second. She had done it to him; pierced him to the heart, penetrating all his manifold armor—and all without really knowing, or trying.

Somack watched her, asleep, and he knew that there was nothing he could do—no way he could avoid the decision. She would have him, or she wouldn't. He would get her, or he couldn't—but it would not be from want of trying—not now.

It was like an after-image; what was left when you closed your eyes to avoid a blinding light. Anna could see other things now, the smaller details and the vague impressions of more, much more, buried just beneath her sight and waiting for her to look. When the pain was gone and when she understood, perhaps then she would look, but not now.

Her power was gone. It was gone and she had never fully understood it —and barely used it. Gone and worse, really, for she could have it back any time and knew that she would always choose not to. The responsibility was too great for her now. The dream and whatever stood behind the dream had shown her how great a power she'd had. And yet there was no way she could cast it off and rid herself of forever having to choose—forever having to deny what she could so easily use.

There was another matter. One her mind tried to slide away from and delay till another day. The dream had given her an order, an order she was slowly coming to understand. She was to pass on the dream—pass it on as only she could pass it on. Oh, if only she could sleep forever. There would be no waking and no facing hard things to face. It would be so easy . . .

"You're pretending."

The sound, so close to her, startled her eyes open and once open there was no point in closing them again. But she covered them with her hand and let the light come in more slowly.

"You tell a hard story," she said, and ended with a sigh.

I AM SORRY.

The words echoed in her mind and she sat up abruptly. "You knew what would happen—you knew and you brought me here. . ." The accusation died on her lips but remained in her eyes.

Somack's smile was saddened. "You remember?"

"Too much," she answered bitterly. "Too much." And it was clear to Somack that she did not remember enough. She did not remember asking him to help.

The sun was low in the sky and Somack muttered something under his breath. He stood up with a jerk and extended his hand to help her up. She let him take her hand and gasped at the speed with which he lifted her. Somehow she found herself very close to him, looking into his eyes, and he was kissing her. She stiffened, but it was too late. He had an arm behind her and he pulled her forward until she pressed against him. Surprise filled her eyes and then they changed. Something happened. The tension in her body was different and she found herself no longer resisting.

Somack saw and felt the change and he kissed her forehead, kissed her hair.

"Let me go," she pleaded. "Please, let me go."

He did, but she didn't seem to know. He rested his hands on her shoulders and she stepped back finally, turning and moving away. Her breathing was ragged and she stood for a long time until it was past. Then she wiped her eyes.

"Why?" she asked without turning to look at him.

"I wanted to let you know," he said, and stepped closer. "I want you to know how I feel about you, and I want you to think about it."

"He wants me to think," she said, and he did not see the ironic smile that crossed her face. "He wants me to think."

She turned to face him and he could not place the expression she wore. "Am I a machine?" she queried. "Do my gears creak so badly?"

He didn't know what to say to her sudden questions.

"What do you think I am doing with my mind? What sort of things do you suppose I think about?" Her exasperation came mingled with something else. "It's hard enough when you're blind—when you won't . . ." She stopped herself and sighed audibly.

"Blind?" Somack said. He stared at her for a long time. "Is that what I am?"

"Yes!" she said, and she couldn't stand the way he looked at her.

CHAPTER 15. LITTLE OR
NOTHING

It had no name. The builders had never given it one. To them it had been a project—an instrument to save them and the universe they lived in. In time it had become their protector and finally, when there was nothing else left, their monument—just as it was the monument of all those whose memory it carried.

To say that it was tired would not be correct. The amount of time it had existed, functioning, was hard to imagine. Much of that time it had spent in the void to no purpose and with no companion save Speaker, who was really just a subset; an altered and miniature copy of itself.

No, it was not tired. Fatigued or slightly run down would be a more accurate description. Deterioration was a slow process with something as well made and intelligent as it was. It was not supposed to decay, but time had taken a slow toll. It knew, deep inside, that it would not survive another time of the darkness—another time of void. Speaker might, for Speaker was so much smaller and so much simpler. But without the memories and without the vast store of knowledge it carried, Speaker would be useless—a toy mouth speaking with no mind behind it.

This was its cause for concern and the reason that it must be certain of success this time.

Once before the planet had been visited by a man, and that had ended in failure. The man had come alone, bringing with him only the *Ambol* and an ambition to turn anything he might find to his advantage. The man hadn't found what he was looking for. But he had found Speaker and through Speaker he had been led into finding the dreams.

The builders' machine was successful in this, its designed purpose. To those who had the capacity it would give the warning. They would know from living experience how great their power and how great their responsibility must be. Telepathy was just the first step—the awakening of a new sense to an invisible world. Newcomers to this world were like moths straining to see without eyes. They were drawn to the strongest light; to the minds of those around them. Only later, when the new sense was fully developed, would they be able to see into the dark corners of matter and space. Later still they would learn not only to see, but to manipulate the very laws by which they lived.

And here lay the danger. It was this manipulation which the builders had tried so hard to control. They had done it blindly, knowing only the terrible effects of the tampering and not the how and the why. The builders could not see the fabric that was being destroyed around them so they did the only thing they could do. They created something to see it for them and in doing so they had come as close as any to producing an artificial life. Their machine could see for them and act for them. That's what they had built it for and that is what it was doing now.

It was thinking back to the first failure it had experienced in dealing with human beings. This failure was something it had to think about very carefully, especially in the light of a possible repetition. That first man had gone away with a full knowledge of his own potential power and the suggestion that he pass on his warning and knowledge. But in attempting to pass it on, the man had died. Even with the *Ambol*—a changed *Ambol* —sent along to protect him, the man had died. Only good fortune had allowed that man to pass along his information to Somack.

It was a lesson the great machine would take to heart. Never again would it rely on so frail a method. A better method would be used this time. A foolproof method; one that involved no danger for those who transmitted the dream.

The solution it had devised was a good one, but another problem was threatening to interfere; a problem which came in the form of a small device: A small black cube. The cube strained space in a dangerous and familiar way. The builders' machine sensed this with the sureness of a well-worn memory. It had seen many devices like this cube in the far-past and their use invariably led to disaster. The cube itself was a primitive Hursk device and the small region of space it strained would return to normal when the cube was destroyed, but there would be larger devices sure to follow. This time there was little danger—except to one very important person: Anna. Already the cube had caused harm and fear, and there was nothing the great machine could do to prevent further damage. All it could do was worry. The cube was small and so far its function had been limited to observation, but it was still dangerous. It could be used for a great deal more than just observation.

The cube had to be destroyed and the use of others like it prevented. The great machine had to do this—and protect the two who now carried its message; all with only Speaker to work with. Large and powerful as it was, the great machine could do nothing because it could not move. When the great darkness had swept over it and the last of the builders had died, so had its power of motion. It drifted helplessly, clinging to half-existence in a new universe. It was capable of thought but not action. All it could do directly was to pass along the dream—and only a few could accept it. It was not exactly helpless but, constrained as it was by inertia and circumstance, the word was a close enough description. It would try to help, but only time would tell.

A nna stood with her back to the sun, casting a long and distorted shadow across a sea of grass which was beginning to stir with the evening breeze. Dark hair rippled against her back and seemed to snare the light, changing it and letting it re-emerge, only in softer, more subdued shades.

"You're angry?" Somack guessed. He'd been watching her, waiting for her to look around or break the silence, but she seemed to be elsewhere, thinking about something serious. She turned at the sound of his question and her eyes slitted a little against the light, or perhaps to see something in his face more clearly.

"Angry? No, not exactly." Her voice was cautious and her eyes continued to search for some answer they could not find. "But I don't like orders."

"Orders? What orders?"

"Don't play innocent with me," she accused. "Stop pretending that you don't know what I am talking about."

"I don't have to pretend that," Somack laughed nervously. "It's hard enough to understand you when you say something straight out, but when you beat around the bush like this—"

"Beating around the bush? Well that's better than you! You trick me here—and you trick me there. I get ordered to bear you children and you pretend not to know!"

"Now wait a minute—wait just one minute." Somack had a flurry of thoughts and suddenly he understood what had happened. Somewhere around here a very big machine had made a very big mistake—and somehow he would have to correct it. The look on Anna's face told him that this wasn't going to be easy.

"There's been some mistake," Somack said lamely.

"You made it," she said, pursing her lips together.

"No. I would never make a mistake like that. If I'd known this was going to happen, I would never have brought you here."

"What do you mean?" There was a sudden note of doubt in her voice and the accusation in her eyes was replaced with something else. She had not expected him to deny—she had not wanted him to deny anything.

"I would never have allowed you to get an order like that," Somack continued. "Not in a thousand years. I would never have allowed a compliment like that to be delivered so impersonally."

"Uoooo!" *Egotistical!* Where did he manage to hide it all! Compliment! Anna was mad and couldn't show it. She was happy and wouldn't show it. It was a happiness that welled up deep inside her and threatened to wash away her resistance. She fought it desperately. He had no right—he didn't deserve to know—not when it would only make him smug and confident.

"You know," Somack said, "your eyes have a way of changing color. It's fascinating to watch. I can almost tell what you are thinking."

Anna closed her eyes and covered them with her hands. What a stupid thing to say and it was worse because she knew it was true. What could she do? How could she think straight when even the stupid things he said made her feel good She opened her eyes again and found him still standing there and smiling at her.

"We'd better be getting back to the *Ambol* now," he said. "The light is starting to go and we're through here. We've accomplished what we came here to accomplish."

"*We?* What do you mean *we? You* have accomplished what *you* wanted to accomplish. No one ever bothers to ask me! I won't go. I'm not going back to that ship of yours—I'm not going—not while you're—not while you think stupid things and grin like that."

Somack suppressed his smile with an effort. "I am sorry," he said seriously. "This is not exactly the situation I had expected. It's awkward trying to cope with a problem you can't fight. I would never order you to do anything—certainly not something likely to make you mad like this. I can't undo what's been done—especially, well . . . I don't want you mad, but I don't know what I can do."

"You can . . ." Anna paused, frowning.

"There is one thing I *can't* do, and that is deny it would be a pleasure to have you—"

"Stop it! I can't think when you say things like that!"

Somack looked at Anna and it knotted his stomach. He tore his eyes away and looked beyond at the trees and the far ridge. The *Ambol* was waiting over there and the sooner he got back the better he would feel. Nothing was more important than getting away from here now. He'd always thought that once he discovered the source of the dream it would be a simple thing to bring other people here and let them see the same things he'd seen. But it wasn't going to be that easy. It was going to be a longer and safer way—one that would take time and, well, one that would take Anna. He studied her eyes and the set of her chin. He was not happy with the way his present predicament had developed. Why hadn't he been told—and why had she? It would have been so much easier the other way around; with her ignorant and with him taking advantage of it, and yet it wouldn't have been right. She had a choice now and she knew the full extent of her responsibility. It was only fair. She must choose to come with him now *despite* being ordered to do so.

"Is something wrong?" she asked, seeing the distant look in his eyes.

"No, nothing is wrong. I was just thinking of how impossible it would be for me to leave you here alone. But I must, if you ask. It's strange having everything tangled up this way."

"Please," Anna pleaded. "I want to think. Too much is happening."

That's for sure, Somack thought bitterly. He couldn't get anywhere with this barrier between them and he was beginning to worry that too much delay would be dangerous. Somack wasn't sure how long Speaker would be able to draw the IXT's and the Quaker's attention. The sooner he got Anna back aboard the *Ambol* the better he would feel.

"We have to go," he said finally. "You'll just have to trust me. This whole mess isn't just a big trick to help me get you alone—and I think you know that. It's making it harder for me."

She knew that, and yet she couldn't go. Not without some resistance —and not without some doubt. There were so many things she still didn't know or understand and so little time to find out.

"I'll go," she said at last, "but only on one condition. That you promise not to talk—you promise not to ask me anything."

Somack nodded his head reluctantly.

"And that you never-never ask me to do anything. Not until I can think."

Somack looked at her puzzled but he agreed. He didn't know that when she spoke of *doing*—she meant doing something with the great potential of her mind. She was frightened. More than anything else, she was frightened of doing something she could not undo—starting something she could not stop. She had seen the terrible results too often in her newly acquired dream memories and they would remain with her always. It was an awful thing to hold power within your grasp and fear to touch it lest it turn on you and destroy you.

Strangely enough, once Somack agreed never to ask, she felt better— as if somehow he was taking the responsibility away from her and she didn't have to worry about it any more. She was wrong to feel this way, but she wanted to. She wanted to feel safe. She wanted someone to protect her from so much power.

Devlon came to an abrupt stop. He put the black cube to his ear and listened. The words from above were reassuring. There were no signs of pursuit within the cube's limited range. Standing at the edge of the woods, this was just the news Devlon had hoped to hear. For the past ten minutes he had been running, heedless of the tracks he left and quite confident that Merrick and his companion would have no trouble following them. Devlon wanted the tracks to be followed. He was tired of being chased and the plan he had worked out would soon rid him of the problem once and for all.

He looked out into the bright light beyond the scattering of trees ahead of him. Off to his left lay a large spoon-shaped valley, gently sloping and surrounded by a fringe of trees. The entire grass-filled plain drained down into the narrow gap just below him, opening further on into yet another gentle valley. With the time he had gained by running, Devlon would be able to cross the narrow stretch of open ground unobserved before either of the IXT men had time to reach this edge of the ridge's covering. He had calculated the move carefully, keeping to the other side of the ridge just to make sure. They would be over there now, following his tracks, while he sprinted through the grass toward the opposite crest.

He ran down the slope easily, gaining momentum at an unexpected rate. He reached the bottom quickly and found to his surprise that there was a narrow gorge about eight feet across and just as deep blocking his way. The gorge was hewn in smooth and slippery rock and water flowed in a steady course over the solid surface at the bottom, springing inexplicably from the turf and deep grass which surrounded the miniature canyon. The deep cut extended several hundred yards in either direction —too long a distance to travel in the time he had allowed himself. He backed up the slope quickly and managed to jump across without a hitch. An exhilaration filled him, something different from the feeling he got hearing a crowd cheer. Here he was—not even a physical type—and he was doing things he had never dreamed of, fighting for his life in a primitive and basic way. It made his blood flow faster and he knew he was going to enjoy killing the two men chasing him.

Devlon sprinted up the slope toward the trees, panting hard by the time he gained his objective. Finally he had time to rest and he paused, breathing hard. A minute or two passed before he was breathing normally again. By that time he had managed to find a rock of suitable size to fulfill his purpose. The edges of the rock were jagged and it weighed a good five pounds, fitting his hand nicely if he didn't grip it too hard.

Now there was nothing to do but wait. The sun was beginning to sink toward the horizon—a perfect addition to the plan. When the IXT men climbed the slope below him, they would be walking directly into the light of the sun. He moved a little further up the slope and settled down to wait, resting his back against a tree and pressing the black cube to his ear. He was facing away from the direction he had come, completely invisible from below, but with the cube he would always know where the enemy was. They should be coming into that device's field of view any minute now.

Merrick and the man with him paused at the edge of the clearing. The tracks were unmistakable. They led off down the slope and up the opposite one and back into the trees.

"This thing could take a long time," the Enforcement crewman commented. "This creep could run for a month of Sundays before he decides to give up. Why don't we just let him go, and get the ones we're really after?"

Merrick squinted into the bright sunlight. "Devlon's just about as sneaky as they come. You don't get to be the head of an organization like the Freedom League without learning a few tricks. If we let up now, the Quaker may decide to come back and pick him up—and clean us out for good measure."

Both men knew how precarious their own situation was. When word had come down from the *Exeter* about the fate of their shuttle they knew what little chance they had depended on their getting their hands on something or someone the Quaker would be willing to bargain for. The only trouble was deciding which the Quaker wanted more: Devlon, Somack, or Anna. Merrick preferred to take no chances and that meant rounding them all up. Devlon couldn't run forever and he must be tiring by now. The man wasn't cut out for this sort of thing. He had to make a mistake or give himself up before too long.

"Let's go," Merrick said, and the two men started down the slope.

They paused at the bottom, taking a good look at the flowing water in its little trench and the signs of Devlon's crossing to the other side.

"He jumped that?" the crewman muttered. His voice betrayed a growing respect for the man they were chasing.

Both of them followed Devlon's example and leaped across the miniature chasm. On the other side the crewman went so far as to draw the needle- nose he was wearing.

"Put that thing away," Merrick grunted. "Devlon isn't even armed. He's no good to us dead."

The crewman shrugged, but he kept the gun out.

"Suit yourself," Merrick muttered. "Just don't get carried away."

"Don't worry about me," the crewman answered sharply. "That torch you've got isn't much good and neither is that poison pen. You people in Justice tend to forget how you got there."

Merrick scowled. The artificial leg he wore below his right knee was something he had grown used to a long time ago. His limp was hardly noticeable and it was something he tended to forget about, but the crewman's comment reminded him. It was an unnecessary insult. Enforcement people tended to think that only incompetents ended up in Justice.

"Very well," Merrick said. "Perhaps you are right and more caution is warranted." He reached into his pocket and withdrew a penlike object. "This may look harmless, but it's as deadly as any needle-nose ever was."

The crewman eyed the small weapon, then shrugged again. "No range," he grunted, "and it only kills—can't disable." He started up the hill without another word.

The tracks were plain in the grass and easy to follow, even easier than those in the duff under the trees. Merrick followed the crewman at a distance of about ten feet, squinting at the man's back against the glare of the sun. It was easier to keep his eyes on the ground and Merrick found himself doing it without really thinking. The first bits of shade were being cast around them by the trees ahead, but the tracks continued up a little corridor of light and it wasn't until the crewman passed the first tree trunk that a leafy shadow fell across their path.

Then it was too late.

Merrick heard what sounded like a meaty thunk and he raised his eyes just in time to see the crewman's head jerk back. The man's knees collapsed, throwing him forward in a sprawl that was unmistakably leaden. Merrick's eye caught some motion and he raised his hand to fire, but just then a breeze shifted the branch of a distant tree and he found himself looking directly into the sun. He squinted, shook his head, and fired anyway—but the aim was imperfect. Merrick threw the expended poison pen away and quickly drew the torch. He fired this just as blindly, but with more effect.

Devlon tumbled to the ground. A streak of burning flesh and cloth marked his back where Merrick's wild shot had gone and Devlon screamed in unashamed agony. But even in his agony Devlon never forgot for a moment that he also had a weapon now. The needle-nose seemed to find its way into his grasp by instinct and he fired in much the same way. His shot was low, spiking a neat little hole in Merrick's artificial leg and toppling him back down the slope.

Devlon scrambled behind a tree, narrowly avoiding Merrick's return fire.

It was all over with the IXT. Devlon felt the blood pounding in his ears as he took aim. But Merrick didn't co-operate. He discontinued his futile firing with the torch and staggered back down the slope in an awkward, jolting stride.

Devlon fired again and watched as Merrick spun on his good leg and spilled headlong down the hill, rolling frantically. Devlon aimed again and squeezed the trigger just as Merrick rolled over a lip of grass and disappeared with a resounding splash.

He cursed. Merrick might still be alive, but there was no way he could check, safely, to find out. But then the one he'd clobbered with a rock groaned and Devlon brought the gun back up to firing position. The IXT crewman struggled to his knees; and the blood pouring from the gash in his forehead was blinding him, causing him to wipe at it futilely.

Devlon laughed. He laughed again after he shot a neat little hole in the man's outstretched wrist. In a few minutes the man would bleed to death. Devlon patted the little black cube which had helped him set up his little ambush.

"Damn it!" Devlon kicked himself for the fool he'd almost been. What had he been thinking of! He held the solution to the Merrick problem right here in his hand. All he had to do was ask the Quaker's crewman above if Merrick was still alive down there in his wet trench. Devlon spoke into the cube quickly.

"You're too far away," the crewman answered. "Move further down the slope—that's better. I see him now. He's lying in the water but—yes, he's still alive."

Devlon smiled. He moved down toward the lip of the gully. He did it cautiously, constantly asking for information from the cube.

"Watch out!" the crewman's voice shouted from the cube. "He's moving —he hears you coming."

Devlon stopped. He was carrying the needle-nose in his right hand and a handy little piece of wood in his left. He threw the wood to his left and moved quickly in the opposite direction. The stick fell near the edge of the drop—among a scattering of grass and soil. It seemed to hesitate for a moment, then slide a ways, dropping over the edge along with a trickle of sand.

M errick shook himself. He was wet and bruised from his eight-foot fall into the rock-strewn watercourse. Blood was streaming from his shoulder, running down both the front and back of his shirt. His mechanical leg kept trying to slip out from under him when he moved. And move he must. He was desperate. He knew he would be dead the moment Devlon got up the courage to come after him. He couldn't run away so he did the only thing he could do. He waited. His only chance lay in killing Devlon first.

He followed the sounds above, keeping as close to them as he could. The pitiful torch he held was his only weapon and it was useless beyond the range of a few feet.

When Merrick saw that branch come tumbling down from above he knew it was his last chance. He reached out with his good arm, grabbed a projecting rock, and pulled himself up. His wounded arm was weak but still strong enough to hold the torch. His heart was pounding and he knew he was moving on adrenalin alone as he threw his arm over the edge and blasted away. He did it blindly, burning an arc in the grass with the fury of his short-range weapon.

Devlon watched the pitiful attempt from a good safe distance. Merrick wasn't even trying to see how his firing was doing—he was just blasting away at an empty piece of real estate. It was fun to watch and Devlon relished every moment of it. He could kill Merrick any time now, but he saw no need to hurry.

"Over here," Devlon said at last.

The words took Merrick's strength away. He dropped, slid and fell back into the water of the stream. It washed over him, cool and comfortable—the last pleasurable feeling he would have. He didn't want to die—not like this, not with Devlon laughing and sneering down at him. He struggled to his knees and his vision cleared for a moment. He saw the water and the only weapon he had was lying beneath it. He reached out, touching it where it lay in the water, and felt something burn his hand. Blood darkened the water, gushing from his wrist, and somewhere above him Devlon was laughing louder. Merrick gritted his teeth. He wanted peace. He wanted to die alone. He concentrated. His hand trembled, but it closed on the torch —depressing and locking its firing stud in place.

Devlon was aiming his second shot—a paralyzing neck shot—when something unexpected happened. Merrick disappeared into a cloud of steam which suddenly came boiling up out of the stream. Steam filled the canyon quickly and began to spill over onto the grass only to be swept up and blown away.

"Damn it!" Devlon shouted. "Damn it! Damn it!" A blind fury filled him and he fired again and again into the billowing cloud of white. The shots were futile.

The steam cleared finally and exposed Merrick to the sky again. He was dead but he had died quietly and he had died alone.

Devlon stood looking down at the body. His anger continued to build slowly and something in his mind began to twist. He'd been cheated —*cheated!* A red haze filled his eyes and the body below him seemed to change shape. It became young and beautiful—it became Anna's body— and he fired into it. He fired and fired and fired . . .

Merrick was beyond feeling the effects of Devlon's madness.

Margy and Jennings waited in a hostile silence. Margy divided her time between watching the two figures on the distant slope and the man sitting next to her. Occasionally she would see Jennings' face tighten at some action he was observing and his jaw would begin to work in a way she was so very familiar with. She knew Jennings was fighting with himself but she was afraid anything she might say would only make things worse.

Finally, when Somack and Anna rose and then began to cross the open ground toward them, Margy knew she had to act. She had to ease the tension or Jennings would take out his frustrations and anger on people who would have no way of fighting back.

"I don't blame you for what you did," she said, and the words seemed to drop into an empty well. Jennings' only reaction was to ignore her and finger the firing stud on his needle-nose.

"Listen to me," she continued urgently, touching his averted shoulder.

He reacted immediately, brushing her hand away and gripping her wrist in a vise of his own.

"I told you to be quiet!" he said through gritted teeth, "and I meant it. If you foul this up too, you'll regret it."

"Too?" Her voice was puzzled and hurt, and her eyes began to mist from the pain of his grip.

"Yes, too! You helped that girl escape once before, and it's not going to happen again."

"I'm glad I did it!" Margy sobbed, and she tugged at his iron grip ineffectually. "You'd never have been able to hold me like this if I hadn't done it. You would have lived the rest of your life a cripple, proudly sticking to the rules of an organization that cripples you first and then won't let you get well. Can't you understand!"

"Shut up!"

"They want you a cripple!" Tears of pain were streaming down her face. "They want you that way so you will hate"—she gasped as he suddenly increased the pressure on her wrist—"hate yourself and everyone else!"

"You finished now?" he asked, releasing her contemptuously. "For someone who can't stand pain—a traitor to me and everyone else—for someone like that you can sure talk awfully high and mighty. You never stayed around long enough to find out how I lost my arms, did you? You ran off, because you couldn't stand the thought of a cripple liking you, loving you."

"No! No! That's not true."

Jennings sneered. "If I had a choice between you and the IXT, I'd choose half a life with them over a full one with you. Is that clear? I don't think I can make it any clearer than that."

There was nothing she could say and no way she could answer the look in his eyes. She buried her face in her hands and shook her head until it disappeared in a veil of beautiful blond hair.

Jennings jerked his eyes away and stared out across the green field, denying the lump that formed in his throat. The business walking toward him occupied his mind and he could gratefully ignore the problem quietly convulsing in the grass behind him. He stood up and moved closer to the edge of light dividing his patch of trees from the meadow and the game he was after.

"That's far enough!" he shouted when Anna and Somack had approached to within a hundred feet of the tree he stood behind. "Don't do anything foolish, either of you." He stepped out from behind his tree and pointed his weapon at Anna. "You can read my mind, so you know that I'm prepared to use this if the need arises."

"I recognize the uniform," Somack said quietly, trying to attract attention to himself, "but I'm afraid the face isn't familiar."

Jennings smiled. "Turn around, Mr. Somack, and raise your hands, and you, little girl, move away from him."

Anna complied and Jennings stepped forward quickly, placing the muzzle of his needle-nose against Somack's neck while he searched hurriedly for hidden weapons. Finding none, he stepped back and circled toward Anna.

"Is that really necessary?" Somack asked, seeing the IXT man's intention.

"I'm afraid so. I have enough to contend with without having to worry about getting shot in the back."

Anna raised her hands but did not turn around. Instead she kept her eyes on Jennings, watching him as he stepped up and placed the cold muzzle against her neck. Her eyes studied his face and caught at his eyes. Jennings ignored the scrutiny and proceeded with his search. But he found the big eyes too much for him and a splotch of color began creeping into his face and his jaw tightened involuntarily.

"Nothing personal," he said, and immediately regretted his apology. He was simply doing his duty and apologies were not in order.

Anna said nothing, and that only made things worse. She could read his mind and that was enough to make any man angry.

"You think I can read your mind," she said, and Jennings jumped at the word, "but I can't—I won't."

Jennings stepped back, finished, and stared at her for a minute. He didn't know whether to believe her or not, and then decided he didn't. "It doesn't really matter," he said. "What has to be done, has to be done. We are all going back to your ship now, and take care of this Speaker of yours. Disguising itself as one of us just isn't going to work."

Somack raised an eyebrow.

"You know what I'm talking about," Jennings growled. "I was aboard the Quaker's ship and saw the thing changing shapes. I know what it can do."

"Then you also know that we left Speaker in the care of your good friend, Captain Merrick."

"Merrick—hah! You had a gun on him the whole time, right up until I started down anyway. I'd be very much surprised if he is still alive."

"He was alive. Very much alive the last time I saw him."

"Sure," Jennings grunted, backing away from them toward the trees. "And that Speaker thing is just a harmless pet; it goes around changing shape just for the fun of it."

"It's no pet," Somack said.

'Well, we'll soon find out. If it tries anything funny, you two will be the first to suffer."

Anna moved over next to Somack again and her hand slipped into his. Somack glanced at her for a moment and then back at Jennings.

"All I can say," Somack said firmly, "is that your organization must be mixed up more than I had thought possible. One minute you're offering me bribes to help you find the Quaker, and the next minute you're in there helping him with whatever dirty work he has planned."

Jennings listened in silence, then motioned with his gun. "We'll leave the Quaker out of it for the moment. He'll get whatever is coming to him once we have straightened out the situation here. Walk ahead of me and don't try anything. Stop when I say stop, and move when I say move."

There was nothing to do but obey. They moved up the hill past Jennings and into the shade of the trees. There was a touch of cold in the air, perhaps from the mood they were in or perhaps from the lowering of the sun in the sky. Jennings walked a few paces behind them and suddenly found himself confronted with the problem of Margy again. She was standing up now and there were leaves and bits of twigs caught in her hair, as well as streaks of moisture on her face.

"What are you doing?" she asked, and her voice carried the same note of despair and wildness that shone in her eyes. She clutched at the small bundle in her hands, the same bundle she never seemed to be without.

"I'm doing what should have been done a long time ago," Jennings answered. "You know that what both of these two have done is punishable by death. I spared the girl once before and all it did was lead to trouble. I don't know how I could be any more lenient than I'm being right now. I would be fully justified in executing them both right now, but I'm not going to. They will get their trial, but if this Speaker turns out to be dangerous—turns out to be a menace to everything we've built, then I'm sure their next court won't be quite as lenient as I was."

"What about me?" Margy asked, stepping closer and dropping the bundle she carried. "What about me? Why don't you shoot me now? I'm a traitor! For three years I've been trying my best to ruin the IXT."

"Shut up!" Jennings snapped.

"No!" she said, and moved even closer.

"Stand back," Jennings said, and his voice was cold as he turned the gun toward her.

For a long time Margy looked at the needle-nose aimed at her and at Jennings' finger hovering on the trigger. Then she looked up into his eyes and they stared at each other for a moment.

"Do it," she said, reaching forward and pulling the gun toward her, pressing it against her heart. "Kill me, and when you've done that, do it to yourself too, because you're a traitor of a worse kind."

"Let go, you fool!" Jennings shouted, and he jerked the gun away and at the same time pushed her with his free hand. There was a flash of light and Margy fell backward toward the ground. Jennings' heart stopped and even though only grass and leaves had suffered from the shot, he sobbed and the gun slipped from his fingers. It could so easily have been her and not the leaves and grass.

"Touching scene."

The voice came from the shadow of the trees above them and sent a shiver through them all. Devlon moved from the cover where he had been listening and watching. He moved like a cat and wore a Cheshire smile to match.

"Young lady," Devlon murmured, turning his smile on Anna, "be so kind as to toss that lethal weapon on the ground up here toward me. I wouldn't want anyone to act foolishly and spoil all my fun."

Anna did as she was told. Devlon knelt and picked up Jennings' needle-nose. "You know," he laughed, "I do believe that this is the first time you have ever done anything I asked you to do. Perhaps our little party here will be more pleasant than I had planned. I can't imagine more delightful company with which to end this happy play. For a moment there, I thought Mr. Jennings would save me the trouble of intervening. But things have worked out for the best after all. A true tragedy was averted and at the same time, plenty of good footage was obtained."

They looked at him blankly.

Devlon swelled inside. He was feeling the power of his position, relishing it and turning it over—contemplating how he would use it. They were ignorant. Four ignorant people who would go to their deaths never knowing why—or perhaps they would know. Perhaps it would be better to let them know—see how they reacted.

"You can't understand, can you?" Devlon asked. "You don't know what I'm talking about, do you?"

"I doubt if you know yourself," Somack said coldly.

Something boiled up in Devlon. For a moment his eyes seemed to cloud over, then he smiled. "You people are lucky," he said. "Any ordinary man could never have taken what I've taken from you four and still remain calm. It takes self-control—iron self-control. For example—"

Devlon tossed the needle-nose he had used on Merrick toward them. It landed at Jennings' feet. They all looked down at it, but no one moved.

"That gun is empty," Devlon continued. "Useless—and yet I had the guts to bluff you with it. I gambled my life. What do you think of that?" No one said anything.

Devlon's smile broadened, bearing his teeth. They were going to deserve everything they got. "Pick it up," Devlon said, motioning at Jennings. "Go ahead, pick it up. You see—the charge is dead."

Jennings complied.

"Now, point it at Mr. Somack," Devlon ordered.

"Why?"

"Just do it," Devlon said patiently. "It's all part of the Quaker's script. Just point it and fire. You'll see what happens."

"Quaker?" Anna cried. "What do you mean? What's the Quaker have to do with this?"

Devlon laughed. The look on Anna's face was too much to believe. She was actually afraid of what might happen to Somack.

"Quaker?" Devlon mimicked, then his voice hardened. "You little brat. What do you think has been going on around here? Who do you think is behind all of this? Who do you think wrecked your little telepathy game! Not me certainly." Devlon fished in his pocket. "You see this? This is what wrecked you and this is what you are playing for right now. Your final moments are all being recorded and in a moment an IXT assassin is going to aim his gun at Mr. Somack and fire. The shot will be fatal."

"You can't—"

"Oh, but I can!" Devlon said, cutting Anna short. "Of course, there may be something you can do to delay that moment."

"What do you mean?"

"Come here, dear, and I will show you exactly what I mean. There is no reason for you to deny yourself the pleasure I can give you in these last few moments of your life. Somack can wait, if you're willing to go first."

The Quaker watched what was happening within the cube's field with a frown on his face. He'd been watching for some time now, debating with himself on the proper course to take. He held in his hand the trigger which would change the cube from a simple observational device into something much more useful. The moment he depressed that trigger the five people down below—anyone who came within range of the cube—would be under his complete control. They would do what he asked, act as he wished them to act.

Still, the Quaker hesitated. There was no turning back. Once he triggered this particular aspect of the cube there would be no backing up. He would control those people down there permanently. Their will would be crushed just as effectively as Anna's telepathic ability had been crushed —and that had been crushed by the mere static, not the full force and proper function of the cube. The cube would capture their minds and crush their wills. They would retain their knowledge, but otherwise they would become vegetables. It was something the Quaker didn't want to do but he needed to know more—he needed the information they held in their minds and he had to act before Devlon put that information beyond his reach forever.

He couldn't wait any longer. He depressed the trigger he held and sighed a little bit in regret.

D evlon blinked. For a moment there his vision had blurred. Something had happened—but what? He seemed to have lost a moment of time. Anna was crouched on the ground, her arms were wrapped around her head and she was rocking back and forth in agony. Why, just a minute ago she'd been standing up. What was wrong?

Devlon looked around. Nothing else had changed. Jennings was still standing there holding the useless needle-nose. Somack was still standing there looking dumb and Margy was still lying on the ground, propped up by her elbows, in the exact spot where Jennings had pushed her. He was imagining things. Nothing had happened—except—the sun seemed a little lower in the sky, and the cube he was holding in his hand seemed a little bit warmer than it had been just a moment ago. Devlon shook his head.

"Get up!" he growled at Anna, not at all pleased with her play-acting or whatever it was. "You get up now and get over here or you'll regret it."

Devlon's words seemed to penetrate and Anna became very still. Her arms unwrapped slowly and she looked up; her eyes dilated and seemed to unfocus as he watched. *She's scared witless*, Devlon thought, and his heart began to pound wildly. The smile on his face spread and he motioned with his arm, *come here, come here*. She did it! She was obeying him, standing up and moving closer. Devlon's eyes darted about. He watched her move, he watched the shape beneath her clothes and . . . he caught a glimpse of dark eyes; a pair of dark wells he could fall into. He shivered, remembering something that had happened once before.

"That's far enough!" he barked. There was an edge of fear in his voice and the gun he held wavered in his left hand as it moved to cover her.

All of a sudden Somack stepped closer. Devlon caught the movement in the corner of his eye. He turned toward it, gratefully shifting his attention from the girl.

"You are another problem altogether," Devlon said, taking careful aim. "How you die is something I've given a good deal of thought to. A shot in the knee will do for a start."

A pressure, slowly building in the back of Devlon's mind, made his eyes water suddenly. He squinted and shook his head impatiently only to find that the blurring of his vision wouldn't go away. He took a shot anyway, missing to the right.

"That was just a warning," Devlon muttered, trying desperately to cover his confusion. "Move any closer and you'll lose your leg."

Somack stood extremely still. He was aware that something was wrong with Devlon. The way the man's head bobbed from side to side, almost as if he were dodging something, and the squinting and sudden uncertainty in his voice; they all pointed to an opportunity and Somack watched for it with all of his attention.

"You look sick," Jennings told Devlon, without sympathy.

"What?" Devlon said absently. He was hardly paying attention. There was something happening to him; something happening to his mind. The people around him seemed to dim in his view and an unearthly quiet settled on his ears.

Somewhere, deep inside, there was an animal cry—like a wolf suddenly released from captivity—and it raced through him snarling in mindless fury. He cried out and the sound of his own voice was frightening. He began hitting himself in the head with the small black cube and the pain helped to keep the wolf back.

"You!" he cried, turning his dimming sight on Anna. 'You are doing this to me!"

She met his glare and he looked too far—he saw what he had only glimpsed before. The sight caught at him.

"Gaaaaa . . ." he screamed, struggling not to see. His face twisted and he threw with all his strength, hurling the black cube at her, striking her down with all the force in his arm.

Fury and hate exploded in his mind—a blinding flash of light caught between two mirrors. Devlon saw himself—*himself*—and his lungs could not contain the scream that echoed in his mind. He stumbled backward a step and his finger convulsed against the trigger it touched. The odor of scorched dirt and leaves rose from the ground at his feet and he covered his eyes trying to block out the sight he could no longer bear.

The needle-nose flashed a second time and the people it endangered seemed frozen by the spectacle of what they were seeing. Only Margy seemed capable of acting and she struggled with the bundle she had carried so long. But she had disguised the shape of Eyeada's pistol too well and it was caught in a tangle of material that refused to yield. In desperation she cocked the exposed hammer and groped amid the padding for the pistol's half-hidden trigger.

The sound of Eyeada's pistol being cocked seemed to penetrate and Devlon's eyes opened, fully dilated, and they were struck by the full light of the lowering sun. It was the last thing his eyes would see and his arms rose spasmodically and he fired at the light in the sky.

Margy pulled the trigger at the same instant and the sound of that shot exploded into the quiet around them. The bullet lifted Devlon into the air and he seemed to float for an instant before collapsing to the ground, twisting once and then lying still.

Somack found himself kneeling over Anna, wiping a smear of blood from her forehead and gently probing the growing bruise beneath it.

"How is she?" Jennings asked. He had not been idle in the few moments following the shot. Already he held in his hands the two things Devlon had so recently held.

Somack looked up and he saw immediately that nothing had really changed. Devlon had merely interrupted a scene that was now going to be commenced all over again.

"It's just a bruise," Somack answered quietly. He knew she was not seriously injured by the blow, but the knowledge failed to lessen his concern. It wasn't her physical well-being he was so very worried about.

"Check Mr. Devlon," Jennings suggested, and his tone showed that while he was still giving orders, they were not the same as before. "I wouldn't want to let him suffer."

Somack did what he was told quickly and returned to Anna's side without a word.

"Well?" Jennings asked.

"He's quite dead," Somack said simply.

The impossible had happened.

For a long second the Quaker sat and simply stared at the void before him, unable to believe that the device he was so sure of had failed. It was built *not* to fail and so heavily had he relied on this property that now he was left without any means of knowing what was going on—no way of influencing the outcome of a situation so important to him.

The experience shook him and for the briefest flash of time he was touched with a sense of impotence reminiscent of a time in the past he hated. He threw off the feeling with a downward twist of his lip and turned to confront Speaker.

Speaker was still standing exactly where he had been standing throughout the Quaker's long session in the observation room. When the Quaker glared Speaker did nothing. It had nothing to say about what had happened.

"You had nothing to do with that?" the Quaker demanded, pointing at the darkening sphere where only a moment before the scene down below had been clearly displayed. The light in the spherical observation chamber was still dying out. Many of the tangled strands which crisscrossed its interior were still glowing faintly and they provided an eerie background, a dying still life, the greater portion of which was blocked from view by the Quaker's bulk.

"I have not done anything," Speaker said. Speaker never said any more than it had to. It answered this question truthfully, just as it had answered all of the Quaker's previous questions, but this time the Quaker was not going to be satisfied with the simple truth and he knew enough not to waste time asking Speaker for explanations.

The Quaker assumed the worst. Since Speaker had not destroyed the cube—something else had. And that something was on the planet below him.

He punched communication to the bridge of his ship and spoke to both his crew and the ship's computer. "Prepare to follow our usual plan of last resort, begin maximum acceleration toward the planet and ready Alpha and Omega for disposal."

"Yes, sir!" came the enthusiastic reply and the Quaker cursed himself for not returning to the planet's immediate vicinity long ago. As it was, he and his ship were halfway toward the planet's sun and precious time would be wasted before he could once again regain complete control of the situation.

"If the IXT ship tries to interfere in any way," he added as an afterthought, "destroy it."

The order was acknowledged and the Quaker began to glide toward the door so that he could take personal command of the operations by the time his ship was in position.

"What you plan to do is a mistake," Speaker protested mildly.

The Quaker paused and turned. For a moment he just looked at the pale imitation of a man. He was disgusted. "You have convinced me," he said finally, "that you, and whatever monstrosity you represent, are far too dangerous to live. Since I cannot kill you, I must do the next best thing—and that is getting rid of whatever does your thinking for you."

Speaker was incapable of understanding an insult when one was offered and it made no attempt to follow the Quaker's reasoning. It simply did what it was made to do, and that was talk.

"Your fear is mislaid," it said. "You must not do what you plan. I cannot allow it."

"Ah!" the Quaker exclaimed. "Now we are getting somewhere. I thought you said that you were incapable of offensive action. If that is true—then how are *you* going to prevent *me* from doing anything?"

"I cannot do anything," Speaker said. "But I can place myself anywhere I please on your ship; delicately, in areas where inert objects are not welcomed."

The Quaker paused, swallowed hard. Speaker's hint, or threat, was well taken. There were any number of places aboard the ship where an unwelcome and indestructible mass would cause serious trouble or worse.

"Very well," the Quaker growled. "You go ahead and do whatever you feel like doing. You may be able to blow this ship apart by sticking your body where it isn't wanted, but that isn't going to gain you much. A million years of floating around in space is certainly not something I would look forward to."

Speaker, having no reason to expound on its age, did not. All it could do was reconfirm the offer it had made earlier. "Within the hour you will see what you have been looking for. But now there are others who must not see. They must be gotten rid of. The IXT must be removed from this area alive. They must go so that none will come again, expecting to find something they cannot find."

The Quaker nodded. He wasn't worried about the IXT. They would be gone before long—one way or another. If Speaker wanted to keep up some pretense that an agreement had been reached, the Quaker had no objection. He really didn't care any more whether he saw what he was going to destroy before he destroyed it.

CHAPTER 16. DEPARTURE

C aptain Kane, Commanding Officer aboard the IXT *Exeter*, witnessed something he did not like. For some time he had been watching and waiting; watching the far-off Quaker's ship—partially obscured against the blazing background of the planet's star—and waiting for it to move. Now it was moving and the time he had to act was reduced to a limited and finite number of minutes.

Delay was no longer possible. Trying to resist the Quaker's ship again was out of the question. There was only one thing he was concerned with now and that was the recovery of his people from the planet below. Those who had not returned on the ill-fated shuttle were still alive down there and they were the only ones left alive who could tell him about the alien being which had been destroyed along with the shuttle. There were others down there too, people who were not members of his crew, and they might be able to tell him even more. But his real concern was for his own men. The others were more of a threat than anything else—an undefined threat which he would probably never understand. The Quaker wanted them and this alone was enough to make them a threat the IXT could not tolerate. Captain Kane considered everything carefully before issuing orders to the crew of the rescue shuttle he was sending down.

"Capture them," he said finally, "if possible in the time available. If this is not possible—kill them."

The captain wished his men luck and then returned to the mending of his wounded ship and the search for those who had not yet been found among the wreckage. It was not a pleasant task.

Jennings put the small black cube to his ear. Nothing happened. He shook the thing and repeated the process. Again, nothing happened. Somehow he had gained the impression that Devlon had been listening to the cube, or perhaps it was just the way he had spoken about it. Devlon had treated it like something special and yet, it seemed nothing more than an inert cubical rock—a piece of cut jade perhaps. Any special properties it may have had certainly weren't revealing themselves now.

Jennings put the question aside for the moment and turned to check on the little group around him. Anna still lay on the ground unconscious and Somack knelt beside her, while Margy stood quietly leaning against a tree. They were all his prisoners, really, but he was beginning to regret the role he had forced upon himself. He was too much of a realist to kid himself about their eventual fates. He hadn't cared before, and his not caring had been a fiction he could see through now. The truth was, he hadn't *wanted* to care before and the anger in him had resulted from his failure to maintain the objective viewpoint he was trained to have. His duty was clear and for the first time in his life he found himself at odds with it. For three years duty had been his whole life, the only thing prolonging a bitter existence.

He looked at the pair of hands he had come by illegally. Duty had dictated the necessity—the breach of a code as old as the IXT. It was a lie, though. Other things besides duty had made him want his hands back. Looking across the clearing at Margy and the sun setting behind her, he could admit that now. It was something hard to swallow and his face seemed grimmer than ever.

"It's time to go," he said, and his voice was hard.

Somack and Margy both looked at him. Neither of them were aware of the change taking place in the man ordering them to move.

Somack lifted Anna into his arms. Her hair flowed in a carefully arranged cascade over her right shoulder and down toward her waist across a gently sloping blouse. It did not dangle toward the ground where it might tangle or catch on something. Coming to his feet in one steady motion, Somack's eyes never left the face that seemed so close to him and the little bruises he wished would go away.

The conflict of his senses gave him a strange feeling. Anna seemed so small in his eyes and yet so substantial in his arms, a solid weight against him. The contrast was striking and yet not wrong. Perhaps in a physical way it was the equivalent of something else, something deeper and more important in its hidden place.

Skirting around Devlon's outstretched body, Somack knew how frightened Anna would be if she could see what she had done. Devlon was dead, but the single bullet wound in his shoulder did not account for it. Perhaps the shock of the blow had been the last straw, but there was something in the staring eyes and bared teeth that told him differently. The real cause of Devlon's death was something Somack was careful not to point out to his companions.

Margy walked in front of him and was careful not to look in Devlon's direction, while Jennings seemed too preoccupied to bother looking. It was a small thing to be grateful for in a game he seemed to be losing. Somack knew something of the IXT and he had long experience with their less powerful cousin governments, planet bureaucracies and port authorities, and he'd learned something from it all. The less important you seemed, the less you threatened their power, the more likely they were to let you alone. They might crush you absentmindedly, but they wouldn't go out of their way to do it. The thought gave him some hope. If he could put something between himself and their power—just a little trouble that they might not consider worth the time and effort to overcome, then there would be a chance for survival.

"You have a ship," Jennings was saying impatiently, and Somack suddenly realized that he had been ignoring the conversation for some time.

"Yes, certainly," Somack answered, and he had a sudden inspiration, along with an insight into the problem he was having in understanding Jennings' ignorance of the situation. "You've been aboard the Quaker's ship, haven't you?"

Jennings answered in the affirmative and everything began to fall into place. Somack could understand a little better now why everyone seemed to be working at cross-purposes and he tried to explain the situation to Jennings. It was an explanation that the other found difficult to believe.

"We'll see," Jennings said. "If you can prove to me that Merrick is still alive and the IXT is in control of everything, and not your Speaker, then I won't have to take any drastic action."

Which means, Somack thought, that you won't kill us on the spot.

D usk was beginning to thicken by the time the party of four reached a spot overlooking the *Ambol*. There was just enough light to make out the ship against the sky and the trees against the far horizon. A vague grayness filled the gentle valley and obscured shapes more than it illuminated them.

Jennings was taking no chances. He held his gun ready in the expectation that he might have to use it without much notice. He scanned the valley for the sentry he'd seen near the ship earlier, but the man was nowhere to be seen. Then a motion caught his attention and he squinted to compensate for the faulty lighting. The sound of a muffled voice came from the left, halfway between the fringe of trees and the *Ambol*.

"Don't make a move!"

The words were a command and the authority in the voice made Jennings hesitate for just a moment, and after that it didn't matter. He dropped his gun—not because he was afraid, but because he recognized the craft which was sitting off to the left of the *Ambol*. It was an IXT shuttle and the dim figures who swarmed around it were combat marines.

"Move out into the open," the voice from the darkness ordered.

Jennings did as he was told and Margy and Somack followed his example. Several men were moving toward them now and in a few minutes they had all been carefully searched.

"Who are you?" the man in charge asked. He was a sergeant but you could tell by the tone of his voice that he wasn't impressed much by the rank insignia Jennings wore, nor Margy's either. Neither of these two officers fitted the descriptions of the officer and crewman he was still looking for. Somack and Anna were the two civilians he was supposed to capture, but these two officers bothered him.

Jennings tried to explain.

"There isn't time for that now," the sergeant said, cutting him off. "What happened to Captain Merrick and the crewman with him?"

No one could answer that question.

"Very well," the sergeant said. He was a beefy man, but he could move quickly and make decisions—especially when time was running out and his own life depended on them. "Move toward the shuttle," he ordered, then began speaking quickly into the microphone around his neck.

Searchlights immediately began to illuminate the area. The shuttle sprouted them like tentacles and they stabbed into the darkness. The IXT shuttle rose into the air and it seemed for a moment as if the lights were the means of its propulsion—pushing it away from the ground. But then it began moving sideways in a rapidly growing spiral away from the *Ambol,*

"O.K.," the sergeant said, "let's get moving. Down toward the *Ambol,* The shuttle is going to make one quick sweep of the area. It'll be back in five minutes to pick us up. Maybe by then you two will have come up with some explanation for your presence." He was speaking to Margy and Jennings in particular, but he motioned for all of them to move.

As a group they moved off toward the *Ambol,* Somack was still carrying Anna and as they approached the ship he could make out a pile of something laid out in the grass. Several men were standing around it as if waiting for some order.

"A shame," the sergeant commented to Somack. "I would like to have seen the inside of that little ship of yours, but I'm afraid we haven't the time. I've heard some rumors about it. A shame having to blow it up like this."

Getting closer, Somack could see that the pile near the *Ambol* was a pile of explosives. He smiled a little bit. The sergeant noticed the smile and he didn't like it.

"You haven't got much to smile about," he said pointedly.

"Depends on how you look at things," Somack answered.

The sergeant paused, then turned away. He was listening to something coming in through his radio headset. The news he heard wasn't good.

"Something wrong?" Jennings asked, seeing the expression on the marine's face.

"The shuttle has recovered some bodies—two of them. The ones we were looking for." The sergeant's expression remained sour. He watched the horizon and shortly the shuttle was returning, lights blazing. It landed as abruptly as it had taken off. "Everyone aboard!" the sergeant shouted.

The men who had been working with the explosives ran toward the shuttle. They piled aboard followed closely by Margy and Jennings. Jennings paused as he entered and looked back at the sergeant. "There's another body," he said quietly, "one you seem to have missed. A man called Devlon."

"There isn't time," the sergeant said and someone pulled Jennings back into the shuttle and away from the entrance. "You next," the sergeant said, turning to Somack.

"We aren't going."

The sergeant turned toward the shuttle and motioned with his hand. Two marines piled out and started toward them. They took only a few steps and then froze. A faint orange light played over their faces and lit the general background in a way that made the hair on the sergeant's neck crawl. He turned back toward Somack and Anna, keeping the aim of his needle-nose well away from them. For the first time the sergeant was getting a really good look at the ship which rose up behind Somack and the girl he held. The orange glow the ship gave off compelled him to look and made it easy at the same time. The glow was evenly distributed, marred only by the many scars and discolored indentations that covered the *Ambol;* scars and indentations from which many tiny filaments were sprouting. The filaments quivered in an invisible wind, seeking who knows what in a random search of directions and finally stiffening. Several of these filaments just happened to stiffen in the sergeant's direction and he swallowed. His tongue seemed to be caught somewhere in the back of his throat and when he finally found it, it didn't seem to work quite right.

"G.A.G.," the sergeant said, his eyes searching Somack's face for the answer. The sergeant was a simple man and watching Somack he found something simple to admire. He saw the girl in Somack's arms, the ship standing behind him, and the grim determination on his face.

"G.A.G.," the sergeant repeated and there was a note of awe in his voice. "A war model, damn it, and I thought they had all been scrapped ages ago. God, what a collector's item."

Somack still didn't answer.

The sergeant didn't seem to mind. His eyes kept wandering up toward the *Ambol* and then back at the two people at its base.

"You're a dead man . . ." the sergeant said slowly, "when—when we catch you again." There was envy in the sergeant's eyes as he stepped backward, then turned and dashed back toward the shuttle. Harsh words flew from the beefy marine as he ran and his two frozen men came to life and piled back into the shuttle ahead of him with a haste that was hard to believe. Strains of a brief argument drifted back from the shuttle as the sergeant boarded. The argument was very brief and the shuttle lifted with every indication that the shuttle's pilot was certainly not one of the people arguing with the sergeant's decision to leave quickly.

The shuttle was gone in seconds and Somack stood alone for a moment in the quiet field. A sudden stirring in his arms made Somack look down again. He was not alone. No, not at all.

M oments later, as the IXT shuttle raced up toward the *Exeter*, Jennings turned his head toward Margy who was strapped in and confined next to him. Her eyes met his in return. There was a calm between them now, like never before. Perhaps they would both die soon, executed. Perhaps—if lucky—they'd earn hard labor and exile together on Hollenglen. These prospects made other problems seem small.

Jennings wanted to speak—say something of what he felt—now that the old life was ended for both of them; they could leave it behind. But the shuttle's engine-noise made talking impossible. All he could do was reach a little with his hand—not far enough. But, then Margy reached too and for an instant they could touch.

The Quaker observed operations from the wide expanse of his control room. Men were seated all around him, each one of them busy at an important task or backing up an extremely important one. They did not have time to do what the Quaker was doing. He was overseeing the operation; correlating information from every source and coordinating the whole. It was something ordinarily left to computers, but the Quaker could do it and his judgment was better than a computer's. The men who served him could only judge this by the success they always had and the fact that they were all still very much alive. There were few complaints.

The planet's disk was finally becoming visible in the forward screen. The Quaker's ship was already decelerating as fast as it could; dumping the momentum it had gained in its rapid return. In moments the planet would grow until it filled the screen. Then, and only then, would the Quaker be in a position to carry through with the plan he was set upon. Speaker would be unable to prevent it.

"The *Exeter* has been located," one of the radar men reported. "She is holding position over the western twilight zone. Not in free orbit; close in and apparently waiting for something from the surface."

The Quaker acknowledged the report, but he wasn't really interested in the *Exeter*. The threat it represented was minimal. The IXT didn't bother him much, because they couldn't. No matter how much they learned of him, they would never be more than a nuisance. Speaker was another matter. Anything indestructible was dangerous, even if it was a machine as he was now sure Speaker was. Indestructible machines were constructed by dangerous people, and there was nothing in Speaker's behavior to reassure the Quaker. It was clear that all Speaker lacked was transportation. Who knows how long the thing had been waiting down on that planet. Perhaps Speaker, and whatever had created and now controlled Speaker, had been waiting years for someone to come along and provide them with transportation. If Speaker and its parent ever managed to get away from this planet and system, there was no telling how much havoc they might wreak. If you could make an indestructible machine which could only talk, you could just as easily make one that could only kill. The Quaker was not a cruel man. He simply did what he thought was necessary. He would destroy this planet and whatever lived down there. That was necessary, and if it failed to disable Speaker, then he would know that Speaker's master had escaped aboard either the *Ambol* or the *Exeter*. He would hunt them down too, if need be.

There was only one thing the Quaker was thankful for in the present situation. Speaker was either a very stupid machine, or the mind controlling it was overconfident.

The Quaker had destroyed planets before. He had done more than his share of destroying Hursk-worlds and some others as well. The action was usually more deliberate and well thought out than the one he was about to take now, but the end would be the same. He liked to make his destruction meaningful. He liked to leave a work of art behind when he did something on this scale, but time and need did not allow. The job would be quick and brutal.

"The *Exeter* is moving away, sir," his radar man reported. "She's moving away rapidly; out toward safety range."

The Quaker nodded. He expected the IXT ship to drop into main drive and head back toward civilization. It had wounds to lick and important information; information important enough to warrant not risking their ship further. The Quaker chuckled to himself. No doubt the IXT would be out here again before long, sniffing around for any clues to the mystery they still couldn't comprehend. But by the time they got back here there would be nothing left except a little interstellar debris.

"Sir," the radar man said, looking up. "There's another object lifting from the planet's surface. I can't tell yet for certain, but it's probably the *Ambol.*"

Speaker, standing all this time just behind the Quaker, finally spoke. "You plan something that is not necessary," it said.

The Quaker turned and faced his opponent, or rather* what he was beginning to regard as his opponent's proxy. "There seems to be some evidence that you can read minds along with your many other tricks," the

Quaker said. He was just talking. He didn't really believe Speaker could read minds. Otherwise the creature would act to prevent what he was about to do.

Speaker seemed to consider the statement for a moment. It answered frankly, "It is not within my power to read minds; however, your actions speak for you. I have promised to reveal the one you seek when the *Ambol* is safe. A few more minutes and that condition will be met."

The Quaker glanced at the screen and the planet growing ever larger before his eyes. The time had come. He looked across the room and in an extreme corner stood a man with apparently nothing to do. The man was watching the Quaker and when the Quaker nodded and raised a hand to his chin the man depressed a small button and turned a key. Nothing could stop what was going to happen now. It was just a matter of time and the Quaker continued talking just to distract Speaker's attention.

In a few minutes the Quaker's ship finally stopped its motion toward the planet and once again began to move away. But there was something else that was no longer connected to the Quaker's ship and it continued to move toward the planet, gaining speed as the gravity below began to pull it on. The computer was carefully programmed and the falling object did not appear on the screen, nor did any of the men stationed around the room see fit to mention its presence on their instruments.

The planet's fate was sealed and as one last precaution the Quaker nodded once again to the man in the far corner. The ship's great engines choked and died. Only a pair of tiny generators continued to operate, just enough power to keep the ship's electrical system in working order. There was no change in the control room. The screens continued to blaze in full glory, but now there was nothing significant Speaker could do; no great power plant its indestructible body could jam up and destroy with disastrous and fatal results for everyone aboard. By the time Speaker realized what was happening it would be too late.

Outside, beyond the screens and hull of the Quaker's ship, an object tumbled slowly in space, on its way toward destruction. Technically the object was a bomb but it was not a human invention. The Quaker had done quite a bit of looking before he had come across a stockpile of them. The race which had perfected the devices no longer had a use for them. They had used far too many of the things on themselves.

Most bombs merely exploded, and for a start this one would do the same thing. There the similarity would end. The plasma bomb, instead of dissipating its energy in an ordinary fashion, formed a cell of convection currents. More and more material was drawn toward the burning heart of its furious reaction and added to the energy and strength of its field. The process was very inefficient. Only 5 per cent of the material drawn in was actually brought to the proper temperature and pressure and most of that was material which simply would not react, but there was more than enough hydrogen to keep the thing going and growing all the time.

The Quaker knew what would happen. He didn't need to watch. He didn't draw any pleasure out of what he was doing, it was simply something that had to be done.

The bomb continued to fall and the men at their stations strained at their instruments. They watched and waited. Finally the bomb plunged into the atmosphere and dropped toward the wide expanse of an ocean below it. It burst. An all-consuming fire roared. The crewman observing the blast on the optics was blinded. Another took his place.

Below, the air flowed toward the holocaust. The ocean boiled and joined its energy to the ever-increasing carnage. The very rocks began to melt and flow.

The Quaker's eyes remained on Speaker. When would the creature react? When would it realize what was happening? Never, it seemed, and the room was tense with waiting men.

Mountains sagged down and began to boil. An island continent shuddered and shook. In seconds it was gone—gone as the whole world would go. No life could survive. Whatever lived down there—whatever controlled or produced Speaker—would not survive. Then something inexplicable happened: the chain reaction ceased. Crewmen at the instruments knew it first and the shock of it kept them from doing more than look on in disbelief. The Quaker suddenly became aware of the stillness of his men. He moved to speak, but an action cut him short.

The crewman at the optical gear saw it first.

"No!" he screamed. "Oh God, noooooo—"

"What is it?" the Quaker demanded.

The crewman slumped back and fell away from his optics.

"He's dead," someone said.

"Sir," the crewman at the radar said, barely audible. "There's nothing there," and then looked back at his set, unable to believe his own words.

"Nothing where?" the Quaker shouted, and he moved forward, almost as if he were intent on ripping an answer from the man.

"The planet, sir. There's nothing inside! It's hollow." The words came out in a rush and the man's eyes darted back and forth between the Quaker and the impossible display on his screen.

The Quaker rolled forward and people leaped from his path. He moved toward the optics and impatiently brushed the dead man aside. He looked at the screen and froze. The bomb had ripped a gaping hole in the planet's crust. Beneath, through the vapor and steam of its destruction, there was nothing. A swirling chasm of black, sucking—sucking him toward it. He fell, fell, fell down into the darkness.

"YOU HAVE SEEN ME," it said and in that second the Quaker did see it. He lived a thousand lifetimes in that second. Information flooded into his mind in a swirling confusion. Then it was over. The vapors condensed and rock began to rain down, obscuring what lay below. The Quaker blinked and for a moment he thought he might die, but then he looked around—at the men and their white faces—at Speaker who did nothing—and he decided not to.

"So," the Quaker said after a long time had passed, "you want me to cart you around with me. You want me as your chauffeur; sort of a cosmic tour guide."

Speaker said nothing. There was nothing it could add to what the Quaker had already seen. The Quaker knew this, but he felt better after speaking anyway. It was one thing to have your mind changed about something and it was another to admit the change—even to yourself.

"Strange," the Quaker said, more to himself than to Speaker or the crewmen who continued to sit and wonder, "strange how things work out. Very convenient for some." The Quaker's eyes dwelled on Speaker and he knew that he had only himself to blame. After all, he had taken the being aboard in the first place—and he dropped the bomb. No one had made him do either, but he was sure that someone, or rather—something—had known that he would do both. Now he was trapped. Now he knew too much to deny that the course laid out for him was the one he would have to follow. Speaker could not compel him to do anything. The Quaker knew that for certain now, but he knew too many other things along with it. In the end he was going to co-operate, but he wanted to make it clear that he was going to co-operate on his own terms; in his own way.

"You understand that, don't you?" the Quaker said, completing his train of thought.

Speaker did not answer. It could not read minds. Such direct communication was left to others. Speaker's job was to speak, and, occasionally, to demonstrate the dangers inherent in doing anything more. With the Quaker's help Speaker could now search for those who needed the warning most. There would be no more waiting; no more helpless hoping that the message would eventually get delivered. The few who were ready and the few who could be convinced would be brought here and shown. There were many races scattered across the sky and time was something that refused to stop.

The Quaker dismissed his men and they left quietly. They could tell that he was in no mood for questions of any kind. The Quaker sat and stared for a long time at the ship's main screen. It still showed the planet as it had once been and not as he had seen it only a few moments before. How lucky these men were, the Quaker thought as he watched them go. They would never know what lay beneath the disturbed surface of that planet. They would never see it as he had seen it.

There was one thing he would never forget. That was the apology in the thing he had seen. He had done his best to destroy the creature and all through the period it had communicated with him there had been a tone of apology. It had apologized for the memories it was giving him and most of all it had apologized for its appearance.

I HAVE BEEN CHANGED.

The Quaker remembered that thought more clearly than all the rest, and he remembered also the impression of a great holding back on the other's part. It was as if the creature was holding something back, containing within itself some experience too terrible to mention or even think about. The Quaker shook his head. He wanted peace for a moment. He wanted time to digest the great change that was being forced upon him. It was too fast. He could feel an aftertaste—a reaction against what was happening to him.

There was one place he could go and think; one place where he was sure to be alone. Speaker remained behind and the Quaker glided soundlessly through the corridors and aisles of his ship. Men turned away when he passed and pretended not to see. They knew where he was going and they dreaded the place. They dreaded the very thought of it.

The lights were dim and the Quaker did nothing to change them. The gloom suited him for the moment and he paused to contemplate. He was surrounded by the relics of his past. The long years of his life, and the dust covered them just as it covered the trophies he had collected.

There were faint motions in the dark and the Quaker knew their source. Years and years and years he had hated that source. Whenever time had dragged—whenever he felt his purpose falter—the Quaker had always come to this room. It contained the horror of the past and the reason for his existence. The Hursk and everything it stood for resided here. And the love he had never had and the friends he had lost so long ago; they were all here too. The long silence stretched into hours and the Quaker cried. No living soul had ever seen him do it and he would never do it again. It was just something that happened and something that he would not try to explain to himself. He let the tears run until they wouldn't come.

"I suppose you're happy now," the Quaker said, and the Hursk only thrashed mindlessly.

The Quaker glided forward in the dark and he felt for something very small. He found it at last and hesitated for just a second before he pressed it. The tiny click echoed in his ears and he knew that somewhere a pump was grinding to a halt; equipment was stilled for the first time in three hundred years.

"Rest in peace," the Quaker said very quietly, and the small echo of his words were his only answer. The Hursk would move no longer.

The Quaker sat for a long moment. He did not know where he was going, or what he would do. Or even if he would do as Speaker wished. But he was not the same. He was like the memory-filled creature who had done this to him. Something deep inside him was changed.

The Quaker closed the vault door when he left. He summoned men to him and he said a few words. "Seal it," he told them. "Seal it tight."

The *Ambol* pushed into high drive and the bright lights of that medium lit the screen around Somack. He had only one interest at the moment and that was to put as much distance between himself and the Quaker-IXT as possible. Fortunately both of these sources of danger seemed to have other things on their minds at the moment.

The *Exeter* had preceded him into high drive and Somack watched incredulously as it disappeared from his screen in a direction that could only mean it was returning to base. The *Ambol* reacted to the sight by moving at top speed in a nearly opposite direction. It was taking no chances that the IXT might change its mind and decide to pursue instead of limping back home. Somack watched for a while and there continued to be no signs of pursuit. Shortly it would be impossible for even the Quaker to follow them and when that time had passed Somack heaved a sigh of relief. He was home free.

A PREMATURE ASSUMPTION, the *Ambol* flashed, and Somack was shaken from his brief feeling of relaxation. He must have spoken his contentment aloud for the ship continued, **THERE STILL REMAINS ONE VERY IMPORTANT PROBLEM**.

Somack felt a moment of irritation and then realized with some humor that there was a good reason why the ship's audio system had been removed. He sat thinking for a few moments and smiling. Then he shook himself. There was no point in putting off the inevitable. He took a deep breath and began to unfasten Anna from the acceleration webbing he had so hastily thrown around her.

"What is it?" she murmured as he lifted her, and then her eyes opened wide. He carried her silently and all the time her eyes darted about, finally coming to rest on his. He avoided the gaze and quickened his pace. He set her down on her bunk before she had time to verbalize the questions in her eyes.

"What's happened?" she asked, sitting up the moment she was free of him. "What have I done?"

"Nothing," Somack said, glad that she could not remember. "Now just lay back and rest. We can talk about it when you've had some rest."

"No, I won't," she said, and pushed his hand away. There was something very determined in the way she did it and Somack stood back helplessly, watching as she probed the growing bruise on her forehead. She touched it gingerly and her eyes widened and then narrowed. Her eyes seemed to blur as she focused them on some point beyond the walls around her. Some of the tautness left her face as she concentrated and for a moment her mouth slackened and formed an absent-minded *oh*.

"Do that again," Somack said.

A sharp look and a frown greeted his meaningless sentence, but he had succeeded in breaking her train of thought. There was time enough for her to remember what had happened. He saw no reason why she had to do it right now. She looked at him, puzzled, and when he said nothing further, something seemed to come home to her. She looked around at the familiar room and listened to the sound of the *Ambol* in the background.

"We're alone, aren't we?" There was a note of resignation in her voice and she bowed her head and stared at the hands she had clasped between her knees.

'Yes," Somack answered. "Is there anything so terrible about that?"

She looked at him and there was something close to wonder in her eyes. She thought of all the things that had happened in the past few weeks and most of all she thought of the terrible responsibility that had been thrust upon her.

"You take it so easily then?" she asked. "You are ordered and you follow. No questions. No doubts. How can you do it when you know what I am; when you know that I have stolen from your mind and have worked to destroy what you have been looking for all your life? Can you still do what you must, like a soldier, or is it just that you don't care?"

Anna ran out of words and looked away. She was breathing hard and Somack watched her until she began to blush.

"I'm going to tell you something," Somack said when he caught her reluctant eyes. "When I first started this trip, I didn't know you from any of the other billions that inhabit the universe. I spent the first half of my life scratching for every penny I could save. I had only one goal in my life and that was to get where we just were. I didn't know what would happen when I got there and I really didn't care. It was something to work toward and that was more than most people had.

"When I first saw you, you were just one more passenger—like the millions I'd seen before—and the only difference was that you were going to be one of the last. The dream I had has changed and grown a lot since then. When I learned that you were going to be a part of it all, I thought I was finally getting lucky; I thought I was going to get something I didn't really deserve. When I learned that there was only one really safe way to pass on the message we both carry, I thought—'What a stroke of luck.'

"I was a fool. It's nothing but a burden. A precious burden perhaps, but a burden just the same. What good is it to be ordered to do something you want to do anyway? At the very least it makes you chafe and wish again for a free hand."

"What do you mean?" Anna asked, and she tried to edge away, but there was a wall behind her. She drew her legs up against her and huddled there watching him uncertainly.

Somack sat down and looked at her. He touched her knee and the chin trying to hide behind it. "No one ordered me to love you. It happened a long time ago."

Anna blinked and her lips quivered. "You're just saying that," she said, pleading for a denial.

"I am saying it," Somack admitted, "but not *just.*"

He loosened the hands she held so tightly around her legs and touched her shoulder. "Lie down now," he said, and she unwound, slipping over and letting her head touch the pillow. Somack moved closer and brushed back the hair which was threatening to engulf her face. "You have very beautiful eyes," he said quietly, "and if you blink again they will overflow."

Anna sniffed. She swallowed the words that would not come and trembled as Somack touched her cheek, moving fingers lightly down and back behind her ear.

He moved closer and her heart would not stop.

"It's not fair," she complained. "I haven't got a chance."

"You weren't meant to," Somack said, and the conversation ended quietly.

S omack lay awake in the night. His mind ran slowly, like a brook through a gently smoking forest. He had never been a greatly troubled man and now contentment filled his very being. Only a touch of guilt clouded his happiness. He had gotten so much, and his troubles—they seemed so little now. What great things had he done to earn this great prize?

She slept beside him now and he never tired of watching. Her face was softened and her hair seemed to fill the universe around him. She was happy in her sleep and he knew, if anything, this was the work he had earned her with.

He touched her bare shoulder with his finger tips. Gently he traced the line of her collarbone and the fine hollow above. He traced it from her right shoulder far over to the left and she purred deep in her throat. She stirred, moving unconsciously close; pressing softly against him. He touched her lips with his and her closeness was suddenly conscious.

"Sneak!" was all she had breath to say.

The next morning Somack sat at the ship's console. His eyes were a little tired with lack of sleep. He was up early and hadn't disturbed Anna.

YOU STILL FACE DANGER FROM THE IXT, the console reminded him.

"I've been thinking about that a little," Somack conceded. "I have another probability for you to consider."

PROCEED.

"As an executive of the Heinmann and Schultz Transport Company, what are the chances that Anna and I will be left alone by the IXT?"

The computer took a few seconds to ponder the question. **PROBABILITY OF DETECTION IN THIS CASE IS 100.00% AS OPPOSED TO 93.68% IN THE CASE OF DERMIFF RETREAT. HOWEVER, ONCE DETECTED BY IXT, PROBABILITY OF ADVERSE ACTION BY IXT IS ONLY 32.46% AS OPPOSED TO 98.85% IN THE DERMIFF CASE. THE H&STC IS A POWERFUL COMPANY. IT SUPPLIES THE IXT WITH BASIC HULLS AND IS THE LARGEST BULK CARRIER IN EXISTENCE. RECORDS SHOW AN EXPANSION TREND IN THE COMPANY. THUS THE IXT MUST TAKE CARE.**

Somack nodded soberly. "I suspected as much. Thirty-two per cent is still too high a risk, but it's not likely to fall much below that."

CORRECT, the ship answered, then fell silent. It still did not like to talk too much when Anna was in the room, and she had just entered. She came up behind him and laid her hands on his shoulders. He turned to look up and she began to massage him gently.

"That wasn't very nice," she said sternly, "waking me up like that."

Somack might have taken her seriously, but for the light in her eyes and the way she strained for a straight face. "I'll never do it again," he promised, letting her face fall a little before adding, "except. . ."

Her eyes narrowed. He was teasing her, and she knew it.

"Except?" she demanded, stepping back and glaring a little.

He swiveled in his chair and stood up. She held her ground and he stepped up close. He let his eyes fall into hers while his finger ran along the line of her jaw and then came away with a tangle of hair. He held it up between them and puffed at it with his breath.

"Except . . . when this stuff attacks me—gets in my nose and wakes *me* up."

She tried to make a face, but it dissolved into a smile. She laughed and her arms flew around him. He rocked her gently against him and stroked her hair. Unaccountably, her laughing turned to crying and he pretended not to see.

She was still in a moment, then said, "I'll never cut it." In her own quiet way, it was a promise she would never forget.

The following is a sample from Robert Enstrom's book *Beta Colony*.
A novel in the IXT Universe.

PREFACE

In the year Alpha-0 (the year all modern history begins) a ship departed from the Earth. In eight years the ship reached Alpha and began the construction of a greater civilization than the one that had gone before. Each fifty years after the first landing another ship would come from Earth bringing new knowledge, new people, and a reminder that home and help did exist elsewhere in the Universe.

In the 250th year of the colony no ship came and Earth was silent. Alpha survived and grew, never understanding the Silence or why it had started. In its own time, it too sent forth ships to populate new worlds. But it never forgot its origins and among its earliest efforts was Beta Colony, the attempt to repopulate Earth.

Over a period of 256 years, 2816 colonists landed in Beta Colony. There are 168 known survivors and/or descendants. Thirty-two of these are in the original area of the island landing site and still reasonably civilized. The rest live in the wilderness portion of the island and have resorted to cannibalism.

PART ONE
The Island
Chapter 1

At age twenty-four Daniel Trevor stood in danger of losing his life. If he was aware of this, he gave no sign. Instead, he glanced around the courtroom—first at those closest to him, then at those further away. In passing, his eyes noted the exits to the room and then paused on a familiar face. A girl's face.

The chains of his leg irons rattled slightly as he shifted position. The armed troopers on each side of him stared fixedly at his face. But he was thinking of something else. His eyes wandered back to the young lady.

His career of crime had been ended by this person in whom he'd placed too much confidence. But he felt no hatred. Perhaps if he had really loved her, he would now be feeling more passion at her betrayal of him. Instead, he simply felt numb. After all, it had been *his* choice to surrender instantly when the state's forces had come for him. He could have fought and died.

He thought of this as he continued to watch with detached alertness. A gavel banged in the background. Massive, heavily padded doors opened and the jury of eleven men and one woman filed in. The judge nodded and one of the jurors fumbled with a small piece of paper. Clearing his throat, the juror read:

"This jury, duly constituted and selected, having been presented with all the evidence, finds the accused, Daniel Trevor, guilty on two counts of the most terrible crime of assassination."

The judge leaned forward. "It is my duty to inform the condemned that, as his crime was most terrible, so must his punishment be.

"As set forth by the law, the condemned is to be allowed the Choice in the manner of his execution."

There followed a long list of sentences that varied in length of time and method of accomplishment but that always resulted in death. When the judge had finished reading he resumed speaking directly to Daniel.

"The Choice was written into the law for good reason. In the early days of Alpha, during the long Silence, religious and other groups were common. Many of these groups placed a great deal of weight on the manner of a criminal member's death. The law recognized the need for this at the time and provided for it. The Choice remains despite the passing away of most of these original groups.

"Most prisoners prefer the quick and painless death caused by the drug MZ 31." For a moment the judge paused. "The law also provides for those who prefer life, any life, to the sentences I have mentioned. At present this alternative would mean taking up permanent residence on Beta Colony."

Having finished, the judge stood abruptly, descended from his high place, and with a swirl of black was gone.

Daniel Trevor sat silently in the tight confines of his "box." He had given himself over to thoughts of the past lately, and now was no exception. He only half heard his state's lawyer speaking from the other side of the glass. Instead, he was remembering the dried-up farm of his youth and the fervent dedication of his father to land that would never yield a fair return for all the back break and tears.

"Why?" Daniel had often asked.

"Because this is *my* land!" his father would snarl back. "No one controls me when I'm on *my* land!"

And that was one lesson Daniel had taken to heart despite all the other anger and resentment between them. No one had ever controlled *him* once he'd understood what his father had been talking about. And the first to learn it was the man who had taught him.

"Get that seed over here!" his father had ordered.

"I'll get it," he'd snapped back, "but I'll get it only because *I* want to get it."

They stared at each other then, for about a minute, both of them turning slowly red and beginning to steam.

"So," his father said at last. "So," he'd repeated, spitting into the dust, looking straight into Daniel's eyes. "You do just that, son, and we may get along yet."

It was one of the most unexpected things, and Daniel could still remember his own surprise, and he could remember the way his hate for that dry land had begun to falter. It was like seeing something change shape right there in front of him—to know that those hateful rules his father forced at him—to know that the old man would abide 'em himself, and the devil take the first to falter.

Daniel smiled at himself. It was kind of funny thinking of all that hate gone to waste. But then again, he'd become a killer soon enough after that to make up for the waste.

It'd been a strange thing to set him off. Just an article in the dusty old *Argosy News*—weeks old by the time he'd happened to read it.

A Trans-Con passenger shuttle crashed today in the mountains west of here, the article had read. *Suspected crime leader Alpho Dury was aboard, along with two members of the Tang-Signet investigating team. The crash was reportedly the result of an explosion, probably aimed at eliminating Dury and any evidence he might have given to the Tang-Signet investigators. One hundred and seventy-two others were killed in the crash.*

"Now, I hate that." He'd said that right loud with no one else around, because he'd been eating lunch out in the fields, just reading that paper to relax by. But now he couldn't relax. It wasn't that he hated so many people dying. He hadn't known a single one. It was just that somebody out there had reached out and taken *control* of one hundred and seventy-two people.

Control, in Daniel's mind, was the same as killing. Once something was controlled, it just wasn't *alive* in the same sense anymore. It could just be killed at a whim. Like he and his father controlled the lives of so many chickens.

And now this. It had been like a sick thing to know that dry land and hard work were no guarantees. His father's dream of being a free man was just a bubble of dust. A killer who would kill you for just sitting on the same shuttle as Alpho Dury might just as well take it into his mind to kill a couple of dirt farmers for some other reason.

Daniel shuddered. *Maybe I never should have walked away from the farm like that,* he thought. His father had never even asked why. That was the kind of understanding they had—two men who did and worked at what they wanted, no questions asked or answered.

He'd gone off to become a killer. No accident, no excuse. His only regret being that he'd never found the man who'd brought down that shuttle.

Once he'd tried to explain why he killed—why people who dedicated all their lives to *controlling* other people needed to be killed. That had been in the early days when he could still feel lonely. But the girl had only looked at him and shrugged. It couldn't have mattered less to her.

Now it was only to himself that he tried to explain.

"Are you sure this is what you want?" his lawyer asked again, breaking in on his thoughts.

"Hm?" Daniel asked, looking through the glass.

"Beta Colony? Are you sure? Once you sign these papers there is no turning back. There is no easy death on Beta Colony."

Daniel Trevor looked at the soft face of the lawyer. "Yes," he said, "I'll be going to Beta Colony."

And even though the lawyer continued to talk, Daniel's thoughts drifted elsewhere. He was a long way from the boy he had been, but the same question still nagged at his mind: How can people want to be controlled? To him, it was the same thing as wanting to be dead. The question haunted him because he couldn't understand why so many had an urge to blend back into oblivion. He was willing to endure anything—to stay alive, even in the hell of Beta Colony—just so that he could go on searching.

Also by Robert Enstrom

Beta Colony, coming soon from NewMythsPublishing.com.

About New Myths Publishing

Publishing the finest in science fiction and fantasy. See our entire collection at NewMythsPublishing.com.